homicide
survivors
picnic

Also by Lorraine M. López

The Gifted Gabaldón Sisters

Call Me Henri

Soy La Avon Lady

Forthcoming:

Limpieza

*An Angle of Vision: Women Writers on
Their Poor and Working Class Roots*

homicide survivors picnic

and other stories

Lorraine M. López

BkMk Press
University of Missouri-Kansas City

BkMk Press
University of Missouri-Kansas City
5101 Rockhill Road
Kansas City, Missouri 64110
www.umkc.edu/bkmk

MAC
MISSOURI ARTS COUNCIL

Financial assistance for this project has been provided by the
Missouri Arts Council, a state agency.

The following stories in this collection have appeared in
these publications: "Homicide Survivors Picnic" in *Alaska
Quarterly Review*, "The Flood" in *The New Orphic Review*,
"Batterers" in *Jabberwock Review*, "Human Services" in *Image*,
"The Landscape" in *Crazyhorse*, "The Threat of Peace" in
StoryQuarterly/Narrative Magazine.

Cover design: Meredith Gray
Author photo: Louis A. Seigel
Managing Editor: Ben Furnish
Assistant Managing Editor: Susan L. Schurman
Editorial Assistant: Elizabeth Gromling
BkMk Press wishes to thank George Hendon, Gary Gildner,
    Jedsen Williams, Jeff Minton

Printed by Walsworth Publishing Company, Marceline, Mo.

Library of Congress Cataloguing-in-Publication Data

López, Lorraine
    Homicide survivors picnic, and other stories / Lorraine López.
        p. cm.
    ISBN 978-1-886157-72-9 (pbk. : alk. paper)
    1. Hispanic Americans--Fiction. 2. Hispanic American families--
Fiction. I. Title.
    PS3612.O635H66 2009
    813'.6--dc22
                                            2009032635

This book is dedicated to and inspired by Louis Aronson Siegel

Acknowledgments

This book could not have been written without the inspiration provided by my husband Louis Aronson Siegel, whose generosity of spirit and wisdom challenges me daily to be kinder and more reasonable with others. I am also profoundly grateful to my astute and patient circle of peer readers: Danielle Alexander, Beth Bachmann, Lauren Cobb, Kathryn Locey, Maura Mandyck, Justin Quarry, Nancy Reisman, and Heather Sellers. Their insights have benefited this work tremendously. My appreciation extends to mis hermanas mocosas at Macondo Workshops, especially Erin Badhand, Angie Chau, Yael Flusberg, Gabriela Jauregui, Daisy Hernandez, Laura Negrete, and Beatriz Terrazas. Further, I must recognize the guidance I have received from my mentors, Sandra Cisneros, Tony Earley, Peter Guralnick, Mark Jarman, and particularly from Judith Ortiz Cofer, whose continued influence shapes my writing life. Gracias tambien to the splendid staff at BkMk Press, especially to Ben Furnish, for seeing the promise in this work and bringing it to print. Last, but never least, I thank my children Marie and Nick; my father Espiridion López; my sisters and brother, Debra López, Kenneth López; Frances López Whyte, and Sylvia López; my dear friends, Lynn Pruett; Meredith Gray; Bryn Chancellor; Blas Falconer; Karen McElmurray; and the entire Siegel and Aronson families—family and friends whose unflagging support and practical help make my writing life possible.

Contents

The Flood

"Auntie," Roxanne says to Lydia in her piercing four-year-old way, the volume of it drawing stares from elderly white men seated near the storefront window. "Auntie, let's sit here." She juts a thumb at the table closest to the seniors. "Okay, Auntie?"

The bakery is capacious and empty except for the old men, the little girl, and Lydia, so there's no reason to take a table near theirs, but Roxanne *likes* people. Already, she's grinning at a gaunt oldster who glares back through thick, distorting lenses that make his gelid eyes strange as those of a nocturnal creature surprised by light.

"Hi, my name is Roxanne," she says. "What's yours?"

Lydia hopes he won't encourage Roxanne, who will likely belly up for a handshake. Luckily, the old man returns to his Danish and Styrofoam cup of coffee.

"Roxanne," Lydia whispers. "Why don't we sit toward the back? There's plenty of room." The bakery's scuffed wooden floor extends back into a deli area that's not yet open for business. The many empty tables and chairs in the rear are invitingly private and offer the opportunity to admire decorative ceramic pigs, trophies, ribbons, and framed black and white photographs of the founding bakers and their employees.

"You don't like this table?" The girl's brown eyes, wide and shiny, threaten to brim. "I picked it out just for *you*, Auntie." So this is another offering. The morning has been full of these—gestures and found objects that Roxanne has presented as tokens of affection—and Lydia cannot refuse too many, especially since she is not really Roxanne's aunt. She's just a cousin to the girl's mother, Shirley. Lydia has reluctantly agreed to keep Roxanne for the summer, while Shirley sorts through some legal trouble. She and Shirley had been close as sisters, growing up in California. When Lydia moved to the South for graduate school several years ago, Shirley trailed after her, though they soon grew apart. Roxanne's father was killed in a car accident before she was born, and the rest of their family still lives on the West Coast, so Lydia's the only relative the little girl knows, apart from her mother.

Lydia sinks into a chair closest to the men to prevent the child from disturbing them too much. Roxanne climbs into the chair before the bottled apple juice and the cream puff Lydia has set out. "Why are those guys so white?" she asks in a stage whisper that is maybe half a decibel lower than her raucous speaking voice. Lydia's certain that even the men with hearing devices embedded in their hairy, oversized ears must have heard this.

"Shush." Against her will, Lydia glances over her shoulder. The men, seven or eight in all, are strikingly white from their balding pinkish pates to their glossy patent-leather loafers, and in the sunshine pouring through the plate glass, they are nearly luminous, ghostly. With beaky noses and hunched shoulders, they huddle over their sweet rolls and coffee like celestial buzzards picking over paradisiacal carrion. These men provide such sharp contrast from Roxanne's dusky skin and kinky jet hair that Lydia's pupils dilate perceptibly when she turns back to their own table. "Maybe they're in a club or something." She sips her coffee, imagining they could be a church choral group getting together after services, though it's only Friday.

"Like on a team?"

"Like that." Though, it's hard to imagine what game they might play—even shuffleboard might prove too rigorous, so maybe mah-jongg or checkers? She unwraps Roxanne's straw, sliding the paper down, coiling it with care. Lydia eavesdrops on the men as she dribbles juice from the straw onto the wrapper, so Roxanne can watch it expand and stretch, writhing wormlike.

"Ooh, let *me* try." She grabs the straw, drenches the wrapper, and puddles the table top.

The old men discuss Michael Jackson, the pop star, his recent acquittal, their voices edged with anger. Next, they are onto Ted Kennedy and Chappaquiddick. Now, they are fuming about divorce and the special dispensation from the pope. Lydia can't follow the connections. Perhaps they suffer some kind of mass senility, a rhythmic call-and-response type of shared dementia. Maybe their white polo shirts and bleached khakis are uniforms of a sort, institution-wear—

"Where are we going after?" Roxanne stretches out her pointy pink tongue, reaching for a dot of whipped cream on her nose.

"After what?"

"After this?"

"Well, if anything's open, like a museum or a gift shop or something, we'll go there." Lydia glances at her watch. Though they meandered as slowly as possible along the flood wall from the hotel to the center of town, it's not much after nine. She'd noticed on the way that the market museum doesn't open until noon, nor does the railroad museum a little

farther downriver, or upriver—how can one tell? And the
County Fair won't admit people until five in the afternoon.

"This sure is a lazy place," Roxanne says, as though
reading Lydia's thoughts. She pops the last bit of pastry into
her mouth and slurps the dregs from the juice bottle.

"Sure is." Lydia wipes Roxanne's sticky cheeks and
fingers with a damp napkin. "They're in no big hurry to open
up." Not for the first time, Lydia questions the wisdom of
this trip. The plan had spawned from a confluence of lucky
coincidence: Roxanne's day camp was closed half the week
because of a Jewish holiday, an advertisement for the fair
appeared in the local paper, and Matt, the man Lydia is dating, had a few days of vacation to use up before the end of the
fiscal year. (Lydia, a comparative linguistics professor, has just
finished a research project, so she has the entire summer free.)
But then, they'd argued—Lydia and Matt—over something
as trivial as song lyrics, and he was then uninvited, though
the hotel room had been reserved, the car fueled, the bags
packed, and Roxanne primed, raring to go to the fair in Kentucky. "Stupid ad didn't mention the fair doesn't open until
five," Lydia says under her breath. Now they'll have to spend
another night in the damp, smoky hotel beside the river.

"Stupid ad," Roxanne echoes. She's at her best in the
morning, Lydia's noticed. The little girl's agreeable personality
early in the day betrays no hint of her intractable, mercurial,
and at times, demonic afternoon self.

"Hey," says Lydia, as she gathers the napkins, plate, and
empty juice bottle, "want to have a look at those pictures over
there?"

They examine the trophies first—Roxanne calls them
"trophy-ohs"—tall and ornate, but tarnished and dust-
furred—before moving onto the grinning ceramic pigs. Then,
they stand before the wall of photos: row upon row of grim

men and women fixed in poses of stoicism and industry, their faces chiseled, Lydia supposes, by hardscrabble Appalachian living.

"Him, him, her, and him," Roxanne says, putting a smudgy fingertip to the glass.

"Don't touch."

"Her, him, him, and him," she continues, obediently pointing from a distance now, "him and him and him, too."

"What?" Lydia asks. "What about them?"

"Them, too." She waves a hand at another photo, a group shot. "All of them, every one of them, *dead*, right, Auntie? *All* dead."

"I suppose so." Lydia reads the dates under the frames. If the people in the pictures Roxanne'd pointed out had lived, they'd be well over a hundred years old.

Roxanne moves along the wall, straining to stand on her tiptoes, jabbing a finger at people in the photos she passes. "Dead and dead and dead and *dead!*"

The old men near the window raise their heads and lift their collective gaze, as though the child has called them to attention.

The River Heritage Museum is the first tourist place to open. Just after ten, Lydia pulls open the heavy door, grateful for the air-conditioned gust that whooshes over them. She digs a wilted bill from her pocket to pay the sharp-featured woman at the register. "Two please—one child."

The woman, wearing a badge that identifies her as a docent, peers at them over her glasses, likely curious about the relationship between the fair-skinned Lydia and the biracial child. "Your momma and you are going have a great old time at this museum," she says, her voice a twanging nasal drawl.

"*She's* not my momma," Roxanne says, dimples deepening. "My momma got put in jail. *She's* my auntie."

The docent looks startled. "Well, then, you and your auntie will sure enjoy this museum." She goes on to explain to Lydia that Roxanne can press buttons at various installations to summon steamboat music and taped narration and trigger mechanized movement from the displays.

Warily, Lydia and Roxanne approach the first exhibit: a model steamboat encased in glass. Roxanne depresses a button near the glass and the paddle blades churn, a flashing red lamp revolves above the bow. Lydia pushes another button, and the music starts up. Roxanne skips into a nimble jig, and Lydia takes her hand, joins her. Just as she's twirling the little girl, a redheaded man, carrying a plunger and wearing a disgusted look on his face, steps into the room. He's dressed in an orange jumpsuit bearing stenciled block letters across the back: *Property of Kentucky State Penitentiary.* Without a word, he passes the dancing pair on his way toward the back.

Lydia leads Roxanne into a side-room exhibit. Together they stand in the dark staring at what appears to be an extraordinarily thick tabletop that is tilted toward them. Roxanne punches a button on the railing separating them from the table top. Thunder rumbles and flashes of light illuminate the display—a relief map of the river area. A tape-recorded narrator warns about the river's strength and fury: *the power to sustain life and ... to destroy it!* Water sprays onto the map from unseen ceiling jets, slicking the model riverbanks before they fill and then spill over, dripping noisily into a drain below. Another thunderclap reverberates, and Lydia realizes that she and Roxanne are holding hands, the child's grip so fierce that Lydia's fingertips grow chilled and numb.

By the time they head back to the hotel, Lydia's head swims from the intense heat, and her stomach rocks queasily. The optical effect of mural sections along the river wall contributes to this touch of seasickness, the scenes scrolling out, expanding with each step she takes, and then winding away like a slowly drawn curtain. Roxanne shields her head with her brown arms as she pauses before images of horse-drawn carriages, women in long skirts, bare-chested natives gutting a doe. The past must seem a distant planet to her, Lydia thinks, these strangely garbed figures, with their out-dated contraptions and tools, as alien and incomprehensible as extraterrestrials. "Who's that?" Roxanne lilts her chin at a flabby-faced man in a black suit painted on the penultimate panel.

"That's Alben Barkley," Lydia says, reading the legend below the mural. "Served under Harry S. Truman as vice president and was known as the 'Veep.'" The muralist has rendered this favorite son as a humorless sort, his eyes narrowed and lips compressed in distaste.

"Veep?" Roxanne says. "What's a 'veep'?"

"It's short for vice president. Says here, 'he coined the term 'New Deal' and assisted FDR in reform of social—'"

"I'm thirsty and hot."

"We're almost there." Lydia's mouth is also dry. She peeks around the wall that ends just before the hotel's vast parking lot and looks out to the green-gray river for relief. The coal barge that blocked their view that morning has inched away from the hotel, so that now it's about to draw up alongside the river wall. It would drive her insane to travel on such a lumbering vessel, but the crew members in their orange life vests had waved in a jaunty, carefree way passing them earlier that morning, as if they were cruising by on a yacht. "We'll have lunch in the hotel, and we can drink whatever we want."

Except a *real* drink, she thinks, which the family restaurant won't serve. She craves an icy mug of beer, nothing better for settling her stomach.

"But I'm thirsty *now*." Roxanne's voice ratchets up a decibel or two.

"Let's get moving then." Lydia reaches for her hand, but Roxanne jerks free.

"I *said* I'm hot. I can't walk no more!"

Lydia checks her watch—too early for a tantrum. "We're here, the hotel is there." She points at the building shimmering in the distance, and she wonders at the delusional optimism that prompted contractors to pave the equivalent of a football field for hotel parking. "What do you want me to do?"

"Just go get me a drink, some lemonade or ice cream." Roxanne's dark face is shiny with perspiration, but her full lips are moist and her eyes clear—no signs of dehydration or sunstroke.

"I can't do that. I can't leave you here while I get you a drink." Lydia hates to scare the little girl, but the steamy heat is a bit much for her, too. "What if someone came along and tried to take you?"

Roxanne shakes her head. "Nah-*ah*, nobody won't take me."

She's probably right. It's much too hot for kidnapping. "Come on, I'm not leaving you, so let's go. You can drink all you want at the hotel. Plus, it's cool there. And the longer we stay out here, the hotter it'll get."

"I can't walk no more." Roxanne folds her arms over her chest. At an impasse, they stand, sniffing the warm fishy breath of the river and glaring now at the last panel, the muralist's representation of the 1937 flood—the pastel blue water submerging light posts, storefronts, treetops. Lydia wipes her brow, counts under her breath. Somehow the barge has chugged past them, heading up, or down, river at a good clip now.

"Carry me," Roxanne says. In the several weeks Lydia's kept her, the girl has filled out. She often eats more than Lydia, and the rigors of the day camp that offers swimming twice daily and sports activities in between have added muscle mass to her large-boned frame. Last doctor visit, a few weeks ago, she weighed fifty-six pounds, a lot for a preschooler, but she's tall, a head taller than the next tallest child in her age-group at the camp. "I can't go no more. I can't take another step."

Just the idea of lugging Roxanne—half Lydia's own body weight—to the hotel in this heat causes the blood to hammer in Lydia's ears. "If you're too weak to walk, oh, well, I guess we can't go swimming later," she says in a mock-patient voice. "Too bad about that."

Roxanne screws up her face and emits a high keening howl that rends the torpid riverbank like a siren's wail. Lydia panics, fearing some well-meaning person will overhear this and report her as a child abuser. She hefts the girl onto her hip. If she favors the side bearing Roxanne's weight, maybe she can limp most of the distance to the hotel.

As the hotel's red awning draws into sight, Roxanne's weeping subsides into hiccoughs. Finally, she grows silent and then struggles to get free. "*Stop*, let me down." Roxanne scrambles out of Lydia's arms and races to pick up a stone, a smooth brown oval streaked with a pale watermark. "Here." She thrusts it at Lydia. "This is for you," she says sweetly. "I picked it out just for you."

Lydia raises an eyebrow, but she holds the stone to the sun, admiring its shape and deep cocoa color. "This stone is perfect." She drops it into the pocket that holds five others, a greenish penny, and a ragweed bloom. Lydia draws the line at feathers, the nasty, germy things. "I have enough stones for now," she says when she notices Roxanne spying a glinting chunk of granite near a beer bottle. "*Plenty* of stones, in fact."

"I think you need one more," Roxanne says.

"Well, maybe *that* one." Lydia indicates a small bit of quartz near the door to the lobby. "That white one and that's it."

At the buffet counter in the dim hotel restaurant, Lydia probes a piece of fried chicken with the serving tongs, producing a hollow rapping sound. "Why, that's petrified."

"What's petrified?" Roxanne asks.

"Really old wood, so old it turns to stone," Lydia says absently. "It also means being scared, super-duper scared." She passes on the chicken for the macaroni and cheese—burnt around the edges of the pan, but presumably chewable—and butter-drenched green beans. "We've got to find somewhere else to eat."

Roxanne slides her tray along the counter. Hoisted on tiptoes, she points out macaroni and cheese, green beans, and something called "sweet potato soufflé" for Lydia to scoop onto her plate.

"Just take what you can eat, dearie," warns the woman carving the roast beef, when Roxanne pushes forward her tray for a slice.

"Oh, don't worry," Lydia tells her. "She can handle it."

"I got good appetite." Roxanne points at her stomach. "Lots of rooms."

Roxanne, of course, opts to sit as close as possible to the only other diners in the place, a professional group, suit-wearing men and women in the middle of a luncheon meeting. While Roxanne tucks into her food, Lydia listens in, soon surmising they are lawyers discussing casework. One of them, an attractive fair-haired man catches Lydia's eye and smiles. After this, she steals glances at him when he's not looking. Despite his ruddy face and pushed-in nose, he strikes her as gilt-edged, even glittery, from his silvery blond hair and his shiny yellow tie to his watchband and his sand-colored loafers. If she had been in the restaurant by herself, she would wait out their meeting and contrive a reason to speak to him. Maybe they would make plans to meet for a drink later.

"Pass me the honey," Roxanne says, but reaches across the table to help herself.

"Please don't pour that on your meat."

"Why not? It's good."

"*Don't.*"

"We handle a lot of methamphetamine cases," the blond man is saying to his companions, and Lydia pricks up her ears. She freezes, her forkful of limp green beans suspended between her plate and her mouth. He shakes his gilded head. "You see a meth user and you know you're looking at a seven-year death sentence."

"Auntie, what's wrong?" Roxanne asks. "What happened?"

"Nothing, eat your food." Lydia drops the fork, pushes her plate away, wishing she could order a vodka and tonic at this family-style restaurant.

As luck has it, Lydia encounters the good-looking lawyer, the golden boy, as she's come to think of him, again in the elevator. After settling Roxanne down for a nap, she takes her swimsuit and Roxanne's to the guest laundry to tumble in the dryer. Though they hung in the bathroom all night to dry, both suits are still clammy and smell, like everything else in their room, of mildew and ashtrays, though Lydia doesn't smoke.

"Hi, there," he says. "Going up?"

"Fourth floor."

"Okey-dokey." He grins, pushes the button. Lydia likes his voice, a low rumble that is both warm and sexy.

"I couldn't help overhearing you," Lydia says. "I'm sorry I was eavesdropping at lunch, and you said something about a seven-year death sentence."

"Yeah, meth addiction, that's what it amounts to." He looks her up and down, no doubt sizing her up against his clients, checking for symptoms of drug abuse. "Why?"

"Someone I know—a relative." Her face hot, Lydia regrets going on this way, except, of course, that she doesn't want him to think *she's* the addict, and because she needs to know if what he's said is true. "Can't some of them *kick* this thing, go into detox or whatever and quit the habit? I mean, a few do, don't they?"

"I never knew one who did. Not one."

The elevator chimes at the fourth floor and the shiny doors slide apart, but Lydia stands rooted. "I thought at first, she was on a diet. She lost a lot of weight. She looked great, you know, had all this energy."

"At first, you really can't tell a thing," he says and holds the doors open, "until the sores appear and the troubles start."

Lydia remembers now the nests of dark red pimples. "She was arrested a few months ago, she and her boyfriend. They had a lab in their garage."

"Do they need representation?" The lawyer fishes a card from his breast pocket.

Lydia shakes her head, steps out of the elevator. "I'm from Tennessee, and she's in Georgia. She has court-appointed counsel."

He catches her hand, presses the card into it. "Keep it. I know some lawyers in Nashville, good ones." He shrugs, winks at her. "Who knows? It might come in handy."

I can't do this, Lydia tells herself. There's no way. A frigid
swell of water slaps her thighs in the wake of Roxanne's dive.
The girl's dark head surfaces, her wiry hair finally as smooth
as a seal's coat. "Come on, jump in. You won't feel the cold."
   "I swam yesterday, remember?" she says. Today, the icy
water feels oily, viscous from the residue of sunscreen, she
imagines, and perspiration, and who knows what else. And
that halved sphere floating toward her, surely not a grapefruit
rind!
   "That's just a little old Nerf ball somebody cut in two," Roxanne tells her, again reading her thoughts. "It won't hurt you."
   "I'm not really a pool person." Lydia mounts the ladder.
Her swimming repertoire is limited to one stroke: a choppy
dog paddle. Plus, she dislikes the water, fears having it over
her head, preventing her from breathing. No, she's not a pool
person, not an outdoorsy type, either, and except for managing
her students and attracting the men she likes to pick up, she's
not much of a people person or even a pet person, for that
matter. And she's definitely not what anyone would call a
kid person.
   Roxanne drenches Lydia with a full-body splash that
spins her off balance in surprise. She slips from the aluminum
ladder and falls deep into the water before clawing and kicking her way to the surface, sputtering. "Why, you *little*—"
   But Roxanne has slithered away, darting underwater like
an eel. Her head pops up when she reaches the side of the
pool. She wags from side to side, taunting. "You ca-an't catch
me. You ca-*an't* catch me."
   "Got that right," Lydia says, holding again to the ladder.
No way can she keep up with Roxanne, who swims so well
she races with the seven-year-olds at camp. Lydia knocks the
water out of her ears, climbs the next rung.

"Where are you going?" Roxanne calls, her voice bouncing off the tiled walls. "Don't go, please don't go. I don't like to swim alone." In truth, the girl doesn't like to do anything alone; she's a pool person and a people person. "Come on, play with me. I promise I won't splash you. I *promise* I'll be good. Please don't leave!" Her voice rises with panic, and Lydia relents, releasing the ladder, tumbling backwards into the water. She forces herself to relax into it, and after sinking momentarily, she is buoyed up. "What are we going to play? What can we play that I can keep up, the way I swim?"

Roxanne wrinkles her sleek forehead. "I know," she says. "Let's play flood."

"Flood?"

"Like this." The little girl stops treading water and descends upright into the greenish water. Then she bobs to the surface and says, "Try it."

"I don't know if I'm comfortable…"

Roxanne inhales deeply and disappears beneath the surface once more. When she emerges, she grins. "There's cars under there, Auntie, and buildings, and trees. You got to look!"

Lydia takes a deep breath and falls stone-like to the bottom of the pool. Water stops her ears, fills her nostrils, and she wills herself not to panic. The chlorine stings her eyes. Tangled on the grate over the drain is a child-sized pair of purple goggles. Gently, the water lofts her back to the surface. "You'll never guess who I saw down there."

"Who?" Roxanne asks.

"Alben, Alben Barkley. He's sitting near the drain, picking on a banjo."

"*Nah*-ah, let me see," and she goes under again.

And this is how they spend the afternoon in Paducah: in the pool, in the flood.

Lydia compares this trip to Paducah to a form of shock therapy—
the unbearable midday heat sharply contrasted with the icy
green pool, and now, here at the fair, she feels as though she
and Roxanne are like body lice, competing with hundreds of
others for breathable air, deep in a foul, sweat-drenched armpit, a *smoker's* armpit; everyone over twelve in Paducah seems
to have a cigarette dangling from his or her lips.

She buys just the half sheet of tickets, so Roxanne can
board a few rides, the safe rides, only those run by people who
look sober and sane. (At a parking lot carnival a few weeks
ago, she let Roxanne ride a child's Ferris wheel operated by
a shoeless teenager who, after starting up the machinery,
slipped into a trance, while the contraption spun faster and
faster without stopping until Lydia and another child's mother
yelled in his face to make him set the brake.) But before
advancing on the rides, Roxanne wants to "play the games."
Lydia's been dreading this: The child has a wickedly powerful arm and a sharp eye. In this soupy heat, she's not keen on
hauling around the stuffed animals Roxanne is sure to win.
Lydia's former guestroom is already crammed with enough of
this garish junk. Lydia glances skyward. The air is so dense
and ion-charged, she expects a downpour to send them racing for the car. But the sky is motionless; the brooding clouds
full, white, and still.

Nearby, the fellow manning the milk-jug pyramids asks
if Roxanne might want to take a practice throw or two. Lydia
shakes her head—not necessary. The little girl topples all
three pyramids, one after the other, and selects a six-foot
stuffed snake as her prize. At the dart booth, Roxanne punc-
tures five balloons in a row, winning a goldfish doll as big as
a calf. Next, she brings the sledge-hammer down so hard on

the child-sized scale that the weighted ball sticks to the bell, won't come down. "I never seen anything like this," says the heavy woman who hands over a huge, inflated plastic parrot.

"Don't you have anything smaller?" Lydia asks. By now, she can't see much over the prizes in her arms. The car is too deep in the field parking lot for her to dash over and deposit these in the trunk.

"I *like* the parrot," Roxanne says in her whiny voice.

"All right." Lydia hasn't a free hand to mop the perspiration trickling between her breasts like a trail of insects. "But no more games, got that? Ride the damn rides."

After the rides, they come to a showdown in front of the ticket booth. Roxanne wants both another batch of tickets for more rides and to be carried to the car because, again, she's worn out, too hot and too tired to take another step. Lydia threatens—in the cool voice she reserves for students who have crossed the line—to leave all the prizes behind, "right here in the dust," if she must, again, lug Roxanne any distance. Roxanne tearfully claims to have won the prizes, "every one of them, just for you." Compromise is reached, though, when they agree to not to leave directly, but to walk, each on her own two feet, over to the grandstands to watch the dirt-bike racing on their way out of the fair.

Though it thrills Roxanne, this kind of racing overwhelms Lydia. The explosive starter pistol and the flatulent muffler sounds pain her ears. She sits on the hard edge of the bleacher, her hand over her mouth, as the three-wheelers shoot around the track. "I can't take this," she says. She feels like everyone's mother—like all those boys on those deadly machines are hers, the way Roxanne is hers. "I can't do this."

"Do what?" Roxanne asks. "You don't have to *do* anything, just watch."

The bikes tip precariously rounding the track, and these

boys are far too young. She's never had feelings like this for strangers. It's as if living with Roxanne has torn off a layer of her skin, exposing a raw subdermal stratum of self, tender and vulnerable as an open wound. A boy sailing around the curve loses his balance in a dusty swirl. She looks away, holds her breath.

Metal scrapes metal seconds before a plosive boom thunders from the track. Spectators gasp, and Lydia shields her eyes.

"He fell off," Roxanne says softly. "I saw him. Then the bike hit that wall."

Lydia longs to dart across the track with the pit crews, to trail after the ambulance now bumping over the dirt ruts toward the wreck. She feels what his mother must feel—shock, confusion, the dread welling like flood waters. That she's not the boy's mother brings no relief. How can she ever have thought this a good compromise, a fine plan for getting Roxanne to the car? She scans the bleachers; of course, Roxanne is the only young child here. Stupid, so stupid, she tells herself, *why* don't I know any better?

Squad cars are now plowing across the track, and the next batch of racers has dismounted and taken off their helmets. They stand about talking to one another and scratching their heads. Lydia gathers up the prizes and manages a free hand to grab Roxanne's. Together they trudge toward the car, Lydia talking the whole way about accidents, mistakes, and being careful, as well as learning to be better, trying to be better. Roxanne says nothing, until she's in her car seat in back and after stopping at a package store, Lydia pulls onto an unfamiliar street, saying, "Why did I do that? I swear I don't know what I'm doing."

And Roxanne tells her, "This is the right way. You *do* know what you're doing."

That night, after Roxanne has been tucked into the double
bed that she's claimed as hers for the trip and has finally
fallen asleep, Lydia has her drink: a large gin mixed with
clouded tap water in one of the hotel's plastic cups. She
nibbles Cheetos from the family-sized bag she bought
Roxanne at the package store for her "treat," while sipping
her drink in the darkened room. Her fingertips grow neon
orange with the salty pollen, and she thinks she ought to have
bought a more nutritious snack for the child, something that
didn't even occur to her until now. She tosses the handful
she's just plucked back into the bag and curls it shut.

Once Roxanne is sleeping deeply, Lydia will hazard flicking on a light, and perhaps the television with the sound
turned low. She leans over the child, listening to her regular
breathing. In the early weeks, when Roxanne first came to
stay with Lydia, she'd thrashed about at night, groaning and
grinding her teeth so noisily that she woke Lydia in the next
room. Those nights, she would enter the guestroom and sit at
the side of the daybed, stroking the child's wooly hair until
she settled into deep sleep. Now, though she snores, Roxanne
sleeps soundly.

Lydia pulls the sheet over the girl's bare shoulder, thinking how odd it is that Roxanne never asks for her mother
and never wonders aloud when she's going home. Surely, most
children aren't this strange. But how complicated it is to handle a child, any child—the tug and pull of relentless negotia-
tion. How wearing and limiting it is, how hobbling, and when
not so tormenting, how stultifying and mundane. Somehow
Lydia's sensed this all along, and she's never wanted a child.
One of her girlfriends has just traveled to China—clear to
China!—to adopt a baby, and another has spent a fortune
on fertility treatments. To her, this is as incomprehensible as

pulling strings to get into prison, angling for an eighteen-year-to-life sentence.

Lydia pours herself another drink and rummages in her purse for her cell phone. She'll call Matt, talk to him about this. Of course, she'll have to apologize first. After she checked her E-mail on her laptop during Roxanne's nap, she'd looked up the song lyrics, and he had been right. Besides, she had been the one to make a big deal out of it.

He picks up after two rings. "'Lo."

Lydia can hear syncopated cheering and horns blaring in the background. She pictures Matt stretched out on his sofa watching a basketball game, a beer on the coffee table before him, as he reaches for the phone.

"Hey, it's me." Her voice is soft, supplicating. "Look, I'm sorry. You were right. It was a stupid fight, my fault really."

He's silent, maybe pausing for a free throw, but then he sighs, says, "It's okay. You're going through a lot. I know that."

When the syncopated roar of the crowd and applause don't resume, Lydia's grateful that he's muted the set. She takes her drink and phone into the bathroom, closes the door. "I don't think I can do this, Matt." Her throat aches saying it. "I'm not patient with her. I don't know anything about raising a child."

"Look, I know it's tough."

"I'm thinking I should find her permanent foster care when we get back," she says. "I can't count on Shirley. She might never be able to take Roxanne back. Maybe my aunt can take her." Lydia considers Shirley's mother, Ida, who lives in a trailer park in Barstow, California. "I can call her, fly Roxanne out there in a few weeks."

"Is that what you want to do?"

"Yes," she says, and then shakes her head. "No. I don't

know. *Anybody's* got to be better for her than I am." She downs her drink.

"Why do you send her to that pricey camp? Why send her there when Parks and Rec has some pretty cheap programs?"

"It's the swimming. She loves swimming. They swim twice a day." Lydia rolls her eyes. Matt knows well that Lydia chose the day camp at the Jewish Community Center for the two pools—indoor and outdoor—so Roxanne can swim in any weather. This is so obvious that she shouldn't have to say it.

"You do it for her," Matt tells her. "You are calling me from where?"

Lydia scans the humid cubicle—the clouded mirror, the mold-peppered shower tiles, the drippy swimsuits hanging from the curtain rod as forlornly as if they'd been executed. "Paducah."

"Ah, beautiful Paducah—you have business there?"

"You know why we're here." Lydia hates when he adopts this riddling savant persona with her. He's so boringly patient and right that she's tempted to break up with him all over again. "We came for the fair."

"For *her*."

"Yeah, but—"

"You do these things for her," he says. "Do you think anyone else who can take her will do what you do for her?"

Lydia remembers visiting her aunt last summer. Ida was wearing a white cotton housecoat printed with cherries, her vein-scribbled legs propped on an ottoman as she stared at *The Young and the Restless*. She could barely lift her eyes from the screen to answer Lydia's polite inquiries about her diabetes and arthritic knee. Lydia flashes on an image of Shirley, the last time she saw her, behind a chicken-wired glass window, speaking into a black telephone.

"Do you?" Matt asks again.

"That doesn't mean that I *have* to keep her."

"No," he says. "I suppose it doesn't." Noises from the basketball game blare in the background, and he says she should call him when they get back in town.

The next morning, Lydia experiences a powerful sense of déjà vu, as once more they hike across the parking lot toward the river walk. Roxanne, again in good form, skips ahead, finding stones and dandelion heads and a rusted toy car to present as tokens of affection. These are accepted by Lydia like ballast, freighting her with guilt, unworthiness, and grief. Lydia's queasiness also has returned, this time due to the gin and the Cheetos and the sleepless night. At the sight of her bloated face and puffy eyes in the bathroom mirror that morning, she'd murmured, "Alben Barkley, I presume."

But the robust Roxanne could be photographed for the cover of *Health and Fitness* magazine. Her dark legs are strong, well-muscled as she skips ahead and trots back to Lydia bearing found treasures. The girl is the forerunner of a new physical type for Lydia's family, which is comprised of gaunt, desiccated-looking men and pale, pillowy women—the lot of them short as jockeys. (Lydia, herself, is a compromise between these types, trim and curvy now, but likely headed toward plush flabbiness as she ages.) At a family reunion picnic, Roxanne would be a thoroughbred colt grazing among stick-like reeds and fat, waxy mushrooms. Why, she could eat them all up.

Roxanne jogs over, offering a dandelion puff. "Why are you such a slow pope?"

"For a pope, I'd say I'm moving pretty fast," she says, and Roxanne dashes off.

She's a bright girl, too, Lydia thinks, not really knowing what other four-year-olds are like. But Roxanne has
an uncanny ability to read people, or at least Lydia, and to
anticipate her thoughts before she speaks them. Roxanne also
has a sharp sense of direction, and she's observant and shrewd.
Yes, Lydia tells herself, the kid knows which side her bread is
buttered on. Roxanne would do fine for herself wherever she
went. Isn't she thriving now under Lydia's uncertain, inexpert
care?

"Close your eyes." Roxanne reappears, hands behind her
back and dancing on one foot, then the other. "I got something
really good here."

Lydia screws her eyes shut, smiling. "What is it?"

"Hold out your hands."

Lydia obeys, and a stiff, fuzzy object settles in the bowl
of her palms. *Not feathers!* She opens her eyes. "Ugh! What is
this?" A rigor-hardened mess of pale down, leathery claws, and
beak tumbles from her hands.

"Don't drop him."

"It's *dead*, a dead chick! Why would you *touch* such a
thing?" Lydia wishes she'd had the presence of mind to heave
it into the river. It glares up at them from the asphalt now, one
beady, reptilian eye wide with disdain.

"Can't we take it to the doctor?"

"Are you out of your mind?" Lydia shakes her tingling
hands, searching about for something other than the murky
river in which to plunge them. "It's dead."

The girl swoops for the bird, but Lydia catches her arm,
reels Roxanne—struggling, kicking, pinching, yowling now
like a feral cat, and trying to bite—into her arms. "Stop it," she
says. "Just stop!" She remembers a public restroom at the edge
of the next parking lot, just past the Farmer's Market. She
tightens her grip on the flailing girl and lumbers for it.

When she catches her breath in the ladies' room, Lydia says, "There are some things we just can't help."

Roxanne, sitting on a counter near the sink and drumming her heels against its cabinet, glowers at her. "You don't love me."

Lydia pumps the soap dispenser in a frenzied way, but only hollow puffs issue from it, so she digs a fingernail for dried soap from the spigot. "I don't always like what you do." This sounds so weak, such an obvious evasion that she follows it up hastily with something she remembers reading in one of those childcare books she's checked out from the library. "But that doesn't mean I don't love you."

"*Do* you love me?" Roxanne asks, cutting to the chase.

"What do you think?" Lydia works a feeble lather into her palms; the hot water is no more than tepid. "You tell me."

Calmer now, they stroll along the commemorative bricks on the way to the National Quilt Museum after again visiting the bakery. Roxanne insists Lydia read the inscriptions on the terra-cotta rectangles, many of these scored with couples' names and sentimental declarations: *My Forever Love, The Power of Love, To God's Glory, Little Buddies, How Good to Share the Path with You, I Love You, Dearest One...* Lydia mouths these in a scornful way. She can't help feeling this kind of emotion is too facile and cheap—there's no struggle reflected here. It's a lie to say only half of what's true.

"Why do they mark the bricks like this?" Roxanne asks.

Lydia shakes her head. "No idea."

"Is it like making a wish?"

"You know, maybe that's it."

As Roxanne dawdles over the bricks, examining them and sounding out the letters she recognizes, Lydia pulls her cell phone from her purse, flips it on to check for messages. One missed call—*Shirley*. She draws in a sharp breath. *Shirley's home?* She doesn't mention this to Roxanne, who's trying to read the inscriptions by herself. The phone chimes in Lydia's hand, jolting her like a live wire. She's tempted to shut it off, disconnect the call, but Roxanne has lifted her eyes from the bricks, watching her now.

"Yes?" she says into the mouthpiece.

"Hey, Lydia, it's Shirley. Can you believe it? They let us out on a whaddayacallit, a technicality. The cops had the *wrong* address on the warrant, so it was an illegal search kind of thing." Shirley's rapid-fire babbling leaves no opening for Lydia to make any reply. "Yeah, it was like unbelievable, like some kind of *movie* or crazy dream or something. Anyway, you got my baby, right? Tell her kiss-kiss-kiss. I'm coming to get her as soon as I can. But now, like, my mama had a stroke, so I got to fly to Barstow, take care of her. Problem is—no money. I hate to ask, but you know how it is, family, and all that. I got to go see her. It was a bad accident. She hit a stop sign. I mean *ran* a stop sign, hit a truck—"

Lydia turns her back on Roxanne, so she won't hear. "You said she had a stroke."

"Oh, yeah, a stroke, too—she's in bad shape, on a respirator. I need like three hundred—what?" Muffled voices chatter in the background. "I need to borrow *five* hundred dollars. Hate to ask."

While Shirley natters on about being out of work, no money, even for groceries, and bills piling up, Lydia peers into a darkened thrift store across the street, the mannequins arranged like dancers frozen mid-step in a waltz. So, she thinks, this is the way Shirley wants it to go—Lydia keeps Roxanne as long as she sends money. And what happens when Lydia runs out of money? What's to keep Shirley from snatching Roxanne then and placing her with the next highest bidder?

As long as her cousin correctly perceives the little girl is her best resource, Lydia knows she will exploit her.

"Listen," Lydia says, interrupting Shirley, who is now complaining about an eye infection she contracted in jail and discussing the possibility of suing the county. "I don't have money. I just don't have it. The best I can do is to take care of Roxanne for you until you're on your feet. It's not easy for me, but I'll help out as long as I can." She doesn't want to push it, but can't resist adding, "If you want to come get her, fine, just—"

"I miss her so! But right now, I can't. I just absolutely can't. Tell her kiss-kiss-kiss. I got to go now. I'll call you later," Shirley says, breathlessly, no doubt anxious to make her next begging call.

Lydia clicks the phone shut, hoping Roxanne won't ask who called. But the girl is bent over a brick, sounding out syllables. "To g-g-get her...for...for—what's that?"

Lydia peers down. "Ever," she reads.

"To get her for *ever?*" Roxanne narrows her eyes.

"It's *together forever.* That's what it says. Come on now. Don't you want to see those quilts?" Lydia's relieved when the bricks give over to the street. She takes Roxanne's hot, dry hand, and they cross.

The Quilt Museum, when they reach it, is—of course—closed. Their reflection in the smoky glass made it seem, for a moment, as though another woman and child approached them from the inside, meeting them at the main entrance. "I thought that was a little girl and her mom," Roxanne says, pointing at the glass. "But it's just us."

Lydia's struck by how similar their expressions are in the dark glass. They both tighten their jaws in exasperation, and Roxanne knits her brows the way Lydia does when she squints at the posted admission times. The place doesn't open until noon, so they resign themselves to revisiting the River Heritage Museum, the other side of the town square. They march there in silence and seriousness, as if fulfilling orders.

The same woman takes Lydia's money. "Didn't get enough of us yesterday?"

"Nope," Roxanne tells her with a smile.

As she returns the change to her billfold, Lydia rifles for the lawyer's card. She files it near her driver's license. Lydia hopes he wasn't just bragging and he can help her find someone in Nashville because what she needs now is a lawyer, a good one.

She snaps her purse shut. The floorboards groaning beneath their feet, they head directly for the side exhibit with the tabletop relief map. Roxanne takes Lydia's hand, as though this is now part of their ritual, before punching the rail button. Again, the narrator's deep voice describes the river's unpredictable power, its dangerous strength, while Lydia and Roxanne stand together in the cool shadows, holding hands and trembling, waiting for the flood.

Sugar Boots

As he bathes three-year-old Beau, Leo Garza thinks about murder. Not about killing anyone himself, and certainly never harming this solemn toddler in his care. Instead Leo reconsiders his lifelong belief that it is wrong to take another's life, and how he never questioned this until his wife Stella's daughter was incarcerated for killing her husband in late spring. Now, as the facts of the case unfold during the pretrial period—his and Stella's worst suspicions about the deceased confirmed and Leo spending several weeks looking after Stella's two grandchildren—he wonders if homicide hasn't gotten something of a bad rap. Clearly, murdering a person betrays a limitation of options, if not lack of imagination. It should *always* be a last resort. But hadn't Micki reached this stage, even gone well beyond it? Divorce could never keep her safe. The memory of her broken face, glimpsed through the glass partition in the prison visiting area, still makes Leo wince, and he wonders if he has other fundamental convictions that are this shakable. Surely, they've never been tested in this way before.

Leo hands Beau a yellow plastic duck, which the child
submerges in the bathwater until the aperture under its belly ceases
bubbling and the water-logged toy bumps along the bottom
of the tub. Beau doesn't talk much, never asks for "mama," or
"dada," or food, for that matter. Instead he whispers, emitting
occasional streams of gibberish punctuated by barely discernible phrases: *Uh-oh, it's the cops. Run. Run!* But mostly, he is
wordless, as he is now in the aftermath of drowning Ducky.
His six-year-old sister Cassandra, on the other hand, rarely
ceases speaking, even in her sleep. Leo overhears her now,
talking for her Barbie dolls in the next room, where she is
supposed to be drying and dressing herself. "No, you wear
that shiny black skirt, and I'll put on these shorts. Ken likes
me to wear shorts because we're going to a barbecue. Oh,
hullo, Ken, I was just saying you like my shorts…"

Leo notices Beau's puckered fingertips and surreptitiously pulls out the plug. The end of bath time inevitably
provokes tantrums. And sure enough, once Beau hears the
water gurgling, he arches his back, flails his pudgy arms, and
wails. Leo catches his head before he crashes into the tiled
wall, but the boy slides underwater, submerging himself in the
several inches that remain in the tub. Horrified, Leo strains
his back hauling the cumbrous, sopping child out. The close
steamy bathroom reverberates with Beau's cries, and Cassandra,
blending her raised voice to create a cacophony certain to
cause permanent damage to Leo's hearing, yells, "Sugar Boots
is throwing up again!"

"Damn it," Leo says under his breath. He wraps Beau in
a Bugs Bunny towel, swaddling him to confine the flailing.
"I'm coming," he calls over his shoulder. The cat, an orange
tabby with four white paws, his "sugar boots," has vomited at
least once a day, sometimes twice, since Micki's children have
moved in with them.

Cassandra appears in the doorway, still naked, her dark eyes avid, eager to impart details of the cat's wrongdoing, and her black hair rising in a crazy nimbus above her head. (Leo will have to brush and braid it fast, before it dries and becomes too wiry to plait.) "There's rubber bands in his throw-up," she says. "Pieces of rubber bands."

Leo rolls his eyes. He sits on the toilet lid, holding the sobbing Beau and toweling his soft brown curls dry. The stupid cat is addicted to rubber bands, his favorite emetic. But in a pinch, he'll substitute any indigestible rubbery material. They have to keep the bathroom doors shut to prevent him from chewing the shower mat.

Before the children arrived, Leo never minded the cat. In fact, he was fond of the languorous tom, whose sole responsibility was to lie in the sunlight streaming from the windows, flicking his rust-colored tail. Stella was the one annoyed by Sugar Boots' indolence. "He never *does* anything," she'd say. "He just sits around, and we have to do everything for him." By "we," Stella meant Leo, of course. Early on, Leo assumed responsibility for Sugar Boots, feeding him and cleaning his litter daily. Once a week, he would brush the cat's fur, swab his pinkish ears with cotton balls, and even dislodge litter gravel from the grooves in his claws with disposable dental picks.

If Stella had her way, the cat would roam freely outdoors, scavenging birds and rodents. But Leo—worried about coyotes, feral dogs, and cars on their busy street near the Hollywood Hills—insisted they have Sugar Boots neutered and kept indoors. He buys an expensive brand of cat food, guaranteed to dissolve hairballs and to keep the cat's urinary tract healthy, and once a year, Leo crates the cat and drives him to the vet to have his sharp little teeth cleaned. The cat was given to them by Stella's agent, Martin, who had gotten her hired as

head writer on *The Benjamins,* a situation comedy on cable
about a gay couple sharing the same first name. So, before the
children came, he catered to the cat like a small furry prince,
illogically hoping Martin would someday notice this and be
sufficiently impressed to represent Leo in his acting career.

But now that the children live with them, Leo can't bear
the cat, that lazy bulimic bastard, the ingrate. On top of feeding,
bathing, and entertaining Cassie and Beau, caring for Sugar
Boots feels like a last straw. Sensing this, the cat perversely
clamors for Leo's attention when he is most harassed. Even
at the best of times, these days the tabby is too much for Leo.
When he drops to the floor to stack blocks with Beau or play
a board game with Cassie, Sugar Boots thrusts himself into
the middle of things, overturning blocks and batting at game
pieces while purring insistently. Leo shoves him away, resist-
ing the temptation to smack his pushy little head. Now, Stella
says, "Nice kitty, nice, nice," as she strokes Sugar Boots, teaching the children to treat pets with kindness.

Hyperventilating, Beau slips free. He streaks from the
bathroom and nearly topples Cassie. In a flash, the boy's shiny
brown buttocks disappear into the hallway. Leo chases
after him, stepping into a pool of warm vomit just before he
rounds the corner into the living room. The telephone rings,
and Cassie cries, "I'll get it!"

"No!" It could be news of a callback, though Leo hasn't
auditioned for anything in several weeks, not since he started
looking after Cassie and Beau. At least the children have
spared him that intermittent humiliation. Leo hobbles
toward the phone, balancing on the heel of the befouled foot
so as not to stain the living-room carpet, a thick handsome
Berber. He lifts the receiver. "Hello."

"Hey, babe, it's Marty. Is Stella there?" Stella's agent has
the habit of calling people whose names aren't important

enough for him to remember "babe."

Leo smiles broadly, baring his newly bleached teeth as if Martin could see him. "No, she's at the studio."

"Really?" Martin says. "I just phoned there, and they told me she called in with a migraine. Her cell's not on."

"Oh, well, maybe—"

"No matter," Martin tells him. "It's nothing, babe. Listen, I can tell it's a little hectic over there, so I'll let you go."

Beau is still howling, though Leo can't see where he's gotten to. Cassie appears at his side and tugs his shirt. "Brother's opening the front door."

"Yeah, I better go," he says into the phone.

"He's getting out. *I'll* stop him." Cassie squares her shoulders and charges off. Sounds of a struggle ensue: slapping noises and more screaming.

"Hey, by the way," Martin says, and Leo holds his breath, hoping hard, as the agent pauses, likely struggling to reel up his name. "How's Sugar Boots doing?"

Leo spies the cat, crouched now at the heart of the Berber. He looks stringy these days and his ginger coat has lost its luster. His languor has been replaced by a persistent edginess. If he were human, the cat would probably take up smoking. Sugar Boots meets his gaze, narrowing his amber eyes as if appraising Leo and likewise preparing to render judgment. After hesitating a moment, the cat retches, spewing a jet of bile between his snowy forepaws. "Great," Leo says, "he's doing just great."

Over the past weeks, Leo's learned there's quite a lot to do with children in Los Angeles. In fact, he and Cassie have become connoisseurs of these venues: the Children's Museum (kind of cool), the La Brea Tar Pits (*bo*-ring), Olvera Street (hot and noisy), the pony and train rides at Griffith Park,

Exposition Park (really great), the Descanso Gardens (good god, *never* again), and so forth. Despite the fact that most of their outings end disastrously, Leo continues to pile the kids into the car day after day in search of the next fun place, as the alternative—confinement at home all day—is too harrowing to consider.

The only son of a conscientious and vigilant mother, Leo's not the kind of caretaker who flips on the television for children while he ignores their presence from another room. Beau's hushed utterances suggest he's been exposed to more than enough TV in his short life, most of it in the form of violent movies and thuggish video games. And though Leo would love nothing more than to work on a show popular enough to be syndicated for daytime broadcast, he's repelled by television before dark. The decadence of the dusty set aglow while the sun is out triggers nausea for Leo, so strongly does he associate it with childhood illness, with lying inert and bilious while a hectoring laugh track blares in the background.

Today, he's driving the children to a play-date with his two sisters and their children at the Granada Hills home of his oldest sister, Beatriz, who has a swimming pool in her backyard. Leo's humming as he unstraps little Beau's child safety seat when they arrive, realizing that he's absurdly looking forward to this get-together, though before the children came to live with him and Stella, Leo invested a good bit of creativity in fabricating excuses so he would not have to see his sisters, even during the holidays. "Their lives are so different from ours," he would tell Stella. Nowadays when either sister invites him to bring the kids over, his breathless response is always, "*When?*"

Beau can't be trusted to walk on his own in an unsecured area, so Leo lugs him in one arm and a duffel bag packed with towels, sunscreen, goggles, and changes of clothing for both children in the other. The late summer morning is unexpectedly fine for Los Angeles. It's breezy and cool—no air quality alerts—and driving across the valley on the 118, Leo could not only make out the foothills, but he could actually discern nubbly brown pleats, the scrub brush, covering them. His step is brisk, even jaunty, as he leads a suddenly shy and speechless (her usual mode for entering social situations involving other children) Cassie up the flagstone walk to the back gate. Leo's proud of himself for not forgetting anything, for his competency in this new role. So long as it is a role, and the acting kicks in, Leo tells himself he can handle just about anything as he reaches to push open the gate.

"Well, he's finally growing some character." His oldest sister's voice resonates above the high-pitched laughter and splashing from the pool and lofts over the tall pine fence with clarity. "I'll say that for him."

"Maybe he'll forget that acting bullshit," Delia, his other sister, puts in. "Did he even *earn* enough to file income taxes last year, or the year before that?"

"I doubt it," Beatriz says. "He's always been spoiled, such a baby. Seriously, didn't *Mamá* have to, like, *die* before he could leave home, before he could get married?"

"And look who he marries."

"*Exactly.*"

"He finds another mamá to take care of him—an abuela, for god's sake."

They both cackle like harpies until Beatriz says, "We better shut up. He'll be here any minute." And their voices are overtaken by shouting, one child complaining and another vigorously voicing denial.

Leo's right hand is still suspended, poised to reach the gate, and frozen in midair. He lowers it now and back pedals a few steps. "I have an idea," he says in a low voice. "Why don't we make cupcakes today?"

"After swimming?" Cassie whispers.

"No, *instead* of swimming." Leo flashes his best smile, the one he used for the latest batch of headshots, a dazzling deep-dimpled grin he's practiced to perfection. (No way does he look thirty-six in those eight-by-tens, let alone anything like a grandparent.)

Beau digs his heels into Leo's ribs as if he is a horse to be spurred onward, and Cassie—wearing a pink swimsuit, oversized plastic sunglasses and an inflated float ring around her middle—gives Leo a look that begins as confused disbelief but quickly sharpens into withering contempt. "You're joking," she says.

"Yeah, I guess I am," Leo says, flatly. "Ha-ha-ha."

"You are not really that funny," Cassie tells him, and she slips past him to push open the gate herself.

"*Get the guns, dog,*" Beau whispers in his ear. "*Get them quick!*"

Now that Leo is a grandparent, a *step*grandfather, he's begun driving like an old man, especially with the children in the backseat. These days, the freeways make him nervous, especially as rush hour approaches—the aggressive drivers, the high speeds, the constant lane-changing and the tailgating fluster him as he tries to deal with the conversations, questions, conflicts, and tears inside the car, so he's tempted to bypass the onramp to the San Diego Freeway and cruise all the way back into Hollywood via Riverside Drive.

As he brakes for a red light, Cassandra asks, "Did you even take the test?"

"What test?"

"The driving test."

"I sure did," Leo tells her. "How else do you think I got my license?"

"You have a *license?*"

"Of course, I do."

A car in back beeps when Leo doesn't stomp on the gas pedal the second the light goes green. People are so impatient these days.

"I would have given you an F-plus," she says.

Leo has no answer for this. Another honking car swoops by, the driver flashing his middle finger as he passes. Leo decides he *will* take Riverside Drive, never mind the twenty or more traffic lights en route and the fact that Beau has dropped off to sleep and all the stopping and starting will surely waken him. Freeway drivers can be far worse, he thinks, than these jerks.

"How come they call you that?" Cassie asks.

"Call me what?"

"Lay-oh-need-us. How come your sisters call you that?"

"That's my full name in Spanish," he tells her, "Léonidas." It's also the middle name of the murderous dictator Trujillo, and Leo despises it. Knowing this, his sisters refuse to call him anything else. Aside from that, the visit wasn't too bad. Beatriz likely guessed he'd overheard their conversation, and to make up for this, she treated him solicitously all afternoon. She even praised his care for the children, observing that Cassie, once gaunt and hollow-eyed, has filled out and that Beau is talking more clearly these days, when the boy hissed, "*Motherfucker!*" in the aftermath of being splashed. Delia, always a bitch, couldn't quite bring herself to be kind to Leo, but at least she didn't pick on Cassie and Beau this time. Whenever his corrosive-tongued sister harps on them, as she usually does during these poolside get-togethers, to pick up their towels or to stop running, he longs to take hold of her face, turn her gaze on the two children, and force her to look, to make her see them the way he does. *Haven't they been through enough already?*

"Are you Spanish?" Cassie asks.

Leo nods. "Dominican."

"Do you speak Spanish?"

"Not that well." Born and raised in the U.S., Leo's Spanish is laughable at best—another source of mockery for his Dominican-born and bilingual sisters.

"Am I Spanish, too?"

"Your grandmother's from Mexico, so yes, you have some Spanish background."

"Can I call you that? Lay-oh-need-us? Instead of Grandpa?"

This is a tough question for Leo, who's embarrassed by the curious stares elicited when Cassie hollers, "*Grandpa,*" to summon him in public. Genocidal dictator versus enfeebled oldster—hard call, so Leo says, "You choose."

She considers this in a silence that stretches into soft snoring, and just as he approaches the familiar turn for Griffith Park, Cassie dozes, oblivious to how close they are to one of her top-rated outing spots. Leo's cell phone buzzes on the passenger seat, and he snatches it up. It's Stella. He's been trying to reach her on and off all day. "Where are you?" he says, his voice low so as not to rouse the children.

"It's Howie," Stella says. "He's been depressed. Dennis broke up with him, just left him for some waiter."

"So?" Leo asks. Howie is another writer on the show, an underling, but also Stella's closest friend for years (no problem getting him a job on *The Benjamins*).

"He talked me into playing hooky today. He seriously needed cheering up." Stella sounds slightly smashed, not

quite slurring her words, but her speech lacks its usual crisp-
ness. "So I took him to visit Micki and—"

"Wait, let me get this straight. You took Howie to the
women's prison *to cheer him up?*" Leo struggles to keep his
voice modulated.

"He's known her since she was a little girl. I thought the
visit might do both of them good."

"And?" Leo hears Cassie stirring now and muttering in
the back. Beau's grumbling, too, gearing into his customary
post-nap crankiness.

"It didn't." Stella's voice wavers, fragmenting. She says
something about "suicide watch" and "really needing a drink,"
but static and silence truncate her speech.

"Take a cab," Leo tells her. "Leave the car and take a cab,
you hear me?"

"I'm losing you," Stella says distinctly before the connection
breaks apart, or the children's voices overtake hers, Leo can't
tell which. He snaps the phone shut.

"I need the bathroom," Cassie says.

"Can you hold it?" Leo asks.

"Um, let me check... *No.*"

An orange-roofed Howard Johnson's looms into sight on
the left, just past a defunct gas station. Leo flicks on the
signal and eases into the turn lane. "Hold it for just two
minutes," he says. "Here's a place you can go."

"I can't hold it no more."

Leo wrenches the wheel and swerves in front of an oncoming garbage truck, slow-moving, but fairly close. He makes the
turn easily. Still the garbage man honks, and his partner holds
up a gloved hand to extend his middle finger. Leo steers up
the drive and swings into the only free space, the one designated for handicapped parking. They will only be a minute. He
yanks up the brake, springs from the driver's seat, and sprints

around the car to release Cassie from her seatbelt.

"Hurry," she says, "hurry, hurry!" She bolts from the car and dances up the cement path and through the glass door, while Leo reaches over to free Beau from his car seat. The boy, too intrigued by this turn of events to indulge in grouchiness, issues an unintelligible stream of whispered phrases.

An elderly man stumping out of the restaurant with an aluminum walker stops to watch Leo, Beau in arms, as he locks up the car. "You don't look handicapped to me," the old fellow says, lifting his chin toward the blue sign. Though it's reached the upper eighties, the man wears a flannel shirt under a khaki windbreaker, and corduroy slacks with a baseball cap. "And I don't see your tag or state-issue plates."

"It's an emergency," Leo says.

"I don't use those spaces myself," the man says, "and I got the plates. I save them for those who are worse off than me." He thumps his walker for emphasis.

"I'll move the car in a minute," Leo tells him, wishing the codger would keep moving and quit blocking the entrance.

"What you ought to do is move it now, son."

"*Whack him,*" whispers Beau, "*Whack him good.*"

"You don't understand," Leo tells both of them.

"Oh, I think I do understand," the old man says. "I understand laziness and lack of consideration real well. I been dealing with it my entire life."

Leo sighs and sidesteps the man, brushing against him as he pulls open the door.

"Think you can push me around?" The man raises his voice so that Leo is sure every diner can hear. "Think you can just push people like me out of the way?"

Inside the restaurant, Leo holds the door closed until he hears the walker bump-rattling off. Curiously, the restaurant doesn't smell of food. There's a trace of coffee in the air, but

Leo can't detect the scent of anything that might be edible. The dining area extends in two directions from the hostess station near the entrance. Both sides contain an identical series of booths with Formica tables. Leo has no idea which direction Cassie took to the ladies' room. The restaurant is crawling with the elderly—no doubt lured by some early-bird dinner special. Several of them mill about the register area waiting to pay. They glare at Leo, their eyes alarmingly magnified by thick lenses.

"What can I do for you?" says the hostess—eighty if she's a day—fixing him with an accusing stare.

Beau mumbles, "*Smoke the mother—*"

Leo cups a hand over the boy's mouth and says, "A little girl, about six, came in here to use the restroom. We're just waiting for her."

"You her daddy?" the hostess asks. She glances from Leo to the toddler in his arms, as if to determine the relationship here as well.

"No," Leo says. "I'm her step-grandfather, actually."

"*Grandfather?*" the hostess repeats. The phalanx of wizened faces registers skepticism and then disgust with this bald-faced liar, this impostor, this shover of old men and unlawful appropriator of handicapped parking spaces.

"Step," Leo says, "*step*-grandfather."

Cassie emerges at last from the women's restroom. Relieved and happy, she skips toward Leo and Beau. "I had to go really bad," she says, edifying everyone. After swimming, masses of her rebellious hair have escaped from her braids to stand upright on her scalp, the sun has toasted her skin a rich shade of cocoa, and her overlarge sunglasses are tilted askew. Still aware of her audience, Cassie steps back to give herself more room and clears her throat. "I need to make a speech, and it's for everyone, everyone but my brother.

Here goes: Old people everywhere, I love you all. You are still beautiful. You have lived a really long time. I'm sad you will die soon. So I want you to know that I love you all." She bows deeply and bobs upright to add, "The end."

Expressions of disbelief and scorn fade into confused amusement. Leo half-expects glasses to chink and a small ripple of applause. In the silence that ensues, he tells Cassandra, "On behalf of old people everywhere, I thank you."

Surprisingly, Stella is home when they arrive. Her car is parked sanely alongside the curb of their narrow uphill street. At the sight of it, Leo releases a sigh so deep it seems to whoosh up from the soles of his feet.

Cassie says, "How come you always do that?"

"Do what?"

"Blow out air like that, like you been holding your breath for two months?" she asks, and Leo does a quick calculation, wondering if Stella has mentioned to Cassie that she and Beau have been with them exactly two months. She says, "It's like you're always worrying too much."

Leo raises an eyebrow. "Is it?"

"And you ask too much questions."

"Do I?"

Stella flings open the door and Cassie hurtles into her arms, while Beau struggles out of Leo's grasp. No one can compete with Stella for their favor. Even so, Leo still feels a pinprick of envy. He catches a sour whiff of wine as he slips past this joyous reunion tableau to take the swimsuits into the laundry room. From the foyer, Leo spies Howie, a bear-like man with reddish gold hair, morosely gazing into an over-sized goblet of Chardonnay in the living room, his ridiculous Kewpie-doll topknot leaning to one side, as if wilted by misery.

Leo averts his eyes, hurrying along the hallway with the duffel. He'd have made a clean getaway, too, if Sugar Boots hadn't shot between his ankles, tripping him and then yowling when accidentally kicked.

"Jesus Christ!" Leo's anger erupts with shocking force.

"What happened?" Stella says. "Are you okay?"

Everyone rushes to his side: Stella, the children, Howie, and even Sugar Boots regard him with alarm, as he raises himself off the hardwood floor.

"I'm fine." He reaches for the duffel, still trembling with wrath. "It's that goddamn cat. He tried to break my neck."

"Sugar Boots?" Howie asks inanely.

"I'm telling you," Leo says looking straight at Stella, "I can't do this. I can't do everything. Something has to give. We should get rid of the stupid thing."

Cassie gapes at him momentarily and then screams as if auditioning—and impressively—for a role in a teen-slasher film. She sustains this for several seconds before dissolving into raucous sobbing. Beau, ever loyal to his sister's emotional extremes, joins in with gusto. Stella stoops to embrace both of them, saying, "There, there. He doesn't mean it," while Howie claps his hands over his ears. Only Sugar Boots, unperturbed, continues to regard Leo with dispassionate, even clinical interest.

"I'm sorry," Leo says. He tucks the duffel under one arm and lifts both hands in mock surrender. "I don't mean it. I guess I'm just tired. I should go to bed."

Mollified, the children grow quiet, but Howie says, "*Bed?* Why, it's not even five-thirty."

"What about dinner?" Stella asks.

"I'm not hungry." Leo chucks the bag in the laundry room and shuffles upstairs to the room he shares with Stella. He splays himself fully dressed atop the bed for a few

minutes listening to the voices downstairs. Then he
snatches up the remote control from the nightstand and
flicks on the set. The screen is blanched by stripes of
gauzy sunlight slanting from the blinds, but Leo lacks
the energy to get up and crank these shut. Instead he
cocoons himself in the comforter, passive and queasy, as
abrasive bursts of syncopated laughter wash over him.

He wakes when Stella turns off the television. It's dark now,
and she's wearing a silk kimono wrap. She's showered and no
longer reeks of wine. Instead, Leo detects sandalwood, spear-
mint, and a trace of Vitamin-E oil when she sits beside him
on the bed. "Are you okay?" she asks. "What's going on?"

"Nothing," he says. "Are the kids in bed?"

"Yes, and Howie is, too. He's staying over tonight." She
shakes her head. "He's in bad shape."

"And Micki?" Leo asks. "Did you see her?"

"No," Stella says. "We drove all the way out there, and
they were moving her into the suicide-watch wing."

"Why? What happened?"

"I guess she said something to the chaplain, threatened to
harm herself." Stella blinks rapidly, bites her lips.

Leo raises himself and pulls her close. "I forget how hard
this is for you sometimes." Stella is so relentlessly optimistic
that it's easy for him to overlook her distress. Before this disaster, she would worry about Micki and her husband Derrick—their bitter fights and dramatic reconciliations—but
she'd console herself by saying, "At least no one's in jail."
And the first time Derrick was arrested for assault, she
amended this to say, "At least no one's committed murder."
Leo wonders how she will comfort herself now. What can she
say? That at least no one has opened fire in the shopping mall

with an automatic weapon?

"Well," she says, "at least—"

Leo interrupts her with a kiss. "Come to bed."

She shrugs off her kimono. "Do you really want to get rid of Sugar Boots?"

"No," Leo says. "It's not that."

"The cat's lost a lot of weight. Maybe we should take him to the vet." This is how Stella frames her directives; "maybe we should" always means "you must."

Leo gives her a curt salute. "Yes, ma'am. Anything else? Wash the car? Pick up your dry cleaning while I'm out?"

Stella cups his face with her cool hands. "What is wrong with you? Tell me."

And the whole humiliating day tumbles out, an uninterrupted barrage of complaint, protest, and recrimination—Leo flashes on an image of the garbage truck he'd cut off earlier, pictures it disgorging its pestiferous load—while Stella listens and listens. No one listens like she does. This is what Leo loves most about her. A teenager when she gave birth to her daughter, who also became a teen mother, Stella is just six years older than Leo. When she was young, she had a role on a popular telenovela broadcast from Mexico City, but she got involved with a bantamweight boxer from the States, a brutal runt, and became pregnant with Michaela at seventeen. Leo's seen videotapes of the serialized drama Stella appeared on, and though she was winsome then, fresh-faced and girlish, he believes she is even lovelier now.

Of course, he was taken with her looks—honey-brown hair, large hazel eyes, high proud cheekbones—when they first met after his audition for a role on *The Benjamins* more than seven years ago, less than a week after his mother's funeral. He had tried out for the part of the macho Latino neighbor, a tough guy who doesn't like the idea of living with gays in the next apartment. But before he opened his mouth to read the lines, the casting director cried, "Next!" Speechless with shame, he rode the elevator down in the company of a stunning woman he assumed to be a star of the new show. When they reached the ground floor, she tapped his shoulder and said in a softly accented voice, "Excuse me. But are you okay?"

"Yes," he'd said, but he shook his head. To his horror, tears flooded his eyes and a sob wrenched from his throat. She plucked a handful of tissue from her purse and persuaded him to join her for lunch. There, in a crowded restaurant on Melrose, over sashimi tuna salads and iced tea, she'd leaned forward on her elbows, eyes wide and alert, and she listened for the first time, really listened to him in the same way she is listening now, quietly and calmly, as if nothing else matters to her in the world.

When he's done and falls silent, she doesn't say a thing. She just rubs the back of his neck and his shoulders, and he says, "I'll take Sugar Boots to the vet in the morning."

But the earliest appointment available isn't until after one. The veterinary hospital is fairly close to Echo Park, so Leo decides to make a day of it—a morning of play at the park, picnic lunch, and then the trip to the vet's. The only problem: he must bring Sugar Boots, confined in his crate, to the playground. By mid-morning it's already too hot to leave him in the car. Always an indoor cat, the tabby detests being out in the open. The one time he wandered outdoors, Sugar Boots suffered something of a feline panic attack. Leo found him in the backyard, his tail puffed into a bottlebrush, his fur standing on end, and his claws sunk into the moist lawn, as if he'd just learned that the law of gravity was being repealed and he had to hang on for all he was worth, if he didn't want to be flung off the face of the planet and hurtled into the galaxies.

Leo tells himself it shouldn't be too bad for Sugar Boots in the crate, a plastic house of sorts with bars so he can see out. He hefts the cat carrier in one arm and Beau in the other as he and Cassie—toting their peanut butter sandwiches and apples—round the lake toward the swing-set and slide. He sets the carrier under a picnic table to provide yet another shelter over the cat's head. But Sugar Boots does not appreciate this one whit. Guttural growling emanates from the carrier and when another cat, a mangy gray shorthair, approaches in curiosity, the entire crate shudders with his fury. Sugar Boots' abhorrence of being outdoors is surpassed only by his loathing of other cats. Leo swiftly shoos off the stray, but long after the other cat is gone, Sugar Boots continues to rock the cat carrier, hissing and spitting from within. Well before noon, Leo decides to set out the picnic. Cassie, sympathetic to Sugar Boots, leaves the playground immediately when summoned to eat, and Beau, always hungry, trails after her. While he chews his sandwich, the little boy casts wary glances from the agitation within the crate to Leo, as if he suspects him of telepathically tormenting Sugar Boots. Maybe if they arrive at the animal hospital early, Leo thinks, the doctor will see them before their appointment.

Though the clinic is open and the young girl manning the front desk is ready with intake paperwork, they must wait until Dr. Thurman returns from lunch. The waiting area contains benches and chairs upholstered with turquoise vinyl, a water cooler with Dixie-cup dispenser, and a basket filled with rubber toys to occupy its visitors. Whether these are intended for children or dogs, Leo can't tell. Beau seems to feel they are provided for his amusement, and he removes one toy after another, examining each carefully before setting it on the seat beside him. Cassie, next to Leo, pores over pamphlets on heartworm, mange, and ticks, intermittently murmuring "yuck" and "gross." Sensitive to odors, particularly those of a fecal and urinary nature, Leo breathes through his mouth as he fills in the forms handed him by the pony-tailed receptionist. She looks no older than fourteen, but her efficiency impresses Leo. She answers phones while filing paperwork and counting pills, and when an astonishingly obese woman enters with a dachshund embedded in her doughy arms, the teenager leaps to her feet with a clipboard similar to the one she handed Leo and greets her in the same way she'd greeted him.

Just before one, the waiting area fills rapidly, and Leo's grateful when the doctor's assistant, another teenaged girl, ushers them into an examining room first. Leo pulls Sugar Boots out of the crate. The cat is so depleted from the morning's trauma and emaciated from bulimia that raising him onto the examining table takes no more effort than reeling up a warm cashmere sweater. Leo berates himself inwardly for waiting so long to bring Sugar Boots for treatment. The doctor, a short bald man with glasses, takes one look and whisks the cat away for blood work and x-rays. "It doesn't look good," he says, grimly, before hurrying out.

Beau's smuggled a squeaky toy—a hydrant-shaped thing— into the examining room and now pops it in his mouth. Leo takes it away to rinse in the sink.

"*Blow your ass off*," Beau whispers.

"What did that man mean?" Cassie asks. "Is Sugar Boots going to die?"

"I don't know what he means," Leo says. "Maybe he just means Sugar Boots needs a shot or an operation." This will likely cost a fortune, he thinks. Stella and he have already talked about selling one of their cars to pay Micki's legal fees, and they haven't put the children in daycare or summer camp because they're waiting to see what these will be after the retainer is spent.

"If Sugar Boots dies, will he go to heaven?" Cassie asks.

"I don't think he's going to die, but if he does, I'm sure he'll go to heaven."

"Will he see my daddy in heaven?" Cassie's brow creases with worry. "My daddy hates cats. Do you think my daddy will find Sugar Boots in heaven?"

"That's doubtful," Leo says. "There are probably separate heavens for cats and for people like your daddy." Where he's headed, her daddy is more likely to encounter the assassinated Trujillo than he is to run into Sugar Boots.

After a few minutes, the doctor opens the door and gestures them into a darkened room across the hall, where an x-ray is displayed on a lit screen. He points to an illuminated spot at the base of the throat. "That's a calcified mass, an obstruction in the esophagus. With cats, I won't operate on the esophagus. I don't advocate this, though I can give you a referral." He goes on to say surgery is too risky and the chances of surviving it are slim. The cat is suffering. He's severely malnourished and struggling to breathe. The vet recommends euthanasia.

"What's that mean?" Cassie asks.

But the doctor doesn't say. He just looks to Leo to explain.

Leo stares at the x-ray, the ghostly mass looks like a thorny clot of smoke, and he's stunned by thickening in his throat, a hot constricting knot.

Cassie slams her hand on the wall. "Somebody tell me what that means!"

"We might have to put your kitty to sleep," the doctor says.

"Is he tired?" Cassie asks.

Leo clears his throat. "Yes, Sugar Boots is tired. He's pretty worn out."

After Leo pays the bill ($324!), the girl at the desk hands him a receipt and a thick cream-colored envelope. He places both on the passenger seat before settling the children in the car. He churns on the engine and cranks the air conditioner to its highest setting. Before pulling out, he flips open his cell phone and calls Stella at work. "We had to put Sugar Boots to sleep," he tells her before explaining about the calcified mass.

"Oh, *no*," she says. "I had no idea he was so bad off, the poor thing. I feel terrible. Does Cassie know?"

"Well, that he's sleeping," he says quietly, "yes."

"She doesn't know he's dead?"

"*No*," he says. And for Cassie's benefit, he adds, "He just needs some rest, a nice long rest."

Stella sighs. "Okay, but she's going to wonder why he doesn't ever wake up."

Before they hang up, Stella suggests they meet at Trader Joe's to pick up some coffee when she gets off work. Afterwards they can stroll across the street to eat at the French-Thai-fusion place, where Beau liked the flat noodles so much last time. It will be too sad, she says, to spend the entire evening home without Sugar Boots around. Leo's surprised this affects her so, but he's agreeable. Neither of them feels much like cooking.

"I was wondering something," Cassie says from in back. "Did we make Sugar Boots tired? I mean, me and Beau, did we wear him out?"

"No," Leo says, "no way."

"Are you sure?"

"Absolutely sure."

"What's in that letter?" she asks.

"What letter?"

"That letter the lady gave you, there in the front seat."

Leo takes up the cream-colored envelope and lifts the flap to remove a card. The hyper-efficient teen has presented him with a sympathy card in order to save a stamp. A rainbow arcs over a grassy hillside on the front and inside it reads: *When a beloved pet dies, it crosses over the Rainbow Bridge into heaven. There, it makes friends with other animals and frolics over rolling hills and peaceful lush meadows of green...*

"Good god," he mutters, imagining Sugar Boots' frenzied horror at this scenario, the ultimate insult it would be for the poor creature, as if dying wasn't bad enough.

"Well," Cassie persists. "What's it say?"

"It's a get-well wish," he tells her, "for Sugar Boots."

At Trader Joe's, Cassie spots Stella first. "There she is, *there, there*, in the wine section!" Leo trundles both children in a shopping cart—Beau strapped in the child seat while Cassie rides in the basket. He wheels them toward Stella in the wine aisle. Her eyes are glassy and her face is flushed. She has two bottles of red in her cart already and is examining a third. As he approaches, Leo glances from her to her cart, and she replaces the bottle in her hands on the shelf before reaching to embrace the children

"Nana, guess what," Cassie says. "Sugar Boots was too tired, so the doctor said he needs to sleep, and then he'll be well, but we didn't make him tired. Nah-uh, it wasn't because of us." She glances at Leo to substantiate this. He nods, his face heating up.

"I'm sorry he's not well. I know it's not your fault, sweetie," Stella says before turning to Leo. "I got here a few minutes ago. Well, Howie and I knocked off early and stopped for a drink and—"

"Did you get the coffee?" he asks, though he can see that she hasn't.

"No, not yet."

"I'll get it," Leo says, "if you'll keep an eye on the kids."

"Sure."

As he turns away, Beau, nap-less and teetering toward a tantrum, grumbles in protest, and when Leo disappears into the next aisle, the boy whimpers. But Leo doesn't turn back. He heads deep into the beverage aisle, pausing before an array of teas, many herbal remedies. There are teas for weight-loss, for sleeplessness, for tension and premenstrual discomfort and stress. Leo thinks of Micki and wonders if there is something to brew for despair. His mother would steep yerbabuena in her chipped blue teapot when he was unwell, and Leo wonders if he can send Micki tea in prison. He should bring it to her himself and take the children to see her. Wouldn't seeing the children be a cure of sorts, a reminder of the future and an antidote for hopelessness? And shouldn't they see their mother—where she is, how she is, and for Beau, young enough to forget, shouldn't he see *who* she is? He finds a package of his mother's tea, tucks it under one arm, and follows the sharp aroma of coffee to the grinding machine.

Leo measures out an estimated pound of Costa Rican to pour into the grinder. The whirring racket makes a satisfyingly angry sound, and when he bags the first pound, he pours in another, Sumatran this time. As he's gristing this, he senses familiar warmth nearby. Cassandra appears at his side. "Beau got away," she says, eyes shining with excitement. "Nana got him out 'cause he was crying and he got away. Now he's lost!"

"For god's sake!" Leo wheels away the coffee in the

machine, the opened bag at its mouth. He races up and down the aisles at one end of the store while Cassie heads off to search another. Luckily the store is not crowded, but the few customers Leo rushes past regard him with alarm, as though he is a madman on a rampage. Meanwhile another child in the front of the store cries, "Mama, Mama, Mama!" Leo experiences a sense of unreality, of being thrust into a nightmare world where all children are imperiled, and he is powerless to save any of them. His mouth goes dry and his heart is pounding in his throat. He thinks of kidnappers, sexual deviants, and senseless brutes who inflict injury for pleasure. How could he have let Cassie out of his sight? And what if Beau escaped from the store into the parking lot? He's so small, he would be impossible to see from the driver's seat of an SUV. Most people are so careless and impatient, always speeding, even in parking lots.

Leo runs up front to the exit to see if he's gotten out, and there, he spots Beau and Stella near a corral of shopping carts and the magazine rack. The little boy is crying with all his might, standing just below a display of the local parenting circular. The magazine's usually cheery cover of pastels and chubby smiling faces is shadowy for this issue, shock-white letters outlined in black spell out a single word: *Autism?* Beau's clenched face is empurpled, blurry with tears, as he struggles with Stella, who looks haggard and lost herself. At the sight of Leo, the boy draws a deep, shuddery breath. "*Mama!*" He pushes away from Stella, who kneels beside him, her tight skirt crumpled and her blouse rucked out of the waistband. Beau twists free, nearly upsetting her balance, and he runs toward Leo. "Mama," he says, pumping his arms as he begs to be lifted. "Mama, Mama!"

"We found him!" Cassie emerges from the candy aisle,

bearing a flat cellophane-wrapped box. "Nana and me, we found Beau!"

Stella rights herself and rises, her face drained of color and her lipstick bitten off. Leo crouches to gather the sobbing boy in his arms. An absurdly pregnant teenager, not more than a child herself with stick-like limbs, knobby joints and wide empty eyes, waddles past. Stella smiles at the girl as if she recognizes her, and panic again squeezes Leo's heart. He jerks his gaze to Cassandra, as Beau, hot and quaking, huddles close.

"Lay-oh-need-us," Cassandra says and she thrusts out the box, containing an array of chocolates—waxy cocoa and cream-colored whorls—shaped like seashells. "Can we get this?" She licks her plump upper lip. "For Sugar Boots, I mean, a get-well gift?"

Leo looks to Stella, who shrugs. "I guess so," he says. He imagines Sugar Boots sniffing at the box before stalking off, his tail high in the air and bent back at the tip, signaling the counterfeit mollusks in his wake. "But not for him." Leo lumbers to his feet, bearing up Beau heavily, as if from underwater, from deep in a sea that disgorges artificially flavored conch and scallop husks, teas for passion and for regularity, rice milk and soy cheese, "exquisite" wines for under five bucks, a busy ocean of things purporting to be what they are not, the murky, flimflam depths of it. Maybe this also, he thinks, is not what it seems, not as bad. Maybe he *can* do this. Leo leans and swoops for Cassie. She clasps a cool hand around the back of his neck, and he raises her, too, whispering in her ear: "We need to talk about Sugar Boots."

The cat is gone, and it's time Leo admits the truth.

The Threat of Peace

Empathy

Stewart sees the kid is just being stubborn now. This eighteen-year-old, whose plump body smells like soured mayonnaise, is the valedictorian type, with a remarkable academic record, but few discernible social skills. He's likely an officer in his chapter of the Harry Potter fan club and an aficionado of complicated internet games involving aptitude in advanced calculus. In other words, he is nothing at all like the teenaged daughters of Stewart's girlfriend, Guadalupe. To his knowledge, her two girls use the home computer only to post suggestive photographs of their pert little bodies on notorious teen sites and to "chat" with people named "Lude," "Octane," and "Smash." They wouldn't give a boring marshmallow like this a second glance. Yet the kid had the spunk to violate his prep school's honor code when he used the internet to access SAT practice problems his teacher was using for a two-day exam.

"I can't understand," the boy says now during mediation with school officials, his voice nasal and his tone prematurely pedantic, "why I can't continue on the honor council. I mean, they're expunging this so-called infraction from my academic record. So it's like it never happened, right? If it never happened, I deserve to be reinstated."

"It *did* happen, though." Stewart has said this at least five times since going into private caucus with the student, after introducing himself to both parties, eliciting agreements of confidentiality, and explaining how the process works. "They are removing the offense from your record as a compromise, so it won't appear on your transcript." But Guadalupe, who is avid to hear about Stewart's cases and who works in admissions at the University of Georgia, has told him there is no way this would appear on a transcript regardless. Stewart doesn't go into this, though, with either party.

He just moves from room to room, holding caucus meetings with one disputant and then the other, wishing that he could rent a better space for mediating these cases when he spies the same green flies keeled over in the window sills, the same cobwebs streaming from the ceiling fans, the same film of dust over the framed nature prints that he noticed the day before and will find the next day when he returns to mediate another case. He makes a mental note to bring dust rags tomorrow, and he says not a word about the fact that the prep school's only concession has no real value.

The fact is Stewart needs this mediation, and the more the kid and the principal go round and round in caucus, the more his hourly fees accrue. The case was assigned to him by Judge Wodji, (Judgie-wudgie, Guadalupe calls him), an aging magistrate, who's been giving him more and more work these days, so while Stewart doesn't mind if this is drawn out, he's anxious for it to resolve equitably and for both parties to report satisfaction to the old man, thus continuing the flow of referrals. Without these, Stewart would have to drive sixty miles from Athens to Atlanta in the hopes of picking up cases from the Justice Center or travel to outlying counties in south and middle Georgia for special education disputes. Once he had to fly clear to Ohio to mediate a case for the US Postal Service, for which he was paid only the minimum rate, plus expenses, but given a denim postal shirt with a single word embroidered over the breast pocket: *Redress.* This spate of local cases finally affirms his decision to leave the small Atlanta law practice, where he litigated for five years with no hope of making partner, to build a mediation practice on his own in Athens.

His stomach rumbles, and he thinks of Guadalupe heating her soup in the microwave of her departmental break room. Every weekday she takes a plastic container of tomato-basil soup to warm for her lunch, and on weekends, she heats the same soup on the stove-top, which she says tastes even better. She keeps a shelf of it, four cans deep, in the pantry. Guadalupe, who's been married to four different men ("the jackasses") and, not counting Stewart, has lived with two others ("the intermissions"), is ever faithful to her tomato-basil soup, and to her girls, who couldn't be more different from the snobbish-sounding prig across the table if they belonged to a separate species.

"But it's like it never happened, see," the kid continues. "If that's the case, I should be reinstated on the honor council, right?"

If anything, the boy reminds Stewart of himself at the same age.

"But it *did* happen. They are only removing it from your record as a concession," Stewart says, wishing he could add something new to this refrain, something more relevant and illuminating, something maybe along these lines: *You will be in your forties, like me, before you have a chance at love with*

the kind of woman you've always dreamed of loving, but by then,
this will be so complicated that you will wonder every day if it is
worth it even to have dreamed such a dream for so many years.
Instead, he tells the kid, "Now, you have to compromise."

Patience

As he drives home, Stewart's throat burns from talking, or
maybe he's coming down with something. He craves honey-
laced tea and then soup—anything but tomato-basil—when
he gets home, and maybe later he'll cuddle on the couch with
Guadalupe and watch *Monday Night Football.* But who is he
kidding? Her girls would no more permit him to snap on the
game than they would spontaneously wash his car for him.
They have their incessant celebrity countdowns and mean-
spirited reality shows to tune in to while they chatter on their
cell phones all evening. Stewart's better off sequestering
himself in the bedroom, armed with earplugs and a book. He
had no way to foresee this when he moved in to save money
for his new mediation practice, but living with Guadalupe
and her daughters these past few months gives Stewart the
feeling he is in a permanent state of disfavor, as though he
is being grounded, night after night, sent to his room after
supper for some offense he can't even recall committing.

He touches his cheek at a red light. The stubbly skin is
sensitive, febrile. His joints feel constricted, his bones stiff
and brittle as the ice-fringed limbs of bare trees he passes
along Prince Avenue before turning on Oglethorpe toward
Forest Heights. Stewart needs rest tonight if he's going to
be on his bean—or "full frijole," as Guadalupe says—for the
mediations Judge Wodji has assigned to him the next day.
Since he's learned to limit his expectations of the home front,
Stewart pulls into the carport alongside Guadalupe's red

Mazda hoping for no more than a hot bath before confinement in the bedroom.

But as he pulls his keys from the ignition, Guadalupe slams out of the kitchen door, her oversized brown flannel shirt (*his* shirt, really) flapping at her sides like russet wings as she rushes toward him, waving a sheet of paper in one hand. The look on her heart-shaped face is both aggrieved and triumphant. She yanks the car door open and thrusts the paper, a letter, at him. "Guess who's suing me now?" she says.

Active Listening

Even though Stewart reads the order carefully and explains to Guadalupe that she is not being sued, she nonetheless phones her two sisters in Los Angeles, beginning each conversation the same way she greeted him, and when a neighbor pops over to invite her to a Tupperware party, Guadalupe again announces that she's being sued.

"My goodness," says the neighbor, a frowsy woman whose thick glasses are smudged with fingerprints. "People can be so ugly." She clucks with righteousness that is undeserved, in Stewart's opinion, as her two teenage boys run with the gang of neighborhood skinheads. Squad cars often pull into their drive, collecting one or the other. Her younger son even has a swastika tattooed on his forearm.

After the neighbor leaves and Delia, Guadalupe's older daughter, returns from track practice, she jumps up to meet her at the door. "Guess who's suing us now!"

And like Stewart, Delia guesses correctly, naming her last stepfather: "Anders."

"Can you *believe* it?" Guadalupe says, fanning herself now with the letter.

"Yes," Delia says in a flat voice, and she pulls open the

refrigerator door. Both girls have the habit of opening the refrigerator to scrutinize the contents when they return to the house, as though they expect transubstantiation to have occurred in its frosty recesses during their absence. They are inevitably disappointed and rarely remove anything from it, but they always check to see, just in case.

"He's not suing you," Stewart explains. "Rule Nisi only allows him to collect his winter clothes and personal effects." And high time, Stewart thinks. The poor guy must have had it rough during last week's ice storm.

"Didn't he have an entire week," Guadalupe says, "a full seven days to do just that when I left him this summer? Remember when we went to Florida while the girls were visiting their father? Why didn't he take his things then? He had *plenty* of time."

"He probably thought you'd get back together," Stewart says. "He maybe hoped you'd work things out. He sent all those letters..." Stewart glances at Delia, who has slammed the refrigerator door, a disgusted look on her face. He doesn't want to say more in her presence. But he remembers well the letters Anders wrote. Guadalupe, impatient with the turgid writing style, had Stewart read them and summarize their contents for her. In these, Anders had offered to go to couples counseling, to take something called *Beano* for his persistent problems with intestinal gas, to look into a penile implant—

"Anders was boring." Delia flips her silky black hair from her shoulders. "He was perverted, too. I never liked the way he hugged us. He used to pretend to mistake me and Connie for you and try to sneak kisses." Delia, with her alabaster skin, high cheekbones, and wide brown eyes, *is* a close ringer for her mother, a willowy taller version of Guadalupe, and her younger sister—shorter and curvier—resembles their mother even more closely.

Guadalupe's limpid eyes flash with anger. "*We* should sue him. We should have him thrown in jail." She opens a low cabinet to step on the shelf and hoist herself onto the counter. From here, she stands on tiptoes to reach a cupboard near the ceiling.

"Where's Connie?" Delia asks.

"Babysitting," Guadalupe says.

Delia wrinkles her nose and stalks out of the kitchen.

Guadalupe pulls a bottle of gin from the topmost shelf of the high cabinet. She reasons that she will not drink too much if it's hard to reach the booze. "The nerve of him suing us."

"But he's not suing you." Despite the scratchiness in his throat, Stewart keeps his voice even. "The guy just wants his things."

"Whose side are you on anyway?" Guadalupe sets the bottle on the counter and climbs down, careful of the glasses, cups, and plates stacked near the sink.

Earlier, while Guadalupe was phoning her sisters, Stewart changed into sweatpants and his postal shirt, and now he rolls up the denim sleeves and turns on the tap, filling the sink to wash dishes. "I don't take sides," he says. "I'm neutral."

"See," she says.

Stewart is mystified. "What?"

"*That's* the problem."

Conflict Style

As Stewart washes the dishes, Guadalupe whisks egg whites for a Swiss cheese soufflé. On rare occasions, inspiration strikes, and Guadalupe pulls out her Julia Child cookbook to break the monotony of broiled chicken or fish and salads she prepares night after night. She's well into her second gin and tonic and whipping the frothy mixture in a fury, as though Anders himself, miniaturized and helpless, is trapped in the bowl. Her cheeks are flushed, her jaw clenched, and now and again Stewart overhears her muttering curses in Spanish.

Stewart has never known anyone like Guadalupe when it comes to facing opposition, and he has a chart he uses for training others in mediation that describes how people react to conflict, a continuum ranging from positive to negative in three categories: evasion, confrontation, and aggression. None of these adequately describe Guadalupe's response, which is close to pure exhilaration. She is invigorated, nearly gleeful in the face of challenges that most others would shrink from. Guadalupe doesn't just embrace conflict; she seems to want to make out with it. The letter from Anders' attorney has infused her with the energy to embark on the soufflé. When it is baking, he suspects she will begin abrading the tub and sinks with a scouring pad, as though these symbolize her opponent's bare flesh to which she is mercilessly laying siege. For this reason, the house is usually immaculate, though Guadalupe, clumsy in gloves and unwilling to ruin her hands, refuses to wash dishes.

As she's folding the egg whites into the batter and Stewart is drying the flatware, the front doorbell rings. They both freeze. Most visitors come to the side of the house, through the carport to the kitchen door. Only strangers ring the front doorbell.

"Probably just some Jehovah's Witness." Stewart tosses the dish towel over the rack to dry. "I'll see who's there."

"More bad news I bet." Guadalupe arches her brow as if to say: *Bring it on!*

They use the front entry so infrequently that Stewart can't open it right away. In fact, he's forgotten he needs a key to slide the top bolt. "Just a minute," he shouts through the thick door, fumbling for his keys. After a few tries, he fits the right key to the lock and opens the door to a stout young man in a sheriff's deputy uniform.

"Anders? God-a-loop?" the deputy reads from his clipboard, pronouncing the name as though it is a ride at a Christian-themed amusement park.

"*Guadalupe*," Stewart says. "Guadalupe Apodaca."

"Apodaca?" The deputy, whose pale freckles and deep-set pebbly eyes are vaguely familiar to Stewart, flips through the pages affixed on his clipboard. "*Apodaca?*"

"She's divorcing and taking back her maiden name." Why Guadalupe, with her track record, bothers to change it each time she weds is a mystery.

"Well, I need to see this person." The deputy holds up his clipboard for Stewart to see through the screen door. The top page is a photocopy of a check for fifteen dollars and twenty cents to ABC Liquors which is signed by Guadalupe Anders. It's drawn on the joint account she had with Anders and stamped: *Account Closed.*

Stewart's stomach lurches. Since summer, he's struggled to bring Guadalupe's chaotic finances under control; he's met with bank managers and spoken to creditors on the telephone, negotiating manageable terms for balancing her various overdrawn accounts and refinancing her high interest loans. Somehow he's missed this one, and he has the sickening feeling this is more serious than it looks, but he keeps his tone light.

"Oh, that," he says. "You see, Officer, Ms. Apodaca *was* married to Mr. Anders. Their divorce is nearly finalized now, but when they first separated, Mr. Anders emptied their joint accounts without telling Ms. Apodaca." Stewart hopes this is the truth, or something near the truth. The check is dated July, around the time they separated.

"I can't discuss this with you, sir," the deputy says. "I need to see the person named here."

Stewart scratches his head. "I'm afraid you've just missed her."

But Guadalupe has crept up behind him. "What's this about?"

"Are you Ms., uh…," He shows the check again. "Did you write this check?"

Guadalupe slips in front of Stewart for a better look. "Yes, I did."

"It was returned from the bank, account closed," the deputy says.

"Oh, no problem," Guadalupe says. "Let me get my purse."

"I'm sorry, ma'am. It's too late for that."

Stewart's hands buzz and his ears burn, as though *he* has drawn the bad check. He knows what's coming, though he says, "We're prepared to pay any fine or late fee."

"I'm sorry, but I have to arrest you, ma'am, and take you down to the station for booking." The deputy purses his colorless lips, shakes his head.

"But, you can't," Guadalupe says in a hot gin-fueled burst. "I never even got the letter! I *always* pay my overdrawn checks when I get the letter."

"They don't have to send a letter, ma'am, if the account is closed."

"*Anders,*" Guadalupe says. "That jackass!"

"I'm sure we can work this out," Stewart says, suspecting there is no way short of bribing an officer of the law, "and you don't have to arrest Ms. Apodaca. If we put our heads together, I'm certain we can come up with something."

"No sir, I'm afraid that's not possible."

Delia appears in the hallway, her cell phone to her ear and a cross look on her smooth oval face. "What's going on?"

"I'm being arrested!" Guadalupe says.

"No *way*," Delia says, her velvety eyes sparking. "I got to go," she says into the phone. "My mom's getting arrested." Delia snaps the phone shut and pushes past Stewart to link arms with Guadalupe. "You can't arrest my mom!"

"Two ways we can do this," the deputy says, reaching now for his handcuffs.

"Officer," Stewart says, "you *know* this is a mistake. We can work it out."

"You can get in your own car and follow me to the station—"

"But I can't be *arrested*," Guadalupe says, shaking her head. Delia, still clinging to her mother, begins sobbing.

"Or I can cuff you and take you in the squad car." He's holding the stainless steel bracelets now.

"We'll follow you," Stewart says. "Just give us a minute."

Guadalupe pats her daughter's arm, murmurs in her ear. Then she turns to Stewart, her brow knitted, her large eyes narrowed, blinking with incomprehension. "How can I be arrested?" She glances toward the kitchen. "What about my soufflé?"

Communication

Stewart dissuades Guadalupe from having a shower and washing her hair, but with a glance at the embroidered word over his breast pocket, she insists on changing clothes, saying there is no way she will go to jail in jeans. Delia, no longer weeping, follows Guadalupe into the bedroom, ostensibly to advise her mother on what to wear for the occasion.

It turns out, the deputy, whose name is Mark Tierney, is a cousin of Tim Tierney, who serves with Stewart on the board of the family services cooperative in town, and he agrees to wait in the living room with Stewart while Guadalupe gets ready.

"How is Tim?" Stewart asks from the loveseat adjacent to the couch, where the deputy is ensconced. Its aged frame dips perilously with the man's weight and the plush green cushions fold in, engulfing him the way Stewart imagines an insect-eating plant might commence slow consumption of a meaty, khaki-clad worm.

"Well, you know they asked him to be Grand Master of the Christmas parade again," Mark Tierney says.

"I heard." Some years back, Tim Tierney had been chosen to carry the Olympic torch through town, and Stewart can't help wondering why honors like this are bestowed on the beady-eyed man whose rumpled shirts and slacks always look as though he has just pulled them from the bottom of the dirty-clothes hamper.

"Never irons his clothes," the deputy says with a laugh.

"Excuse me?"

"My cousin Tim, he never irons." He shakes his head.

"Really, what about his wife?"

"What? No, nobody in that house irons." The deputy settles more deeply into the maw of the couch. He gestures toward the bedroom and points at the framed school portraits of the girls hanging over the fireplace. "Are they movie stars or something?"

Only in their own minds, Stewart thinks, but he says, "No, they're just girls."

"Good-looking girls, the mother, too," Mark adds. "I hope you don't mind me saying, but she's a real looker. I kind of hate to arrest her."

"Well, maybe we can work something out," Stewart says. His throat burns and his ears pop painfully when he swallows.

"Sorry," Mark tells him. "Not my call."

And they sit silently until Guadalupe reemerges, looking like a stunning Quaker in a long skirt and dark shawl. All she needs is a black bonnet. She instructs Delia when to take the soufflé from the oven and to toss a salad for her and Connie's dinner. Then Guadalupe embraces her, as though she's about to embark on a long journey, until Stewart says, "Sooner we straighten this out, sooner we'll get back here."

On the way to the courthouse downtown, Stewart follows close behind the squad car, but they are separated at a traffic light on Broad Street, and when the light changes, a dingy white Volkswagen cuts in front of Stewart's car. The VW's bumper sticker reads: *Rapture? So leave already!*

Guadalupe reaches across Stewart to toot the horn. "That's Rodney's car," she says. "Rodney Pharr."

Pharr is Guadalupe's supervisor, an emaciated man with a shaved head. Stewart met him at a Halloween party to which Rodney, appropriately, came dressed in a Day-Glo skeleton suit. The thin man had monopolized the conversation and peeked, when he thought no one was looking, down the neckline of Guadalupe's low-cut vampiress costume. "You'd think he could afford a better car than that," Stewart says now.

Guadalupe waves at her boss. "Pull up alongside him, will you?"

They cruise into the left lane, side by side with the Beetle at the next red light, Guadalupe rolls down her window and so does Rodney, grinning like a skull. "Hey, Guadalupe, what's up?"

"I'm being arrested," she says. Stewart cringes, wishing the light would change.

Rodney laughs as though she's telling a joke he doesn't quite get.

"No, *seriously*," Guadalupe says. "A bad-check charge. See that squad car up ahead? We're following it to the courthouse."

"My lord," says Rodney. "Anything I can do?"

Stewart doesn't remember the light at this intersection ever taking this long to turn green. Maybe the thing is broken, and they will have to cross tentatively against the red. He inches the car into the crosswalk.

Guadalupe shrugs. "It'll be okay. Stewart knows a judge."

The light changes, and Stewart stomps on the gas pedal, screeching away from the intersection while raising the automatic window.

"What are you *doing?*" She often nags him about his risky driving. Guadalupe, the woman who blithely writes bad checks for booze and has never heeded her marital vows, honors traffic regulations as though they have been engraved on stone tablets. She even minds the ridiculous speed limits for parking lots, enraging other drivers as she crawls along at five miles per hour looking for a space at the Super Wal-Mart. "Are you trying to get us killed?" she says. "Isn't it bad enough I'm getting arrested?"

"You don't have to tell the world," he says through gritted teeth. "You don't have to tell the whole world everything."

Negotiation

At the courthouse, the waiting area is empty except for them and Ed Tonka, a superannuated hippie who heads the Legalize Marijuana Now group in town and has just been led in by a patrolman. The officer un-cuffs Tonka and orders him to take a seat while he files the paperwork. Guadalupe, whose third husband, O'Meara, was an aspiring actor, knows Tonka from her involvement in local theatre productions. Recently, they both had small parts in *A Midsummer Night's Dream*, so they throw their arms around one another the way close family members might after traumatic separation. Ed pulls back to regard Guadalupe's attire and says, "No one even *bothered* to tell me they were casting for *The Crucible*." She explains her outfit, and they exchange arrest stories. (Tonka committed some minor traffic offense on a bicycle and "resisted citation," he says, curling two fingers on both hands to simulate quotation marks.) They console each other until the policeman reappears to escort Ed out for the photographing and fingerprinting.

"You should call Judgie-wudgie," Guadalupe tells Stewart once they are alone.

"I'm not calling Judge Wodji," Stewart drops his voice to a whisper.

She turns to stare at him. "What's wrong with you? You've been acting strange ever since I got arrested."

"It's *strange* to get arrested," Stewart explains. "People are not themselves during an arrest. That's why they call it arrest because you are supposed to stop doing what you're doing, stop being the way you are, and try something different."

"How come you're whispering?" she asks.

"My throat hurts." He fingers tender lumps the size of apricot pits under each side of his mandible. "It's been hurting all day. I think I'm getting sick."

"*Poor Stewart*." Guadalupe's voice is thick with emotion. She presses a cool palm to his forehead. "You're feverish. You should be in bed."

"How can I be in bed, Guadalupe, while you are here, being arrested?"

"Why don't you just call Judgie-wudgie and we can both go home?" she says. "I'll make you some hot tea with honey."

She puts an arm around him and draws him close, her breath warm in his ear. "You like hot tea with honey?"

Stewart nods, closes his eyes. His eyelids prickle.

"Just call him, and we can go home, tuck you in bed with your hot tea and your honey." She nestles closer and strokes his shoulder.

"I'm not calling the judge," he says softly.

A round-bottomed policewoman appears, saying, "Follow me."

Guadalupe rises, smoothing her skirt. "Is this really necessary?"

"Why, yes, ma'am, I do believe this is *really necessary*," the officer says, before pivoting to lead the way. Eyes downcast, Guadalupe trails after her. They both disappear around a turn down the long corridor. After a few moments, Stewart imagines he hears the iron bars clanging shut, and he bolts from his chair to find a phonebook.

The old man's voice is raspy. He tells Stewart he's ill, but he will drive to the courthouse to help him out this *one* time, and Stewart expects he can kiss the steady stream of cases from Wodji's bench goodbye. When he arrives, the judge's skin looks papery and crumpled, his eyes ringed with sooty shadows. Seeing this great ursine man stooped over his cane with illness reminds Stewart of his father who died of pneumonia. Like him in the last days, Judge Wodji's haggard, colorless face resembles that of a pretreated corpse. Now the old man can't stop sneezing into a stiff, balled-up handkerchief, and Stewart's throat burns and tickles. He starts coughing. The two of them sink into nearby plastic chairs, sneezing and coughing until the spell passes, and when it does, Judge Wodji shakes his head and laughs. Stewart joins in, faking a few chuckles until the old man abruptly stops.

"What are we doing here?" He stamps his cane on the floor and says, "*Fools.*"

But the judge draws himself up to arrange for bail, so Guadalupe won't have to spend the night in lock-up. Stewart thanks him profusely, but swiftly, to send him along before Guadalupe reappears at the end of the corridor. He doesn't want her thanking the judge with her gin-fume breath or accidentally calling him Judgie-wudgie.

The first thing Guadalupe says when she sees Stewart is, "We need to get you home. You don't look well." She entwines her arm with his and leads him out of the courthouse, tucking his wool scarf into his coat before she pulls open the door. Sleet falls outside the courthouse, and Guadalupe guides Stewart down the slick concrete steps. "What are you thinking, coming out on a night like this?"

Impasse

Stewart staggers to bed—no soup, no tea, no bath—while Guadalupe regales her daughters with "The Story of Being Arrested." Like all of Guadalupe's tales this is rendered with equal parts of indignation and high hilarity, entertaining enough to preempt television shows and phone calls, but Stewart can't bear a minute of it. He shuts the bedroom door on their laughter, kicks off his shoes, and stumbles into bed fully dressed.

Stewart doesn't feel as though he's slept a full minute when a pan of light splashes in his face. Bleary-eyed, he lifts his head. Milky luminescence floods the sheer bedroom curtains. Someone has activated the light sensor in the yard. Stewart checks the digital clock on the bed stand: 2:14 A.M. Guadalupe snores softly beside him. Rustling noises issue from Connie's bedroom across the hall. Stewart nudges Guadalupe. "Someone's broken in," he croaks. He's lost his voice, so he tries again in a whisper. "Someone's here." The outdoor light shuts off.

Guadalupe raises herself on an elbow. "What is it? Are you feeling worse?"

"No. Yes, but that's not it," he says. "Listen. I think someone broke in."

The sounds from Connie's room are unmistakable now: more movement and a deep, unfamiliar voice—a *male* voice. Both Stewart and Guadalupe lunge from the bed. They tear across the hall, and Guadalupe shoves open the door. They discover Connie, in pajamas, lying on her bed in the arms of a young black man.

"*What* is going on here?" Guadalupe says.

"You have to leave," Stewart says in his non-voice, a hoarse honking thing that startles him. "Go on," he tells the kid. "Get out of here."

"Unh-*unh*," Connie says, her dark eyes ablaze. Of the two girls, this one is most like her mother when it comes to volatility. "You can't talk to Darren like that."

"Like what?" Stewart squawks. He's just told him to leave, and from his expression, this seems to coincide with the kid's deepest desire at the moment.

"You'd better go home," Guadalupe tells him. "This isn't a good time to visit."

Darren scrambles out of the bed, jabs on his shoes, and heads for the window.

"We like guests to use the door, please," Guadalupe says, pointing. She follows and flicks on the hall light to show him the way out.

Connie, cheeks flaming, remains on her bed, tense as a coiled snake.

"What were you thinking?" Stewart asks her.

"You shut up!" She leaps up to slam the door in his face. "You're such a fucking jackass!" she says from behind it.

No, he wants to say, not yet. He's still an intermission.

Reality Checking

In the morning, Stewart nearly calls to postpone the day's mediations. He's still feverish and hasn't much voice. Over breakfast, Guadalupe says she plans to take a personal day off from work. She didn't sleep well after the episode with Connie, and she needs to take care of some business, she says in a cryptic way.

"Good idea," Stewart tells her in his whispery voice. "Things are getting a little out of hand here, aren't they?"

"What the hell do you mean by that?" she snaps. "I'm taking care of things. I always take care of things. That's what I do."

"Last night," he says, holding his swollen throat now.

"What about last night?" she says.

Stewart just shakes his head and sips his coffee.

"I'm dealing with it," Guadalupe tells him.

The girls—dressed, coiffed, and made up as if on their way to star in salacious music videos instead of Central High—file into the kitchen and toss disdainful glances at the breakfast offerings. When it's Connie's turn to give her mother a peck on the cheek, she says she's going to the mall with friends after school, and all Guadalupe tells her is not to be late getting home. A car pulls in the drive and beeps, and both girls rush out the kitchen door.

Stewart says, "Is that it?"

"Is what it?"

"You're not going to ground her or anything?"

"Why would I ground anybody?"

Stewart's breath is constricted, his blood throbs in his veins, and his eyes burn. "If you're not careful," he says evenly, "those girls are going to turn out just like you."

"And *what*," Guadalupe says, eyes blacker than Stewart

has ever seen them, "is wrong with that?"

After this, there is no way Stewart can stay home with Guadalupe. He's determined to whisper his way through today's cases. *The Dispute Whisperer*, he thinks, considering possibilities for a movie or television drama. He wishes he weren't angry with Guadalupe, so he could amuse her with this, but he doesn't say anything to her. And as she clears the table, Guadalupe's not even looking at him. He sets his dishes in the sink and heads to the bedroom to dress.

On the stand near his bedside, he finds a mug of cold syrupy tea.

The morning case is another landlord/tenant dispute, this time involving a divorced couple. The man, the property owner, wants to evict his ex-wife and children from the basement apartment of the building he also inhabits. The former wife is often late with rent and occasionally asks him to deduct this from child support, resulting in confusion about who owes whom what. The man reasons he could get more rent for the place, and reliable payment, from another tenant.

One on one with Stewart in caucus sessions, each disputant is dull-eyed and washed-out looking. They both have low inflectionless voices and tend to stare off at some focal point over his shoulder. They could be fraterna-twin zombies. But when they come together, they bristle and seethe. Their voices rise, their ashen faces flush, and their eyes shine with welling tears. Stewart relies heavily on individual caucus meetings for this one; the atmosphere they generate in the same room is too thick and heated for clear communication.

When he has the ex-husband alone, Stewart reminds him he may be ordered to pay more child support if they live at separate residences as he will have less time with the children, and he will incur the cost of transporting them for visitation.

The man's mouth drops open.

Stewart says, "Imagine what your life will be when they are gone."

Common Ground

The dispute settles in favor of automated bank transfers for both rent and child support, and the couple exits the office for their separate cars. As soon as they drive off, Stewart uses the phone in the rental office to call the court and reschedule the afternoon's mediation. Wodji's clerk tells him the judge has already reassigned that case, though he is out sick, and he's left a message for Stewart to meet with him Monday morning. "Oh, and bring all your case files," the clerk tells him before they hang up. Stewart re-cradles the borrowed phone and collapses into the desk chair, doubling up as if he's taken a blow to the solar plexus. The confetti-patterned linoleum beneath the desk is woolly with dust, yet somehow pocked with fresh heel marks.

On the drive back to the house in yet more sleet, Stewart thinks of Anders, a burly, bearded man whose eyes brimmed with bitter tears both times Stewart has encountered him. He'd been a woodworker, a cabinet-installer by trade and an ardent fixer of things in his spare time, Stewart can tell from the repair work he's noticed in Guadalupe's house: a new toilet in the main bathroom, unfinished shelves in the laundry room, taut screens fitted over all the windows, and the fireplace rebricked. After a year with him, Guadalupe has mastered some home repair skills, and she now replaces washers, unclogs drains, and has even built a handsome spice rack in the kitchen with the tools Anders left behind. Guadalupe, Stewart sees, is in the business of educating herself, graduating from man to man, after she masters what she can.

And the jackasses and the intermissions offer themselves and their skills up willingly, one by one.

How radiant with pride Anders must have been when he walked arm and arm with Guadalupe, absorbing the admiring glances of others like sunshine, just as Stewart does now. (The last date Stewart had before meeting Guadalupe was with a stout, good-natured paralegal who had been mistaken by their waitress for his mother.) A lurching, homely giant like Anders would have glowed—cheeks shining and eyes twinkling—with a beauty like Guadalupe at his side. Stewart pictures him now, coatless and hatless, in this weather, ice slivers needling his un-protected skin, tinseling his brown beard.

Stewart shakes off the image as he pulls into the carport. Despite the weather, the kitchen door is propped open with a terra-cotta planter, and a stumpy man he's never seen be-fore is lugging a carton over the threshold. "Who are you?" Stewart asks.

"Clay," says the man as he brushes past with the box.

"Clay?" Stewart says, thinking there couldn't be a better name for this ruddy gnome with heavy feet. "What are you doing here?"

"Helping out a buddy," Clay says over his shoulder.

"Where's Guadalupe?"

"Kitchen." Clay bears the box down the drive to a van parked on the street.

Stewart finds Guadalupe seated at the kitchen nook beside a heavy-set African American woman whose gilded hair is woven with black beads. Both women have bowls of tomato-basil soup and full martini glasses set before them.

"*There's* Stewart," Guadalupe says with a wave. "I was just telling Lavonne about you. This is Lavonne, Darren's mother."

"Pleased to meet you." Eyes narrowed in suspicion, Lavonne looks anything but pleased by the interruption.

"We're having a serious discussion," Guadalupe tells him, and Stewart wonders how it is possible to have a serious discussion over martinis with someone in a lamé hairweave. Guadalupe points at the shaker on the table. "Want one?"

There's a rumble from another room, and at the same time Clay reappears at the kitchen door. He stamps his boots on the mat and trudges to the back of the house.

"Who is that?" Stewart asks. "What's he doing here?"

"That's just Clay," Guadalupe tells him. "He's Anders' roommate. He came over to help him move his stuff."

"What? *Anders* is here?"

Guadalupe nods.

"But you don't have to comply with that order for ten days."

"I know," she says. "I called Anders and said he could come today. I felt kind of sorry for him in this weather." She turns to Lavonne. "He left his winter clothes behind with the other stuff."

Lavonne shakes her head, beads clicking. "That's no good."

"You want to join us?" Guadalupe asks Stewart. "I can put on some tea, heat another bowl of soup."

A booming sound reverberates from the back of the house followed by cursing.

"Don't pay attention to him," Guadalupe says in a lowered voice. "He's been thrashing around like King Lear for almost half an hour now."

"Dumped the trash out on the floor." Lavonne gives Guadalupe a wink.

"That's right," Guadalupe says. "He wanted one of the plastic bins in the laundry room, so he throws the lint and dryer sheets all over the floor. I said, 'What do you think you're doing? You can't just throw trash all over the floor.'"

"And," Lavonne puts in, "he goes, 'Why not? That's what you done to my life.'"

Both women cup their hands over their mouths, erupting with laughter. In the background, Stewart overhears Clay placating Anders. "We got shampoo, man. You don't need to take theirs."

"You want to sit down with us, Stewart?" Guadalupe says. "Or you can lie down in the bedroom. They're done in there, I think. I'll bring you some tea."

Stewart shakes his head. No way can he rest with this commotion.

"You can keep an eye on Anders," Guadalupe says, "if he's making you nervous."

The women at the table wait for him to decide before resuming their serious discussion. Stewart is tempted to bolt from the kitchen, jump in the car, and zoom away, returning only after the others are gone. But even with the visitors gone, there is no peace for him in this house. And outside of it, there is nothing but peace, vast stretches of it, extending like uninterrupted dunes all the way to the horizon. He imagines himself trudging the expanse of it, robed like a Bedouin or a lost monarch, his richly dyed robes snapping with sandy gusts, as his form diminishes to the size of a punctuation mark—a period—before vanishing altogether.

("So peace, people getting along and whatnot," Guadalupe observed when they first met at the Taste of Athens benefit last spring and after Stewart had described his nascent mediation practice to her, "can be disastrous for someone like you.")

He shrugs off his coat and drapes it on the back of an empty chair. Then Stewart steps to the cabinet to grab a glass. He pours himself a generous drink from the shaker and settles into the dinette chair before pulling off his glasses to rub his weary eyes. The side door slams and outside the kitchen window Stewart beholds a blurry image of Anders stacking plastic patio chairs for removal. The guy is only a cabinet-maker, Stewart thinks, used to working with wood, not people. How was he to know he'd be cast aside after Guadalupe had gotten from him what she could? Stewart knows better; no way will he be blindsided by dismissal. And Stewart—a lawyer, a mediator, a *trainer* of mediators—has so much more to offer, things that took him a lifetime to learn.

Guadalupe pats his knee. "Stewart here had a problem with what happened here last night. Well, we all did. Am I right?"

"Got that right," Lavonne says, her voice deepening with sternness.

"Darren seems like a good kid," Guadalupe says. "But it's not too safe for him to be climbing in and out of windows in this neighborhood. People are not always that friendly around here. You know what I mean?"

Stewart leans in on his elbows, pursing his lips and nodding with the two women, when he glimpses his own face reflected in the kitchen window, which is odd because the kitchen light hasn't been switched on, so as to illuminate his image in the glass. He reaches for his glasses. It is Anders holding up a cracked and plaster-splattered tool. His mouth moves. "What happens to me now?" he seems to be saying.

Stewart shakes his head, wishing he had more to offer the poor dope.

Insistent, Anders holds aloft the tool, shouting now, so Stewart hears him distinctly. "What's happened to my trowel?"

Guadalupe rolls her eyes. "Just ignore him. He'll go away," she says and turns to Lavonne. "You first, and then we'll hear what Stewart has to say."

But he scrapes back his chair and rises.

"Where are you going?" Guadalupe asks.

Stewart pauses. He looks from Guadalupe's brow,

pleated now in bewilderment, to Lavonne's squinting eyes and clenched jaw. The refrigerator hums and then ticks, and outside Anders resumes gathering patio furniture and tools, making muffled clattering sounds, like a blunt knife gouging traces of peanut butter from a plastic jar.

"Stewart?" Guadalupe says.

It hasn't happened often in his experience, but some cases won't settle because the disputants are too fixed in their positions to meet one another halfway or else the mediator's interests compromise neutrality, sealing off all options, but one. Stewart smiles, and then shrugs, as if to say, who knows where? And in a moment in which he will later—much later—take immense pride (though he will have no one to share this with for a long time), Stewart steps over the threshold and out into the stinging cold. But unlike Anders those many months ago, he remembers first to grab his coat.

Homicide Survivors Picnic

Ted climbed into the back seat and slouched down as far as possible. His mother glanced at him over her shoulder and asked, "Why are you wearing my sunglasses? Give me those." She reached behind for the dark glasses that she said made her look like Jacqueline Kennedy Onassis, but Ted ignored her. She gave up with a sigh. As she backed the car out of the garage, Ted caught sight of his reflection in the rearview mirror. The shades made him look a bit like Jackie O., too, or at least a fourteen-year-old boy version of her.

"He's got my *Young Life* cap on, too." His older sister Tina, wearing *his* new gray flannel shirt with snaps that strained to close over her breasts, was a fine one to talk. She adjusted the radio to find a station playing rap music and rolled on one hip to pull out the bandanna—a red and white do-rag thing Terrell had given her before he'd died—that she kept stuffed in the back pocket of her Levis. She lifted it to her nose for a whiff.

"Okay, that's it." His mother stopped the car right in front of Danny's house. Ted sank deeper in his seat. She turned to stare at him. "What's going on, Teddy?"

"*Ted.* Can't you remember to call me Ted?"

"Ted, then, what's the matter with you? Why are you wearing that get-up and hunching over like that? Are you sick? Is it another headache?"

Tina cranked up the volume on a song in which the vocalist shouted a pulsing series of hoarse accusations. "He's incognito, Mom." She folded the bandana in a careful triangle, set it in her lap.

"*Incognito?* Why?"

A curtain fluttered in the front window of Danny's house, and the sprinklers shot on. A prism-tinted mist darkened ant mounds erupting on the neighbors' lawn. "Drive, Mom. *Please* just drive."

"It's Danny," Tina said. "He's hiding from Danny."

"Not that cologne business." Ted's mother faced front, shifted into drive, and inched the car away from the curb. "You paid for those *weeks* ago."

But Danny (Ted's former best friend) was still furious. Red-faced and puffing, Danny had cornered him on the basketball court at the Baptist church just the day before. He'd grabbed Ted by the shirt front, practically lifting him off his feet and promising to "break every stupid bone in your punk-ass body" the next time he saw him. That Danny hadn't simply killed him on the spot struck Ted as a lucky oversight. Now, his neighbor's burly, neck-less shape emerged from the screened door to stand on the porch and pound a fist into his palm. With another sigh, Ted's mother steered toward the stop sign at the corner. Did she have to drive so leisurely? Ted was sure that if Danny wanted, he could jog over, kick in the car window, and yank Ted out, without even breaking a sweat.

"All that fuss," his mother said, cruising with insane slowness onto the cross street, "all that fuss about some pretty awful-smelling stuff, as I recall."

"*Expensive* awful-smelling stuff: Aramis, Calvin Klein, Brüt..." Tina counted off the brands on her fingers.

How Danny's eyes had shone in the thick slab of his face when he showed off the shelf cluttered with ornate bottles—all filled with rich amber-colored scent. The sight aroused in Ted a cold, clammy envy that slithered like a snake, an invisible boa coiling up from his feet to his chest before engorging to constrict his lungs so tightly he could barely breathe, could barely utter, "Cool, man."

That had been the night before he was scheduled to catch a plane for L.A. to spend the summer with his father, "Evil Visitation Eve," as his mother called it, superstitiously alluding to the bad behavior that overtook Ted and Tina (back when she still visited their father) just before such trips. But that was in no way connected to Ted's surreptitious removal of all the colognes from Danny's bedroom, which he wrapped in socks and jockey shorts so they would not clink in the duffel he brought for his last sleepover before heading west. The desire for what was Danny's, come to think of it, also had little to do with the squat, well-shaped bottles that ended up breaking in the overhead luggage compartment and making his duffel reek so powerfully that he had to throw it away in the dumpster behind his father's apartment.

"I can't believe you boys are still fighting over that. Danny's nearly sixteen, almost ready to drive. You'd think he'd grow up a bit. And you, you'll be fifteen next month, son. Can't you go over there, Teddy, and talk to him? Apologize?"

"Nope."

"Well, I can't say I'm sorry. I didn't really like him as a friend for you. 'Danny'—what kind of name is that, anyway?

It's shorthand for a thug's name, a criminal's name."

Tina shot Ted a look over her shoulder, arched an eyebrow. Daniel was their father's name.

"Give me those sunglasses. I can't see a damn thing." His mother groped for them again.

Teddy handed her the shades, though she drove so sluggishly that she didn't really need to see. If she hit anything at this speed, they probably wouldn't even feel it. Driving was about the only thing his mother did with maddening calm. Usually, she buzzed around the house, doing five things at once—grading papers, drinking coffee, talking on the phone, folding clothes while fixing the vacuum cleaner—and sometimes getting so tangled up in her long wiry limbs that she tripped over herself.

Without the dark glasses, the midday sunlight, even in the car, about blasted through Ted's eyeballs like laser beams drilling clear to the base of his skull, and he prayed this wasn't the onset of another migraine. When they struck, he felt flattened, as though he were a cartoon character felled by a falling safe or piano. His mother would have to lead him like a zombie to his bedroom, crank the blinds shut and settle him in his bed fully clothed, where he would ride out the nauseating waves that pushed him through a dark canal of pain.

Come to think of it, he didn't remember getting these headaches in California.

Since he returned to Georgia two days ago, he found himself making mental notes, pro and con lists, for no reason at all, really, except that this summer, his dad had been kind of cool, not all touchy and pissed off like usual. Most of the time, the old man was kind of volcanic—bubbling and seething with hot undercurrents of anger that spewed forth in unexpected rages. But this visit, his father kept himself under control, even dropping the tirades against Ted's mother, the long monologues detailing her shortcomings that would last until two or three in the morning. He'd even taken Ted to some baseball games, bought curtains and stuff to decorate his room, and played video games with him this visit. And he'd mentioned he wouldn't mind if Ted moved out to live with him. Ted didn't have a single headache the whole summer.

California was a heck of a lot cooler than Georgia, too. Even if it didn't level Ted with migraine headaches, the Georgia sun in late summer felt cruel as a blow as soon as he stepped out of the air-conditioning into it. And the smothering humidity that cupped the heat in made him feel like a fly trapped in a giant, sweaty fist. *Headaches, heat, humidity. And Danny, don't forget Danny.*

"Tina, get the map will you?" Ted's mother said. She hunched over the steering wheel, her shoulders set in a grim, determined way. "We're supposed to find the highway to Conyers somewhere."

Ted entered another item for the cons column: *always getting lost.* How many minutes, how many hours, how many days, even years if you added it all up, had they spent roaming the San Fernando Valley and now Northeast Georgia, lost as a trio of lunatics who'd wandered from the asylum to find themselves inexplicably rattling around in a used Toyota Corolla? And *Tina* in charge of the map? Ted loved his sister, but the girl had trouble navigating the halls of their small high school to find her homeroom. Now, pregnant and in mourning for Terrell, she was even more vague, distractible, and uncommunicative. Practically all she'd said to him since he returned from California was, "Hey, can I borrow that shirt?"

"Let me have the map." Ted's temples pulsed in a warning way, and he swallowed hard. "Wait, there's a sign. Mom, get over to the right. Now, *now!*"

"Gosh, don't yell." Of course, she missed the exit and had

to pull into the entrance to J and J's Outdoor Swap Meet to turn around. An array of weather-battered gray booths and rusted folding chairs stood vacant on a paved slab just beyond the drive. "Hey, don't your girlfriend's parents own this place? What was her name?"

"Jerrica," Tina said, pushing the map over the seat. "She gave you that cat, remember?" The familiarity of being lost seemed to have a relaxing effect on his sister, who turned to smile at Ted. "We should stop so you can say hello."

"Are you nuts?" Ted leaned forward. "They sold the place months ago."

"That was one mean kitty." His mother spun the steering wheel, so the tires lazily sputtered gravel into the wheel wells. "I suppose the feline leukemia made him act out."

The black kitten, Gregory, had been Ted's first pet, his only pet. Yes, he'd been a little vicious and strange, prone to pouncing out to bite bare ankles and stealing newspaper to rip to shreds in the laundry room, making sounds like he was wrapping gifts in a fury. Ted raked his memory for a warm remembrance of the tense knot of fur, razor teeth, and needle claws. The one time they'd left the cat alone for a weekend when they took a trip to Jekyll Island, they returned to find Gregory's food and water untouched and the cat listless and skeletal, its wide yellow eyes staring in mute accusation.

"Remember how we held him while the vet put him to sleep?" he said at last.

"Poor thing," Tina said. She had been at track practice the afternoon they took him to the vet but had heard the story a few times.

That afternoon, Ted had been strolling home with Danny from the Golden Pantry, where they'd lifted two-liter bottles of soda, candy bars, chewing gum, and a few loose cigarettes from the pack open on the counter while the clerk was in the restroom. When his mother found him a few blocks from the store, she already had Gregory in the backseat, trapped in a cardboard box, to take to the vet. With uncommon tact, she didn't mention the poorly concealed soda bottles under their jackets; she'd just opened the passenger-side door for Ted and told Danny they'd see him later.

"Remember how he wouldn't die," Ted said. "The doctor injected some kind of sleeping drug, and Greg just wouldn't go to sleep."

"He had to use that cardiac stick," his mother added.

But the vet, young and inexperienced, had missed with that and blood spurted on his blue scrubs, spotting the Formica table top. Gregory had stared past the nervous doctor straight at Ted, as if to ask, "Why are you doing this to me?"

"We were all crying by then, even the vet and the vet's assistant," she said.

"Not Gregory." Ted bit his lip. "He was sure tough."

Tina turned sharply to stare out the passenger side window. She covered her mouth with the red square of cloth. Ted couldn't see her face, but her shoulders quaked and he could feel the heat rising from her back.

"How stupid," his mother said. "We shouldn't be talking this way."

"My bad." Ted stared down at the map, blurring his vision to imagine seeing it the way Tina did, the way his mother did—a random webbing of vein and artery overlaid with the irregular grid of county lines. But he found himself reading it, finding their location and plotting the next turn. "Mom, you have that address?"

The picnic was held in a small park located between the white-domed courthouse and the public library in a small town called Centerville, just outside of Conyers, the city where people made pilgrimages to the house of a woman who claimed to have visions of the Virgin Mary. Ted spotted a few bumper stickers urging him to "Eat, Drink, and See Mary" in the parking area. He hoped his mother wouldn't notice these. She had plenty to say on the subject of religious belief, and Christianity in particular, though this was not what most people in small-town Georgia wanted to hear. In truth, Teddy mostly agreed with his mother's opinions and even admired her for speaking out, but he didn't enjoy the arguments she started, the hot feelings these sparked, so he had to add religious fights to the bottom of the cons column. His mother tipped her Tupperware bowl of macaroni salad at one of the bumper stickers, already tossing her head in contempt. "Hah!"

Tina meandered at her side, not seeming to notice the bumper stickers, the cars, the parking lot, the heat, or even her mother and her brother. She reminded Ted of a grazing animal, shuffling forward in a blind, instinctive way. As they approached the huddle of picnic tables and clusters of other sad, slow-moving people, he wondered if she would feel at home among them. *He* sure didn't. And that banner hanging between two arthritic oaks—did they have to make the lettering so large and clear, for all to see the depressing circumstances that brought this group together?

His mother set her macaroni salad on a picnic table covered with red and white checked oilskin and laden with buckets of fried chicken, platters stacked with bologna sandwiches on white bread, bowls of potato and fruit salad, peeled hardboiled eggs, cookies, and deep-fried clumps that Ted couldn't identify. He made an entry for terrible food in his cons list, well above religious fights. Ted wrinkled his nose at the sulfuric stench emanating from the eggs and rancid tang of mayonnaise left too long in the sun, and he stepped back, but his mother lingered, eyeing the food in a wolfish way. For a bony woman, she could sure pack it away. But it wasn't time to eat, and bold as his mother was in most other situations, she hesitated to be the first to dive into the buffet.

An older couple beckoned them to join their picnic table, and Ted's chest grew tight, his bones heavy. Wherever he went, elderly people glommed onto him. Ted worked for a short time as a volunteer at a senior center, but he had to quit. It was too much. He felt like a rock star besieged by groupies. The wheelchairs, walkers and canes surrounded him, cutting off all avenues of escape and making him feel short of breath, feeble, and a touch geriatric himself. He had no idea why they were drawn to him. His mother said it was his smile, an unfortunate habit he had of grinning warmly when he was most distressed and confused. And here he was now, beaming at a scarecrow of a geezer and his plump, balding wife.

"How're you doing, sir?" Teddy clasped the old guy's scaly claw and pumped it a few times. "I'm Ted."

"Drew Colson," he said, "and this is my wife, Vivian."

"Ma'am, pleased to meet you." He nodded, taking the woman's puffy hand to shake, but released it when he thought he heard bones cracking, like he was crushing a mouse. "This is my mother and my sister Tina." Who'd made him the master of ceremonies, he wondered, as his mother and sister shook hands with the couple.

"I'm Elaine," said his mother, who didn't like to give her last name.

"You're all welcome to sit here with us. This is our first time, so we don't know how these things work," Mr. Colson said.

"I imagine it works like any picnic." Elaine sank onto the bench, her pale knees jutting from her khaki shorts, knobby as a stork's. Tina sat beside her in silence. Ted nodded, grinning at an overweight redhead in neon yellow stretch pants and a red and white striped T-shirt that draped her like a circus tent.

The redhead took this as an invitation and joined the group. She lowered herself beside Ted, causing the table to dip with her weight. "Hope you don't mind if I barge in. I'm Glenda, you know, like the good witch."

Everyone, but Tina, exchanged introductions again. More people arrived to fill in the picnic tables, and some spread blankets on the grass beside these. A few young children tagged along, but the group was mostly comprised of middle-aged women and old couples.

"So what happens now?" Glenda had a doughy face, blue eyes, and an upturned nose that reminded Ted of Jerrica's pet potbelly pig, Hamlet, who had broken his neck when Jerrica accidentally dropped him from a top bunk. Ted struggled to suppress the memory, grinning with such force that he could glimpse his cheeks bunching below his eyes.

"Well, it's a picnic," his mother said, "so picnic things, I suppose."

"I don't think we'll have water balloon tosses and wheelbarrow races under these circumstances." Mr. Colson shook his head in a slow, sad way.

As if on cue, Glenda latched onto Ted's elbow, digging her fingers into his arm in a painful way. "It was my daughter Sienna, almost a year ago. She had already *separated* from him. She got a *restraining* order. I was the one who found her on the basement stairs." Her eyes filled, the flanges of her nostrils reddened.

"There, now." Vivian wrapped a clumsy arm over Glenda's shoulder. Mr. Colson pushed a handkerchief at her. Elaine fixed narrowed eyes on Glenda until the distraught woman released Ted's arm. Tina surveyed the lot of them and yawned.

"I'm okay. I'm okay." Glenda dabbed her eyes with the handkerchief. "But I just don't get it. I mean, she *had* a restraining order. They were *separated.*"

Unable to come up with anything else, Ted said, "That's terrible."

"Yes," she said, "*yes*, it is." She looked to him with relief and gratitude, as though he'd finally explained something she had spent nearly a year trying to figure out. "*You* know what it's like. Who did you lose?"

Ted swallowed and tugged at the neck of his T-shirt. "Well, my sister—"

"You lost your sister?" Glenda glanced at his mother.

"No," she said, pointing at Tina. "My daughter's right here."

"My sister's boyfriend, actually," Ted explained. "He died a few weeks ago."

"He was killed, right?" Mr. Colson asked, likely ferreting out whether or not Ted and his family were at the picnic legitimately, as though he suspected they might be the kind of people to crash picnics for homicide survivors just to keep company with morose strangers—having nothing better to do on a Saturday afternoon.

"He was shot in the neck, dragged through the woods, and left there to die by this guy he thought was his best friend," Tina said in a flat voice. "I can't talk about it." She spread the bandana on the table and nested her head on it. In a minute or two, she'd be snoring. This was her newest habit—sleep—at any place, at any time. Ted's mother refused to let her drive these days, so she was the one to ferry her to and from her job at the consignment children's clothing store, appointments at the midwifery clinic, grief counseling sessions, and gatherings like this one that, she confided to Ted, she hoped would help Tina move forward, and prepare herself to care for the fatherless baby she insisted on having. "Because," she'd said, "there's no way I'm raising another child." But she'd said this in such a way that he knew she could hardly wait for the baby to be born, so she could begin doing exactly that. Ted shook his head, as though to dislodge insects, wondering what would happen if people weren't allowed to speak unless they said what they meant. He imagined a delicious silence unfurling like a beach blanket on sun-warmed sand.

"How hard for you," Glenda said, searching his face for grief since Tina had, in effect, folded her hand.

"Well." Ted hadn't actually met Terrell. Tina saw him at clubs and parties and didn't begin dating him seriously until after her brother had decamped for California. Outside of reciting the bare facts of his death, so far his sister hadn't talked about him at all. When he'd asked his mother about Terrell, she'd only mentioned that he'd had very thick calves, and, by the way, they had done a pretty poor job of embalming him. It was hard to miss the guy with these few details, but Ted was sorry for his sister, and he was lonesome for her, too. Before his trip to California, it was like they tramped along together on the same path—here he thought of the Appalachian Trail that he'd hiked during his short-lived Boy Scout days—but when he returned, she'd somehow managed to stumble on a switchback. Now he couldn't find her. And he was afraid to call her back, to call her name. So he was alone with his mother, who was already hunting down changing tables, highchairs, cribs, and sheets printed with ducklings, lambs, and rabbits at garage sales. "It's hard losing him," he said, "because he loved my sister."

Ted didn't think there were too many other people in Northeast Georgia at this moment writing messages on helium-filled balloons to dead guys they'd never met. This kind of thing was a selling point for his mother, who liked to brag that she bet that no one else in *all* of Georgia was raking clay with a fork to make a ceramic box that resembled a walnut or writing a haiku on rice paper in a tree or having tabbouleh and lemonade for breakfast or whatever other bizarre thing she'd talk him into. (Ted remembered staring at parsley-punctuated clumps of bulgur and the sweating tumbler of bitter juice and hoping, for the rest of Georgia's sake, she was right about the tabbouleh and lemonade.) She gave him a look right now, and a wink, as though to say, see, I bet no one else is doing this right now, like it was some kind of a plus, like he should be thrilled to do things no one else in his right mind would do.

The scent of the felt-tipped marker stung his nostrils. He pressed the tip to the white balloon he'd been given and it popped with an explosive sound. A few people gasped, and someone screamed. "Sorry." He raised his palms. "Sorry about that." At least he wouldn't have to write on the stupid thing, he thought. But Glenda swiftly passed him another balloon, this one as blue as her own weepy eyes. He touched the pen to it, lightly and experimentally; it stayed intact. He'd write something short. His mother had already written her first balloon and was pestering the woman who manned the helium tank for another. Tina, surprisingly, perked up for this activity. Her cheeks were flushed, her hands ink-splotched. She'd covered her balloon's red skin with sentence after sentence. From where he stood, Ted could just make out the question marks followed by exclamation points she'd scrawled on it.

Someone called out that it was almost time to release the balloons, so Ted quickly wrote: *Terrell, I never met you, but I guess you were alright. Sorry you had to die. Ted.* Then he glanced over his shoulder to see if Mr. Colson was spying to expose him as an interloper because he'd never known the murder victim. At the toot of a whistle, most people released their balloons, too few for a colorful canopy, but still they bobbed upward in a pleasant way. Tina kept writing in a fever. But Ted's mother set her second one, the postscript, free with a giggle. How out of place she looked with her bright black eyes, shiny dark hair, and happy smile among these dull-eyed, stunned, even shell-shocked survivors. It was as though she didn't know any better.

"You're a cheerful young man, aren't you?" said Mr. Colson, who appeared at his side as soon as the balloons were lofting on warm air currents toward the clouds. "You and your mother."

"No, we're just nervous." Ted capped his marker with care.

"You remind me of my son. Doesn't he, Vivian? Doesn't he remind you of George?"

The pudgy woman peered into Ted's face. "Why, *yes*, I can see it. Of course, George had blond hair, and he was tall, over six feet and he'd just turned fifty. But there *is* something."

"Was he …"

"He was killed in that Bonus Bonanza Burger in Atlanta. You hear about that?" Mr. Colson asked. "These kids—not much older than you—tried to rob the place. They panicked or something and opened fire in the restaurant."

"Our son was the manager." Vivian's lower lip quirked.

"Now, Mother," Mr. Colson said, and he produced another handkerchief. "That was a long time ago." He turned to Ted. "You know, we go to the prison to see him the last Sunday of every month, rain or shine."

"Your son?"

Mr. Colson gave him a sharp look. "He's dead, boy. He's not in prison."

"He respected the law," said Vivian in a quavering voice.

"We go see the boy who killed him."

Vivian trumpeted into the handkerchief. "We pray with him."

"Every month, the last Sunday, we drive over to the prison and get on our knees with that boy for a couple of hours." Mr. Colson nodded.

"Sheesh," said Ted, hugely relieved not to be *that* kid.

"See, we believe in healing and forgiveness. Even started a ministry at the women's prison near where we live."

Ted scanned the crowd to find his mother. This would be a very bad time for her to enter into the conversation with her excited pronouncements on how she is agnostic because she just doesn't have the time these days to devote to atheism, how Christianity is the sure root of all mental illness, and how if there is a heaven she'd refuse to set one toe in it if it mirrored the patriarchy that governs most churches. She could go on and on making this kind of joyful noise until she nearly got into fistfights over it. But now she was standing at a safe distance with Tina, her arm around her. She seemed to be coaxing her to release the balloon and offering her another, a green one. The helium tank lady, a severe-looking black woman, loomed in the background, glaring at both of them.

Before too long they'd head this way to retrieve Ted, so he had to work quickly to change the subject. "And what kind of work did you do, Mr. Colson, before the ministry, I mean, well, before your son died?"

The old man grinned for the first time, wrinkles webbing his face like roads on his mother's map of Georgia, and he began to tell about the work he'd done for NASA. "You've heard of NASA, haven't you, son?" Mr. Colson had been a scientist; he'd been in the control room when John Glenn had been sent into orbit. Good, thought Ted. NASA, scientist, control room—all perfectly safe topics to discuss with his mother, who had such trouble comprehending where she was on this planet that the idea of more space, *outer* space, stupefied her into rare and beatific silence. Teddy relaxed, idly preparing a few questions about rockets and jet propulsion, though the old man was on a roll and probably wouldn't need any prompting at all.

Over his shoulder, he heard a familiar voice insisting, "And I don't get it because she'd *separated* from him. She'd gotten a *restraining* order…"

Later in the car, his mother flipped up the visor and churned the ignition. "Well, that was certainly…"

"What?" Ted wanted to know her take on that absurd gathering.

"Goddamn boring," Tina said, burrowing in the bandana. "Don't bring me to anymore of these things, Mom. They don't help."

"I thought it was kind of interesting," Ted's mother continued as she steered out of the parking lot. "That old NASA guy and Glenda, the good witch wandering around like the Ancient Mariner—"

"That doesn't help, Mom. In fact, things like that make me want to puke."

They drove along for several minutes in silence before Tina cupped a hand over her mouth. "I'm serious. I'm going to chuck. Pull over, Mom, here, *here.*"

"Use a plastic bag. Teddy, reach under your seat and hand her a bag."

Ted plucked a grocery sack from the tangle of these his mother had stashed probably just for this purpose. He balled it and tossed it over the headrest. Tina coughed and then retched, heaving into it. A thick sour smell filled the car. Ted cranked the window lever before remembering the back windows had jammed permanently shut winter before last. "Um, Tina," he said, "how about opening your window a bit?"

She wiped her mouth with the top of the bag, ignoring him.

"Hang on." His mother turned the steering wheel, and the car crept across two lanes before bumping onto the right shoulder. "Are you okay? Do you want to lie down in the back seat?" She stroked Tina's bushy black hair from her brow. "We'll stop here until you feel better."

Ted threw open the door and sprang out. He'd been holding his breath and now gulped lung-fuls of hot, soggy, but sweet-smelling air. His mother had pulled alongside a kudzu-filled ravine that thrummed with insects. The late afternoon sun burned fiercely, glinting on the ticking car and shimmying above highway. The front doors chunked open, and Tina and his mother stood beside the car, blinking as though they'd just emerged from a darkened movie theater. "What do I do with this?" Tina held aloft the knotted plastic bag.

"Here, I'll put it in the trunk." Their mother reached for the trunk release lever. "We can throw it away later."

Tina handed her mother the bag. "I'm going to walk around a little, clear my head. Teddy, you want to come."

He nodded. "Sure."

"Don't go too far, okay?" Elaine opened all the car doors wide and sank into the passenger seat. When Ted glanced over his shoulder as he and Tina strode along the ravine, he could see his mother shuffling through the contents of the glove compartment, reorganizing the many maps she could not read.

"Hey, I know this place," Tina said after they'd walked some minutes in silence.

"You do?"

"Terrell brought me here one time in that red Eclipse I had. He called me the Eclipse Girl 'cause he saw me parking in the lot of this club downtown, and he didn't know my name, see, so he asked some friends of mine who the Eclipse Girl was." Her smooth cheeks dimpled and her full lips stretched into an unfamiliar smile.

"Why'd he bring you here?" Ted asked. "This is pretty much nowhere."

"He had some champagne, and we were drinking it in these Styrofoam coffee cups. I had to wipe the coffee out with my T-shirt, so it wouldn't taste too bad." Tina stooped, grunting, to pick up a fallen branch. She began tearing twigs and dusty leaves from this, fashioning a walking stick. "He liked to drink. I guess we were driving somewhere. *He* was driving. I don't remember where. He got mad about something, jealous or whatnot and he just, like, yanked the steering wheel and we came down there." She pointed the stick at a mud-rutted slough trailing down into the ravine.

"Wow! What a weird coincidence." Ted was amazed.

Tina gazed at him, her brown eyes moist, shining. "Maybe this isn't the place. Maybe this just looks like the place. Anyway, I spilled champagne all over myself, cracked the bottle on the windshield." She frowned and shook her head.

"What happened?"

"He was still mad, said I didn't love him, but I told him I did. He wouldn't believe me no matter what I said. He said I had to prove it, so he ran across the highway blind, like this." She cupped a hand over her eyes. "Cars were honking and swerving. But he got across. Then he shouted for me to follow him. Dude was totally drunk, you know, but he said if I loved him, I'd follow him blind."

Ted stopped walking, took his sister's arm. "You didn't do it, did you?"

She wrenched free and continued to walk, pointing again at the mud rut. "*That* ruined my car. The battery or something came loose, and that was the last of it." They came upon a fire-ant hill, and Tina prodded it with her stick, causing the mound to ripple and tremble as the insects scrambled for cover. "No more Eclipse and the last of the Eclipse Girl."

They continued in silence, and Ted struggled to puzzle it out. To him, Terrell sounded a lot like the wreck he'd caused, a guy who could be voted most likely to create misery. His sister was surely better off without him. Yet these days, after Terrell, she moved so gingerly that you'd think she had just come through a major surgery, like a heart or lung transplant, with no great chances of surviving her recovery. "You must have loved him a lot," Ted said at last, chalking one mystery up to another.

"Is *that* what you think?" Tina squinted at him in astonishment. "I didn't love him nearly enough to prove it. Maybe he'd still be here if I did." She pivoted, heading back to the car, taking long, swift strides.

Ted hurried to keep up. "But that doesn't make sense. That friend of his killed him. You weren't even there." For the first time, Ted wondered what it had been like being led into the woods by a friend, someone who'd been to Terrell like Danny was to him before the business with the colognes, someone he trusted and joked with and punched in the arm when they both said the same thing together, and then an explosion, a burst of light, a gurgling sound from the throat. Ted swallowed hard, fingered his neck.

The traffic on the highway had thickened that Saturday afternoon with semi-trucks speeding through to make up time lost during the week, Ted supposed. Danny's father drove such a truck for Con-Agra, and he said he was always in a hurry on Saturdays to finish his route. The steady whoosh from the highway stirred a warm breeze, and Ted was grateful for it. He stole a look at his sister, who was again pulling the kerchief from her pocket. After hearing about Terrell, Ted wished she'd leave it alone. It was exactly the kind of thing the Crips or the Bloods flashed around in South Central Los Angeles to show their gang affiliation. Not something he liked to see his sister sniffing at every few minutes.

This time she pulled its corners in both hands and whipped it into a roll. Then she wound it over her eyes, knotting it at the back of her head.

"What are you doing?" Ted asked, blood drumming in his ears.

She didn't answer, but bolted from the shoulder into the highway before he could grab for her. Tires shrieked, horns blared, and there was a sickening scrape of metal. Ted was afraid to look, but when he did he saw that his sister had made it to the median, where she'd sunk to her knees in the blue wildflowers and tall grass, the kerchief still fastened over her eyes.

"Tina! *Tina!*" Ted's mother raced to his side, shrieking, "What the hell happened? What is she *doing?*"

The cars and trucks continued whizzing past, not even slowing to look at the blindfolded girl kneeling in the median and shouting something no one could hear.

Ted swayed from side to side, watching the blur of trucks, all trucks now, for a gap. A cold drop of sweat trickled onto his lip, and he licked it.

"Oh, *no*, you're *not*," his mother said. "We'll *drive* over there from the other side. It won't take two minutes."

Ted glanced at his mother. She'd torn her sunglasses off, her cheeks flamed, and her eyes were round with fright. Even if he made it across how would they ever get back? The best he could do, *if* he made it, would be to hold his sister, hold her there in the flowers while his mother drove around to collect them both.

"Ted, please, *please*, listen to me."

Across the highway, Tina swayed on her knees, sobbing now; he could tell by the way she held her own shoulders, quaking and dipping her head like she was begging or praying. His mother clasped his arm, tried to reel him close, but he shrugged free.

"Ted, no. *No.*" Despite the heat, her teeth chattered.

He looked from her to his sister. How did he ever think he would get away? These two were too good at this. They would tear him apart like they said they would do to that baby in the story of King Solomon, and his father wanted a piece, too. That was clear from bland niceness the old man had layered on his temper this summer like plywood stacked over the mouth of the volcano. Ted only wanted what even an idiot like Danny could have—people who left him in peace, who gave him cologne instead of complaining the heavy kid smelled like rotting meat, who didn't even expect him to mow the lawn, let alone to step up and be the one to love them more than they bothered to love themselves. Ted couldn't even take care of a cat, but they kept after him anyway. They wouldn't let up. He rocked on the balls of his feet, took a deep breath, and then another, wondering what would happen if he just turned his back, stepped away, headed down the highway until he could hitch a ride somewhere, anywhere but Georgia or California. "That might be cool," he said to himself. Then he screwed his eyes shut and he plunged.

The Imam of Auburn

The imam is missing! Mona must tell Nathan, warn him really. Nathan knows the imam, so maybe he can help. This is why she's barged into the Mexican bakery meeting room—two dozen or more health and social service providers gathered here for the monthly meeting of the Auburn Family Services Coalition. And there's Nathan up front, addressing the group on the benefits of mediation for divorcing parents. Last month, he conducted the weeklong conflict-resolution training that Mona had attended for her work with the mental health agency, and she'd admired how calm and patient he remained despite the trainees' blundering practice mediations. He had not even raised an eyebrow after Mona's one outburst that week. Nathan, spare and dapper in his sand-colored linen blazer and gray slacks, now lists the merits of divorce mediation on an easel pad before turning back to the group to explain these more fully. Mona catches his eye, and he gives her a swift nod and a polite look that nevertheless says: *You? What are you doing here?*

Then he arcs his gaze over her head as though looking for someone, to whom he transmits a brief nonverbal message before glancing back at Mona, all the while enumerating the benefits of mediating matters of child custody and support. Why won't he wrap it up, so Mona can swoop to his side and tell him the news? Perhaps this is serious enough that she can push to the front and—

A husky voice murmurs in her ear: "Mona."

Mona starts, swings her head. It's Juana, Nathan's wife, at her side. "I need to speak to Nathan," Mona says, and she tucks a few wayward hairs behind her ears. Something about this woman makes her feel unkempt, even unappealing, though Mona, at thirty, gauges she must be ten years younger than Juana and definitely more attractive, despite the fact that she does not pluck her eyebrows or wear makeup of any kind. But the intensity of the older woman's gaze rattles Mona's confidence in her looks. "I have some important news for him."

"Come on," Juana says now, still whispering. "Let's get some coffee while we wait for him to finish." She clutches Mona's elbow and steers her from the deep-coral meeting room, through a curved doorway that is strung with decorative piñatas. The entire bakery, opened this month by enterprising immigrants, strikes Mona as overdecorated, nearly claustrophobic in its effusion of wall hangings: woven ojo-de-dios ornaments, watercolor landscapes involving burros and cacti, rhinestone-studded sombreros, and bright serapes. It's the setting for a fitful dream one might have after a second helping of enchiladas and way too many margaritas. And the smell, the sticky odor of yeast and sugar glaze, suffuses Mona's nostrils and coats her tongue. She gazes over her shoulder at the puzzled glances rippling through the assembly in their wake. These prevent her from wrenching free and insisting: *No, it cannot possibly wait!*

She follows Juana to the front counter. Nathan's wife orders coffee in Spanish from the red-faced cashier, who produces two steaming Styrofoam cups. Juana pays him, and the women sit at a vacant table before the window. Juana blows thick curls of steam, like escaping ghosts, from her cup, staring as Mona fumbles with a stirring stick, two packets labeled "whitener," and another containing granulated sugar.

Mona first met Juana at last month's training, when the woman had arrived at noon to take her husband to lunch on the last day's session, and Mona, surprising herself, asked if she could join them. The three of them had dashed across the street to a Japanese restaurant where, over black-lacquered Bento boxes, Mona discussed her background in forensic psychology, her work with the local mental-health agency, the grant she'd received to aid Muslim women who are victims of domestic violence, and the imam. It turned out that Nathan knew the imam from a mediation he had facilitated between the police and Muslim leaders after a copy of the Koran had been defecated on and the local authorities were slow to respond. Mona remembers how intently Juana had watched her arguing with Nathan—who'd voiced respect for the man—that the imam could not be trusted.

Lipstick, blushing powder, sooty eye-shadow, kohl pencil—Mona now counts at least four cosmetics on Juana's handsome face, and she catches a whiff of a citrus scent emanating from the woman's sleeveless silk blouse. "Do you think he's done by now?"

Juana glances at her watch, shrugs.

"I need to speak to him," Mona says. "There is a serious problem."

"What is it?"

Mona regards Juana's wide brown eyes, the gentle look on her face, and wonders if she can be trusted. "I need some help

with my divorce." This is not entirely untrue. Her husband from
whom she separated months ago is behaving insufferably.

"But Nathan doesn't practice anymore. He never even
took the bar in Alabama."

Mona glances at a handwritten sign taped to the bakery case, directing people to the meeting in back. "Divorce
mediation," she says.

"I don't know if he can do that," Juana tells her. "You see,
he *knows* you, and that might be perceived as a problem."

Mona is positive now that Nathan has told Juana about
her episode during the training. Her face heats up just
remembering it. The topic had been respect for cultural
diversity when mediating, and Nathan had said something as
innocuous as, "We all know what it's like to be an outsider."
Mona, who sees things others can't even guess at, had lunged
to her feet, heart thrashing in her throat, to sputter: *"You
don't know anything about it. You can't ever imagine what
this feels like! You have no right, no right to speak of this!"*
And she'd bolted, sobbing, from the seminar room. Luckily,
this had been just before the lunch break on that first day of
the training, so she didn't have to return to face the others for
more than an hour, but when she crept back into the room,
she spied the one-eyed, retired judge from Tuscaloosa, his
hefty back to her, drawing air circles near the side of his head
and chirping, *cuckoo, cuckoo.* This was when Nathan had not
even raised his eyebrow; he'd just shaken his head to censure
the old coot and given Mona a sympathetic smile.

"Maybe he can advise me, though," Mona says now.

"Maybe," Juana says. "What's the problem?"

"It's to do with ..." Mona imagines scanning a long list
that unfurls—like a bulky roll of cash register tape—trailing
out the door, bumping along the streets, heading for Interstate 85 all the way to Montgomery. "Cat support."

Here, Juana lifts her eyebrow. "Cat support?"

Mona nods. "And custody."

"Support and custody of a *cat?*"

"Yes, and he doesn't even *like* the cat," Mona says, indignation rising in her voice. She doesn't disclose that neither of them can stand the cat, a pushy tabby that bites without provocation, sharply enough to draw blood. "He's just being obstinant."

"Obstinate," Juana says. "You mean 'obstinate.'"

"Forgive me, I was born in Germany." Mona pronounces it *Churmany* and omits mentioning that she was born on a US Army post to American parents—the fact is: she has never belonged anywhere, ever. "I don't speak perfect English."

"I was born in *ciudad juarez, méjico*," Juana says, neatly trumping her. "So my English is also not perfect, but I think that word is *obstinate.*"

"Okay, obsti*nate*, then. He won't let me have the cat just to create problems, and now he wants to claim cat support."

"Nathan and I have a cat." Juana knits her smooth brow, her skin the same shade as Mona's coffee plus two packets of "whitener," and she leans forward on her elbows. "It doesn't cost much to feed it. Is this a hardship for you?"

"Food, no," Mona says. "Therapy, though, is very expensive." The damned little beast has been diagnosed with feline dominance aggression and prescribed desensitization techniques to practice—with a professional trainer—that may take months, even years to take effect, in conjunction with daily doses of costly anti-anxiety and anti-depressant drugs. These are remedies that Mona and her husband would have laughed off in the early years of their marriage, before dispatching the cat to the pound, but they are now part of the arsenal of grievances they levy against each other during their separation. "The cat has a few problems."

"I *see,*" and Juana's nod is all too knowing for Mona's tastes.

"Look, that's only part of it," she says, the words jumbling out like clothes shaken from an overturned drawer. "My estranged husband is a very powerful man, and he's gotten to them, gotten to them all, all the lawyers. No one will take my case. He and his friends, they all say the same thing, like a script. They're trying to change reality this way. He's a Texan, loaded with money. You can't possibly understand. He has me followed, he's tapped my phone. Can't you see he's just *using* the cat? He's trying to destroy me, destroy my credibility."

"Calm down," Juana tells her. "Lower your voice."

"No one believes me," Mona whispers.

"Look, there's Nathan." Juana lilts her chin toward the arched doorway. She summons her husband with a flutter of fingers, the long nails painted like bright pennies.

Mona cranes to see, and a wave of relief crashes over her as Nathan, lean and loose limbed, ambles toward their table. "I have *got* to talk to you," she tells him.

"Is the meeting over?" Juana asks.

"Not quite. Leoncio's wrapping things up." Nathan pulls out a chair and sits near his wife, facing Mona. "What's going on?"

Mona decides to trust Juana and blurts, "The imam has vanished. There's no trace of him. We have to do something."

"But that's absurd. I just spoke to him on the phone yesterday."

"That was probably a tape recording." Mona can't believe Nathan is this naïve. "They can splice together anything to make you think whatever they want."

Nathan pulls a cell phone from his pocket, flips it open and presses in a number.

"Don't," Mona tells him, reaching for the phone, but Nathan turns away, his striped tie swinging to dangle between his knees, as he listens in silence. Then he leaves a message and number for the imam to call him later.

Mona shakes her head. "You should *never* have done that."

"Why not?" Juana asks.

Mona emits a puff of breath that lifts the bangs from her forehead. "Now they've got *your* number. They can listen in on your calls."

"Who are *they*?" Juana says. "Your husband?   His friends?"

Mona wonders, is the woman stupid? "No, of *course* not. This has nothing to do with him. This is about the imam. The people who took him, that's who *they* are. They can take you away, take anyone away, throw you in a cell, never bring charges, put a hood over your head, bring in snarling dogs, and taunt you and beat you until you say whatever the hell they want you to say."

"Settle down," Nathan says, but in a kind way. Mona likes this about him, the way his ice-blue eyes grow round and moist and how the angles of his narrow face soften with concern. She should have married him instead of that puffed-up blowhard, that phony cowboy. Mona gives Nathan her wry, helpless smile.

Juana sips her coffee, shoots her a look that says: *Oh, no you don't.*

Mona lowers her voice, tries again. "They suspect he's a terrorist. Don't you get it? They've taken him away. We're the only ones who can help him."

"But I thought you had some problems with the imam. You said he couldn't be trusted," Juana says. "Why is it so important to you to find him?"

"Even if he can't be trusted," Mona says, impatient about having to explain something as obvious as this, "*we* have to be trusted, and we have to help him."

"How do you know he's missing?" Nathan asks.

Mona says, "I just know it. That's all." She doesn't want to admit that the fact of it came to her in the middle of the night. It thumped on her chest like a fist, and she bolted from bed, sweat-drenched and quaking, and she *knew.*

"So we don't even know if he's really gone," Nathan says. "He'll probably call me back in a few minutes."

"He's not calling you back."

A gaunt man in a greasy raincoat shambles into the bakery, approaches the counter, and asks for stale goods in Spanish. But under the grime and the silvery whiskers is a face Mona recognizes with a jolt. She grabs her handbag. "I have to go."

"Mona, wait," Nathan says. "Just—"

"I have to go."

"Where are you going?" Juana asks.

"To the mosque, of course. Someone has to help the imam." She turns to Nathan, clutches his forearm. "Will you come with me?"

"*No,*" Juana says, before Nathan can open his mouth to answer. "He has a meeting," she says. "I will go with you."

Nathan looks at his wife. "Really, honey, I don't think—"

"If there's a problem, maybe I can help." Juana stands, smoothes the front of her navy pencil skirt.

Mona knows Juana's words to Nathan are encoded, but in a harmless way, possibly to mean: *the woman's a lunatic, some-one needs to keep an eye on her, and I happen to have some spare time so...* Fine, Mona thinks, releasing Nathan's arm, Juana can believe what she wants. The imam is in trouble; he needs all the help he can get.

"Give me the keys, will you?" Juana holds out her palm to Nathan. "You can get a ride with Leoncio, right?"

"But I can drive," Mona tells her. "My car's just out front."

Juana shakes her head, takes the keys from Nathan. "They know your car."

"That's right." She regards Juana with grudging respect. "They *do*."

"Call me," Nathan says to Juana. "Call me, if... Just call me, okay?"

"I will," she says, and the two women head for the door.

"Are you a spy?" Mona asks, as they exit through the heavy glass door.

Juana tosses her head back to laugh. "I guess you could say that."

In Juana's car, as they thread through the steamy, magnolia-lined streets of Auburn toward the mosque, Mona slips out of herself for a moment. Once in a while, she has these episodes wherein she can pluck herself out of the kaleidoscopic tumble of ominous clues, arresting images, and startling recognitions. Despite her degree, Mona has no aptitude for psychology, forensic or otherwise, and never even applied for certification, which is why she took the position with Mental Health, writing grants and overseeing a gaggle of social workers. Still, vestiges of her training—snippets from textbooks and lectures—occasionally bob to the surface of her thoughts, enabling her to zoom away and regard herself with clinical interest. Now, she sees a petite blonde sitting rigidly beside Juana in a compact car—her face contorted with strain, her shoulders clenched, her neck muscles taut and corded, her head bowed as if anticipating a blow, and her sensibly shod feet pressed to the floorboard as though there are gas and brake pedals on the passenger side and she is stomping both for all she's worth. And Mona wonders if there's a chance what she believes could be somehow ... *wrong*.

"But that's exactly what he wants me to think," she says, over the hectic crescendo of wind instruments from the classical piece playing on Juana's car radio.

Juana gives her a sidelong glance. "Who?"

"My husband. Who else?"

"What's that?" Juana twists a knob, turning the volume down. "What does he want you to think?"

Mona struggles for patience. "He wants me to believe what I think is wrong, what I see is false. I told you, he's trying to change reality this way."

"Mona, I don't understand. Why does he want to do this?"

"So it suits him, like a distorted mirror that makes him seem taller and stronger than he really is. And if I can't see things this way, then I'm delusional or disloyal."

"*Disloyal?*" Juana turns to face her.

"You're not really taking me to the mosque," Mona says, slyly. She's sure Juana will pass it by and take her who-knows-where instead. She has that familiar and sickening feeling of being set up for betrayal, the sense of an elaborate charade hatching to prove she is mistaken and guarantee her humiliation. "Are you?"

"Yes, I am. There it is, up ahead on Armstrong." Juana points left at the domed spire just above the minarets on the plain but stately structure shimmering in the early afternoon sunlight. She presses the blinker to turn into the parking lot, her face unreadable. "Where should I park?"

So Juana knows how to find the mosque, but not where to park? Mona suspects this is part of the trick and directs her to the men's section of the lot. And she has another little test: they will enter the men's entrance to the mosque, just to see what Juana has to say about this. "Why did you come with me?" she asks.

"If the imam is in trouble, if he is missing, I'd like to help. He's a good man." Juana pulls a tube of lipstick from her purse.

"He can't be trusted," Mona says, in reflex. "Do you even know him?"

"Yes," Juana says, astonishing Mona. "I met him at a city council meeting. He cares deeply for the Muslim community, for the women, their well-being—"

"He was spying," Mona tells her. "The only reason he was there is he's a spy."

"Well, in a way," says Juana, gazing in the rearview mirror after applying a few metallic slashes to her lips, "so am I."

Mona leads Juana toward the front of the mosque, past the hedge-lined courtyard and the fountain that sounds like a giggling child as it gurgles into the rectangular pool near the entrance designated for men. Mona knows this from her first visit months ago, for grant purposes, when the muezzin, a short, badger-like man, had scuttled towards her, as he is doing now—clutching his turban cap to his head—to order her to exit the mosque and reenter through the proper door. "You cannot come in this way," he says this time, blocking the doorway with his thick body. "The women's entrance is at the rear of the building. And you must move your car. You have parked in the men's section."

"I'm sorry," Juana says, retreating from the threshold. "I didn't know."

The muezzin points at Mona. "*She* knows."

"The imam is missing," Mona tells him. Surely, news of

this magnitude exempts them from having to use the back door like servants. "They've taken him away."

"That is not true." The muezzin narrows his eyes at Mona, shakes his head, and places his hands on his hips. "Why do you say such a thing?"

Juana tugs Mona's arm. "Come on, let's go out and come in the right way."

"He's in on it," Mona hisses in Juana's ear, and she turns back to the muezzin to say, "You're jealous of the imam. But I have news for you: even if he is banished from this earth, you will never step into his shoes! You aren't fit to carry his jock—"

Here, Juana claps a cool hand over Mona's mouth and muscles her away from the entry, saying "so sorry" to the muezzin and "meet us on the other side, please." She practically lifts Mona, who struggles, but in a weak way. The past twenty-four hours, she hasn't consumed more than half of a cold baked potato and a few sips of that over-stewed bakery coffee, so Juana has little trouble forcing her toward the nearby car. "Get a hold of yourself, will you?" She opens the passenger-side door and pushes Mona into the seat.

"Where are you taking me?"

"To the other part of the lot, the women's part, in the back," Juana says.

"What a cheap trick," Mona says when Juana sits beside her, churns on the engine. "That muezzin, if he really is a muezzin, always pulls this stunt."

"What stunt?" Juana eases the car from its slot and steers around the mosque. Sunlight floods the car, momentarily blinding both women like a camera flash.

"Men's entrance, women's entrance—what baloney! He's just like the imam, but the imam is even worse. I know. I was there when we tried to interview the women. We had to arrange to meet them in restaurants in Opelika and Phenix City, and then half the time they wouldn't show up, or they'd send someone else, a 'friend of a friend,' and everything they said was framed in the hypothetical. '*What if* I know someone whose husband threw boiling water in her face?' and '*what if* my friend's thirteen-year-old daughter is kept, day and night, in a locked closet.' That kind of thing."

"What are you talking about?" Juana parks near the rear entrance, pulls the key from the ignition, and turns to stare at Mona.

"The *grant*. We were supposed to interview the victims, victims of domestic violence, women in the Muslim community. They have no rights. Their fathers, husbands, and brothers treat them no better than convicted criminals. They listen in on their conversations, have them followed—"

"Like your husband?"

"This is different, much different," Mona says, not sure she can explain how. "You think the imam is just a nice man in a *shalwar kameez*. Well, I have news for you. Those women would freeze up during the interviews, practically turn to stone. 'He's here,' they'd say. 'I just saw him.' And the imam *always* wanted to see our field notes, *always* kept his finger in the pie—trying to find out who said what about whom."

"If you think that about him, why are you so concerned that he is missing?"

Syrupy heat fills the car, dizzying Mona, but she holds herself upright. "Even if we don't agree with the imam, we have to help him." She opens the car door to let in cooler air, clear her head. "He needs our protection."

"Why don't you let me talk to the muezzin? He seems to upset you." Juana says. Her powdered skin is pore pocked, gritty as potting clay in the unflattering light.

Mona shrugs. "Do what you like."

They reenter the mosque, and the muezzin meets them in the cool, blue-tiled vestibule. "You cannot come in farther," he says. "Your arms are bare."

"Again, I apologize," Juana says. "This is my first visit, and I didn't know beforehand that I would be coming here."

"Hmmph." The muezzin glares at both women.

"We're concerned because my friend here says the imam is missing."

Friend? Mona marvels that Juana can lie so smoothly. She must really be a spy. "They've taken him away," Mona says, "for questioning. They don't have to charge him, and they can keep him and keep him until he's a dusty heap of bones."

"The imam is *not* missing," the muezzin tells them in a stern voice. "You must stop saying this. He was here this morning for *Dhuhr*, and he will return shortly for *Asr*. You can see him for yourself." He wags a thick finger at Mona. "You are not helping things by spreading this untruth. Excuse me, I must prepare for the call to prayer."

"Don't you have a recording for that?" Mona says, eager to catch *him* in a lie.

"Yes, and I must turn it on. You may not come in any further." The compact man pivots away from the women, disappears into a doorway.

"He's lying," Mona says, shaking her head.

Juana opens her handbag and pulls out her phone.

Mona's shoulders tighten. "What are you doing?"

"I'm going to call Nathan. I told him I would call." She punches in a number and turns away from Mona. "Hi," she says into the phone. "We're at the mosque... No, not yet, but the muezzin thinks he's on his way."

The *salat*, a throaty wail, rumbles through the mosque, buzzing in Mona's bones. Her arm snakes out and she snatches the phone from Juana. "Nathan," she says. "It's Mona. Tell me what does your wife do? Where does she work?"

"She's works for the *Montgomery Independent*," he says. "She's a reporter."

Dread engulfs Mona like flood waters. "A *writer?*" Mona drops the phone, which cracks on the sky-colored tile. She points at Juana. "You t*hief!*"

The muezzin hurries out. "Keep your voices down or you will have to leave."

"I'm sorry." Juana crouches to gather up pieces of the phone.

"Listen," the muezzin says, putting a finger over his lips. "That is his car."

But there's a rush of engines, several car doors chunking shut from the other side of the mosque, men arriving for *Asr*. "What kind of car does he drive?" Mona asks.

"It is a Ford Bronco," the muezzin tells her. "The muffler needs work. That is how I know the sound."

"The imam drives a Bronco?" Mona says, trying to picture the brooding, bearded man behind the wheel of a truck. "What color?"

A door yawns open, and the imam appears at the end of the long corridor. He strides toward them from the shadows, as smoothly as a figure gliding forth in a dream, his long coat flapping with each soundless step. "But that *can't* be him," Mona says.

Juana sighs as though worn out. "It is, though. He's right there."

"You?" Mona says to Juana, her voice a squawk of alarm. The whitewashed entry shudders and then whirls, like a scene taped by a video recorder being relinquished in a struggle. Mona stumbles toward the muezzin, reaching for his sleeve. The last thing she remembers: the blue-tiled floor slamming against her cheekbone like a sledgehammer.

Weeks later, Juana arrives, without Nathan, to visit her at the Facility, and Mona wonders if the woman has forbidden her husband from seeing her. Triggers, Mona thinks, remembering what the doctor has said. Seeing Juana, this time wearing an olive green pantsuit—*silk?*—with tapered sleeves and pearly cuff buttons, spins Mona back to that strange time just after she was fired from Mental Health. And she wonders if she should refuse the visit. But no, she's much stronger now. If she can recognize that this might be a trigger, she can resist it. Besides, Juana will be only the second visitor to come see her, and Mona wants the others to know she has people on the outside, people besides her husband, who care enough to come and see her in this place. So she hopes to flaunt Juana somehow, lead her through the Facility for all to see. Too bad it is midday and most are lingering over lunch in the dining area.

"How are you?" Juana asks.

Mona shrugs. "Do you want to go to the game room? It's too noisy here," she says, though they are standing alone in the lounge near the front desk, where a solitary receptionist reads a needle-craft magazine in the gray wash of fluorescent lighting.

Juana follows Mona to the recreation room, where Mona points out shelves on which board games are stacked. Disappointingly, the room is vacant. "Do you want to play Aggravation or Sorry?" she asks. "How about Scramble?"

"It's Scrabble," Juana says. "I don't want to play games. I came to talk to you."

"Oh?" Mona tries to raise an eyebrow, wishing she had practiced this beforehand in a mirror. "What about?"

"First, I want to know how you are doing." Juana sits in a gray folding chair at a card table. She settles her purse on her knees.

Mona sinks into the seat across from her. "I'm doing much better. I'm on medication." With a sweeping hand, she indicates the empty room, as though it is filled with others like her. "We all are."

"Your divorce?"

"Why would I get *divorced?*" Mona asks, surprised no one has bothered to bring the woman up to speed. "I love my husband. He cares about me, wants what's best. Do you think I could afford a place like this on my own? Without him, I'd be sleeping in the streets, begging scraps from the bakeries." Last week, her husband had taken the very chair Juana now occupies, sunlight from the open windows reddening his oversized, hirsute ears. "There she is," he'd said when she smiled at him. "There's the pretty little gal I married." The metal seat groaned with the bulk of him as he leaned forward to peer at her over his glasses. "I sure hope you're getting better," he'd added. "This place is costing me a fucking fortune. One thing I do hate is a bad investment."

"What about the phone-tapping? The following?" Juana persists. "The cat?"

Mona cups her mouth with one hand and whispers, "*None of it was real.*" Then she sits upright and says, in a normal tone, "Except the cat."

"What happened to the cat?"

"We found the perfect place for it." Mona flicks her fingers, a magician's gesture for making objects disappear. She pictures a dustpan full of ash whooshing into a bin, spume rising in a smoky gust.

"Well, that's good." Juana glances around the room, and Mona casts herself in her visitor's perspective, scanning the dusty television mounted near the ceiling, the bookshelves lined with almanacs, dictionaries, and encyclopedia sets—a few volumes missing, creating gaps like yanked teeth—the dull linoleum floor, the sagging wheat-colored divan, and the folding chairs and card tables. Not that shabby, Mona thinks.

But Juana takes the room in and takes it in again; she's hesitating. "I also want to tell you something. The imam really is missing now. I had been interviewing him for the paper. We were supposed to have our last meeting at Starbucks last Tuesday, but he never showed up. He's disappeared. Not even his wife knows where he is. She's very distraught." Juana studies Mona's face, her inky pupils darting back and forth as though she's viewing a tennis match.

"Are you recording me?" Mona points at Juana's handbag.

Juana's waxy red lips form a small *o* of surprise. "No, of course, not."

"Open that, if you don't mind. Let me see."

Juana clicks the clasp and upends her purse into her smooth green lap: wallet, keys, lipstick, compact, tampons, cell phone, pocket-sized writing tablet, hairbrush, pen, glasses case, receipts, and an opened roll of mints spill out.

"You wear too much makeup," Mona tells her. "Let me see that compact."

Juana hands her the tortoise-shell disk. "How did you know he'd be missing?"

"Preconfigured," Mona says. She opens the compact, examines her face.

"Do you have any idea where he might be?"

Mona huffs onto the mirror. Her moist breath fogs the reflective disc, but the condensation shrinks away, forming the shape of two Caribbean islands: one kidney-shaped and the other tiny as a speck. "Here," she says, handing back the mirror.

"Tell me what you know about the imam. You had some theories before." Juana snaps the compact shut and tosses it with the other items back into her bag. "You might be able to help us find him."

"I've told you everything I know. I even told you things I didn't know." Mona rises from her seat to show that the visit is nearly over. "In case, you hadn't noticed this is a certain kind of facility. It's voluntary, true, but I'm here because I had problems with perception, Juana. Now, I'm getting better. I'm taking my meds, talking with my doctor. Deep down, I've never been disloyal to my husband."

"*Disloyal?*"

Mona wonders what it is about the word that trips the woman up. "Look, I appreciate your visit, but I'm not at all who I used to be. I don't see things that way anymore. I was sick. I was wrong, dead wrong. That's all you need to know. My husband forgives me." She remembers how he stroked her hair before leaving and rubbed her under the chin. Mona laughs. "You really don't need to know that, though."

Juana stands, steps toward Mona, and draws her close in a tangy aromatic embrace. "Just because you were ill and maybe confused about some things, doesn't mean you were not also right." Her breath is warm, minty, and moist in Mona's ear.

Mona pulls away, her gaze ransacking now the four corners of the room. Surreptitiously, she runs her fingers under the card table. *Gum?* They can do anything these days, anything they want. *We*, she reminds herself, *we* can do anything they want. "Listen to me. You are being very, very … *hazardous*," she tells Juana. "But I understand. See, I used to be like that, too."

In the foyer, Mona presses against the alcove window and with her index and middle fingers, separates the blinds just enough to watch Juana striding toward her compact car. Inside the car on the driver's side, Mona spies a lean form—*Nathan*. He's unfolding a road map while Juana slips into the seat beside him. She speaks to him briefly and lifts the cell phone to her ear. Mona's not much surprised Juana's made her husband wait in the car. Really, the woman is insecure to the point of paranoia. And can Nathan be *that* submissive? These two are no more capable of finding a missing imam than they are of overthrowing the government. They're much better suited to well-mannered mediation trainings and mild bakery presentations.

A chunky redhead, the mother of a young man admitted a few nights ago after a botched suicide attempt, clatters toward the door on absurdly high heels, like some hoofed creature desperate to escape. She holds a small bouquet of pink tissues to her mouth as she reaches for the knob. Deeply involved in stitch-craft lore, the receptionist doesn't even glance up, and Mona slips out in the distressed woman's wobbly wake.

She sprints across the parking lot and raps on the window of Juana's car. The couple stares at her, open mouthed. Before they can activate the car locks, Mona pulls open the back door and scoots into the seat, slamming it behind her.

"What do you think you're doing?" Nathan says, rotating his torso so fully that Mona suspects he is double-jointed—calm, kind, *and* double-jointed.

Juana says, "But you can't—"

"We've got to help the imam. Even if we don't agree, we have to help him." Mona scrunches down in the backseat, so those on the outside will not suspect she is now inside. "Just drive," she says. "We can talk later."

Batterers

Ellis warned himself against getting involved with a married woman again. The last time this happened, it ended badly for him. He had fallen in love with the woman, and when she broke it off, he'd sunk into a gloom that lasted until he joined the Peace Corps and departed the country for the Dominican Republic. Because of that fiasco, he worried now that he thought about Caridad Bausch more than he should. He reminded himself to keep a cool distance from his colleague, who was not only married, but also the mother of two children.

But Ellis, weary of the solitude of his small bachelor's apartment in Atlanta, much enjoyed the time he spent with her and Micah, another coworker. The three of them passed long hours at the prevention resource center kidding each other and mocking their boss, the odd and controlling Ms. Hilda Cogswell, whose fear of being overshadowed by her staff drove her to confine them to the chilly basement office. There, they reviewed videotapes and teaching materials on substance abuse prevention and composed a weekly newsletter sent to other human service agencies. As Ellis saw it, their salaries were a total waste of public funds. His conscience would have forced him to quit, if not for Caridad Bausch, who now glanced over her computer screen, thesaurus in hand, to ask: "Ellis, what do you think of the word *triumvirate*?"

"Triumvirate?"

"Yes, as in the Center offers a triumvirate of services." Caridad was charged with composing text for the informational pamphlets Ms. Cogswell planned to order.

"How about *tridential* services?" Micah suggested, without looking up from his computer screen, on which he played game after game of minefield.

"Isn't a trident the devil's pitchfork?" Caridad frowned. "I don't know if that's what we're going for here."

"The Center offers a sharply pronged, satanic selection of services," Micah said.

"What three services do we offer anyway?" asked Ellis.

"Well, I'm not sure, but there are three of us. We must do three things."

"At least three," Ellis assured her.

"We just don't know what they are." Micah exploded a mine with a blipping sound.

Despite his pleasure in Caridad's company, Ellis felt he ought to eat lunch on his own now and again and leave work on time instead of lingering in the parking lot to chat with her through the rolled-down window of her car. The previous week he'd stood leaning over her car so long that sun blisters erupted on the back of his neck. And so, though he'd considered the idea, he decided not to ask her to speak to his batterers group on Saturday. Without Ms. Cogswell's knowing it, Ellis facilitated weekly antiviolence sessions for a small group of men who were ordered to attend as a condition of release from jail time on domestic assault charges.

No, he definitely would not invite Caridad, though she was the perfect choice. The long drive together from Northeast Georgia to south of Augusta, the chance for her to see him in a new role, the possibility for drinks and maybe dinner in Augusta—all of it too tempting for Ellis to contemplate with a comfortable conscience. So despite Micah's privately offered suggestion ("You ought to get her to talk to those guys. I think her second husband knocked her around some."), Ellis determined not to ask Caridad to speak to his batterers. Besides, he had to be in Columbus, Georgia, all the way across the state near the Alabama border, on Monday to mediate a special education dispute, also behind Ms. Cogswell's back. He'd be far better off taking a hotel room in Augusta on his own than ferrying Caridad hundreds of miles back and forth.

Yet, as he and Caridad struggled with the coffeemaker in the break room, improvising a filter from folded paper towels—Ms. Cogswell kept the filters, stirring sticks, and Styrofoam cups, though not the coffee, locked in a file cabinet—Ellis heard himself sigh and say, "I don't suppose you'd consider speaking to my batterers group on Saturday afternoon."

"Sure," she said. Her flushed cheeks were streaked with tears of hilarity—they had just taken turns imitating Ms. Cogswell's crowing voice and hectoring manner as they devised the makeshift filter, their employer being safely ensconced on a plane headed toward San Francisco for a conference. Caridad rubbed her eyes with her fists and grinned. "I would very much like to do it."

"That'd be great." Ellis switched on the coffeemaker with a deft stroke. "The court doesn't pay anything, but maybe I can take you to dinner afterwards."

"Fine," Caridad said. Then she cleared her throat, stretched her slender neck, and emitted a rooster's screech that would have been the envy of Chanticleer, but was such a dead-on impression of Ms. Hilda Cogswell summoning Micah that their coworker bolted—in reflex—to hide in the men's room. And no matter how many times Ellis tried on the drive back to Atlanta and later that night, alone in his apartment, he couldn't come close to echoing that sound.

For the next few days, Ellis spent his time imagining, and embellishing in his mind, the forthcoming trip to McDuffie County with Caridad Bausch. He planned a few things to talk about and hoped they would be able to speak some Spanish which, he told himself, was another good reason to take Caridad along: she could help him practice his Spanish. Before she had become Caridad Bausch or Lindley or anything else, she had been Caridad Villalobos, born in Jalisco, Mexico, and a native speaker of the language in which Ellis hoped to be fluent one day. It had been several years since he lived in Santo Domingo, so he sorely needed to exercise his Spanish. *That* was really why he asked her to come.

But his sister, Amanda, all the way in Austin, found reason to dispute this within two minutes of their weekly telephone call. "Bullshit," she said. "You expect me to believe you're taking this woman almost three hundred miles roundtrip to work on your *Spanish*. You could order some fucking tapes for that."

"I told you she's going to speak to my group—the batterers. She's had some history of domestic violence—"

"Worse and worse." Amanda clucked her tongue. "Sounds like you've fallen for some married chick with a *ton* of baggage. How many times has she been married anyways?" Ellis's

sister was a trial lawyer for the D.A.'s office with such a repu-
tation for shredding witnesses in cross that defense attorneys
counseled clients they *knew* to be innocent not to take the
stand against her. "*Well?*"

Here, Ellis was tempted to cry, *Objection!* Instead, he
grumbled, "I don't see how that's at all relevant."

"Does she have any children?"

"Just two."

"Where are they?"

"With the father for the summer—visitation," Ellis said.
The previous week, Caridad had been uncharacteristically
withdrawn and unsmiling. Ellis had taken her out for a beer
after work one night and even held her hand—plush and
warm as a silk undergarment—while she told him about putting the children, a teenage girl and an eleven-year-old boy,
on a plane to visit their father on the West Coast. He had
been the abuser, their father.

"You're in trouble, my brother, and you don't even know
it," Amanda told him.

"That's not true," Ellis said, because he did know it.

Helmut, Caridad's husband, opened the door when Ellis arrived to pick her up on Saturday afternoon. Ellis had only
spied him twice before: once from the office basement window where he had a close view of Helmut's thick calves, light-
colored socks, and tennis shoes, and on another occasion he
glimpsed a figure in the driver's seat of a pickup truck at the
end of the day. Ellis had not been wearing his glasses—he
wore them less and less when Caridad was around—but he
could tell the driver was human and not a side of beef as
it first seemed. He couldn't make out much more than that.
Now, he faced the man directly, and Helmut loomed larger

than Ellis expected, blocking the door frame and casting a hulking shadow across the threshold.

Helmut admitted Ellis into the narrow hallway dividing a dining room and parlor. "So you're taking my wife."

"Just to Augusta to talk to my group," Ellis said, minimizing the distance and his intentions, "the batterers."

The man didn't respond, made no eye contact, so Ellis regarded him freely. Helmut reminded him of a shambling building, a condemned property moldering in a vacant lot. His eyes had receded into his puffy lids, dim windows behind rain-swollen shutters. His face was overgrown by a bushy beard and a tangled pile of brown hair. And were those bed-spread marks scoring his ruddy cheeks? Ellis doubted the man did an honest day's work. In fact, both he and Micah privately speculated that Caridad—sweet, funny Caridad—was the breadwinner here, while Helmut supposedly studied divinity, working toward a ministry degree after a failed career as an actor. Ellis had rarely thought about Helmut the past few days, though he caught himself mouthing variations on his name while navigating tricky patches of traffic: *Hell Mud, Hell Mutt, Hell Mate.*

"We'll be back by this evening," Ellis said.

Helmut sucked his teeth, looked Ellis dead in the eye. "You are so blond, *so* blond for a Jew, even the hairs on your arms."

This was when Ellis noticed a fist-sized crater in the folding door to the parlor, a fine sifting of plaster on the polished wood floor, and his stomach turned. Intimidation—raised voices, slammed doors, damaged property—he knew well from his training, was the first sure step toward spousal abuse, though how was he to know who struck the door, how it happened? "Well, not much to say about that," he said. What he wanted to say was, "And you are so blockheaded, so dense for a human being." But he had no desire to start a fight, ruin his date, because it was a date now. Caridad deserved better than this bloated bully. "Where is she? Where's Caridad? We don't want to be late."

She appeared from a corner of the hallway. Had she been listening the whole time? "I'm ready to go." She smiled, her teeth gleaming in the shadowy hall. "Goodbye, dear," she said to Helmut and opened the front door without kissing or embracing the large man. Ellis raised his eyebrows, wondering if these also struck Helmut as inordinately blond, and pulled his keys from his pants pocket.

"Good luck," Helmut said, and he shut the door after they stepped on the porch.

Ellis unlocked the passenger door first for Caridad, who was wearing jeans and a sleeveless dark blouse that made her seem slimmer, slighter than she did in her office skirts and blazers. As she slipped into the front seat, her thick, ropy braid brushed his wrist. Ellis suppressed the urge to grasp and stroke it, cup the back of her head, draw her close for a kiss. Instead, he shut the passenger-side door, stepped around the car, and climbed into his seat.

"Is Helmut okay?" He churned on the engine. "He's not upset about this, is he?"

"Helmut." Caridad pinched her lower lip, wrinkled her brow. "Helmut is … *depressed*. He suffers from depression. And I cannot comprehend it. It is like a person who is colorblind trying to understand blue. Do you know what I mean?"

"I do," said Ellis, who was truly colorblind and couldn't tell blue from purple, or green, for that matter. He had to sort his socks when he bought them into labeled shoeboxes.

"If he had cancer or malaria, then I would know how to cope with that."

"What about leprosy?" Ellis pictured oozing sores on the man's thick calves.

"Then he would have to go to a colony, no?"

Ellis glanced at Caridad's blouse and wondered if it were red or purple. "You know that's what I've got."

"Leprosy?"

"No, colorblindness. I'm colorblind. Achromatopia, it's called. It's to do with being able to see color rods. Some people can't see blues or yellows or reds. I've got the rare kind." He laughed. "I can't see any rods."

"So what do you see?"

"I guess, or I've been told, I see what you see when you watch a movie in black and white. I see light and darkness, shades, that's all."

Caridad touched her warm fingers to his wrist. "You cannot see blue?"

Ellis shook his head. "Not blue or red or purple or green."

"No colors." Caridad's voice was thick with emotion, as though she grieved this.

"But, hey, I've never seen color, so it's okay." He didn't want her to feel sorry for him. "If I don't know what I'm missing, it's not like I'm missing much, right?"

Caridad went silent and stared out the window, perhaps appreciating colors anew. Before they made it to the highway, she produced a smaller bag from her capacious purse. "I have something for you."

Ellis's heart plummeted—the cliché was true: one's heart could take on sudden ballast and sink. Ellis disliked gifts or favors, especially from women; these tokens freighted him with unbearable encumbrance, implicating him as surely as if he'd accepted bribes. Ellis once went home with a woman he met in a club who'd asked him after sex what he liked

for breakfast. And he'd murmured drowsily, "Trix. Trix are
for kids." In the morning, he woke in an empty bed, pulled
on his pants and wandered into the kitchen, where she'd set
out a table that exactly replicated the picture on the back of
the cereal box, including the checked tablecloth, the orange
juice, crisp bacon slices, the pat of butter half melted on the
toast, and of course, the brimming bowl of Trix. "Excuse me,"
he said. "Will you excuse me, please?" And he scuttled back
into the bedroom, where he remembered a large window, the
sun pouring in. He jammed on his loafers, threw on his shirt,
scooped up his wallet and keys, unhitched the screen, and he
fled.

"This was given to me, and I don't want it, so here." Caridad handed Ellis a mechanical pencil, a cheap disposable
thing. "You like pencils. Here is one for you."

Ellis's aversion to pens was the subject of much teasing
from Caridad and Micah, who chided him for his "inabil-
ity to commit," even to setting his notes down in ink. Soon
Ms. Hilda Cogswell ferreted out Ellis's preference for lead
and thus kept boxes of new pencils, and the pencil sharpener,
sealed in the safe behind her desk.

His heart lofted. "It's perfect. I love it."

"A *pencil?* How can anyone *love* a pencil?"

He clicked the lead, and predictably, it splintered off,
bouncing to the floorboard. "Thank you," he said. "This is
great."

The best way to get to south Georgia from Athens, Ellis
had discovered—in the brief time he was allowed to investi-
gate his territory before Ms. Cogswell's obsessions forced her
to limit the staff to the frigid basement in Gainesville—was
to take the long-winding Highway 78, in no way a fast drive,
for one could get stuck behind a wide load, such as a moving
house, that blocked the road in both directions. This hap-

pened to Ellis once, causing him to crawl along the highway
for what seemed hours. But usually the drive offered many
bucolic, even quaint sights—barns with wrought-iron weather vanes, black and white cows in paddocks, the occasional
herd of frolicking goats, and acres of alfalfa, some of it har-
vested and rolled into large, hairy spirals. Now, after a recent
rain, the fields and lawns they zipped past struck him as ag-
gressively brilliant, nearly neon with color he couldn't identify
but assumed to be green.

As they departed Lexington in Oglethorpe County for
the open road, a flock of oversized dark birds ringed a vibrant
splotch of road kill on the other side of the highway. These
were too large to be crows; in fact, they looked like stumpy
men in dark dusters. "What on *earth?*" Ellis said, slowing as
they passed.

"Those are the turkey vultures. They feed on the dead.
When attacked, they vomit up the stomach contents onto the
predators." Caridad turned to face Ellis, her dark eyes wide
in her oval face. "Tell me about your group. What are they
like?"

"Well, you'll see when we get there." Ellis didn't want
to predispose her toward them based on his feelings about
the men. He especially had no desire to mention Ayo, the
Nigerian, whose certainty about the intellectual inferiority of
women led him to question their basic humanity and to place
them on a personally conceived evolutionary scale somewhere between dogs and cattle. This would surely put her off.
"They've all had some bad luck. I guess you could say they've
had their problems."

"I am really looking forward to talking to them."

"Speaking of talking, ¿quieres hablarme en español?"

"Claro que si," she said, but slowly and carefully, the way
she always spoke Spanish to him, like he was an impaired

five-year-old. "I will tell you about the colors in Spanish, so you will know them more, what they taste like, what they smell like, okay?"

Ellis nodded, wishing he had not mentioned his debility. "¿Que es azul?"

"El azul es como hielo," she began, and they limped through a discussion of the sound of purple, smell of green, taste of brown lasting all the way to McDuffie County.

As Ellis pulled into the parking lot of the Baptist church, where the group met in a small bungalow just behind the church, he spied Ayo, always first to arrive, dropped off by his wife, his only family member with a driver's license. She had the habit of bringing Ayo early and leaving him long past the time the others departed, sometimes arriving as Ellis loaded the teaching materials into his trunk, the dimples deep in her round, shiny face as she collected her husband from the shadeless, shimmering gravel lot. Ayo already looked as stiff and dehydrated as a wrung-out washrag. He shook himself before taking choppy steps toward them, and Ellis wondered how long she'd punished the man this time, the woman whom her husband deemed somewhat smarter than a cow, but not quite as clever as a hound.

"Is that one of the men?" Caridad asked in English.

"Yep, that's Ayo," Ellis told her. "He's from Nigeria."

"Nigeria," Caridad said, stretching out the word in a dreamy way, as though picturing herself there—or so Ellis imagined—wearing a striped robe at a bazaar, haggling over breadfruit... "He must have a hard time here."

"You could say that," Ellis admitted. He parked alongside the handicapped space nearest the entrance to the bungalow and popped open the trunk, where he'd stored the dry-erase board, the file case, plastic cups, napkins, a box of graham crackers and a Styrofoam cooler containing two family-sized bottles of soft drinks and a bag of ice.

Caridad helped him unload the trunk into the small classroom. Ellis set up a snack table under a bulletin board posted with a warning—punctuated by many exclamation points—against tampering with the air-conditioning. Ayo lingered at the threshold until Ellis greeted him and introduced Caridad, who hung back, neither offering her hand to shake nor making eye-contact with the Nigerian. Ayo seemed satisfied, even pleased with her reticence. He took his customary seat at the head of the table, put his hands behind his neck, stretched out his legs, and cast his eyes up at the rust-stained ceiling. "My wife is being very foolish today," he said with a sigh.

"Let's wait, okay, Ayo? Let's wait until the group gets here to start." Ellis removed the papers he needed for the workshop and snapped the file case shut. Once Ayo got started on his grievances against his wife, little could be done to stanch the flow from the wounds he picked open.

Caridad poured herself a cupful of sugar-free cola. "Would you like some?" she asked Ayo. "It is refreshing."

"I *never* touch caffeine or alcohol," he said.

"There's water." Ellis pointed at a cooler in the short hall leading to the restrooms. He arranged the attendance sheets on his clipboard.

"Water would be fine," Ayo said, without making a move toward the dispenser.

Caridad sipped from her cup. "Where is the restroom, Ellis?"

"Down that hall, take a left." Ellis noted that Lavender Howell was scheduled to graduate next week; he'd have to remember to pick up doughnuts at the Bi-Lo. P.J., though,

missed last week's session. Ellis scribbled a reminder to himself about P.J., the additional workshop to be assigned.

As Ellis made his notes, Lavender, Buck, and even P.J.
filed into the room. P.J. grabbed a napkin and loaded it with
as many graham crackers as he could freight to the table, and
then he returned to the snacks to pour two Solo cups full of
sugary cola. Ellis was pretty sure the nineteen-year-old was
a user: the sweets, the long-sleeved flannel shirts, the unex-
plained absences. But unless he arrived to the group meeting
stoned and disruptive, that wasn't a concern, really. In fact,
Ellis risked losing the kid if he mentioned his suspicions.
And how would that help P.J.'s girlfriend and their baby?

By the time Caridad returned and took her seat beside
Ellis, the men had settled around the long worktable and
pulled out their homework notebooks, cheap spiral-bound
tablets Ellis had presented to each one at the first session.
After eight weeks, Ayo's still looked new, though he filled it
regularly with page after page of elegantly scripted complaint.
P.J. had lost his, and now its replacement looked grubby and
abused, as if he used it for place-kicking practice. Lavender's
notebook was nearly as neat as Ayo's, though this was because
he rarely used it. Somehow, the cover of Buck's tablet had
gotten charred and then burnt again, several pages scorched,
as though the man routinely carried it with him into hell.

Ellis asked the men to introduce themselves and explained
to Caridad that in so doing, they would discuss their progress
on last week's homework assignment: action steps for changing their lives. "P.J., why don't you start?" he said, mindful of
the young man's trouble concentrating. "And then we'll move
on to Lavender and Buck. We'll hear from our speaker, and
have Ayo report after that." After the first few sessions were
hijacked, dominated by the Nigerian's long-winded grousing,
Ellis resorted to having him speak last, when the session was

nearly over and the others impatient to leave. Rather than cut Ayo short himself, Ellis had the group let him know when his time was up.

P.J. sniffled, rubbed his nose with his sleeved wrist. He opened the tablet to a page, which was translucent with grease and tattered, but blank. "My name is P.J. Taylor. It says here I'm going to change my life, and I took steps."

"What steps?" Ellis asked.

"I went to the Shell station to use the payphone and called up my mama last night, told her I was coming to stay with her."

Ellis leaned forward, squinting at P.J., who continued pretending to read.

"If I stay with my mama, I can't get in no more trouble with Shondra and all that. Plus, Mama cooks a whole lot better and the house don't stink like pee."

Ellis controlled his urge to sigh. "What do we call that?"

"Avoidance," Ayo said, separating the syllables with such precision that it sounded more like a phrase: A *boy dance.* "That is avoidance."

"Is this a good strategy?" Ellis asked.

Caridad frowned oh-so slightly, and Buck, taking the cue, cleared his throat to speak. "That ain't a good strategy on account of you can't avoid ever thing 'less you die. I mean, you got to deal with shit, am I right, partner?" He faced Ellis, but his wayward eye traveled toward the ceiling rust, while the other eye focused on his own right thumbnail, the blackened one he said he'd smashed in the door of his truck.

"Not only that," Ellis said, "but we're here to talk about problems we have relating to women and taking advantage of women—"

"Male privilege," Ayo put in, but he rolled his eyes when he said it.

"Exactly." Ellis ignored the eye-rolling. "You're not going to break this pattern if you merely take it to another house and expect your mama to do for you what you need to do for yourself."

P.J.'s mouth hung open, his dark eyes empty. He reached for a graham cracker and thrust it between his lips.

"Think about it, at least, will you?" Ellis turned to Lavender. "How about you, Lavender?"

Lavender flinched as though from a mild electrical shock. Usually, he enjoyed a certain degree of invisibility in the group, Ellis had noticed, through silence and stillness. Now, he flipped the pages of his notebook until he came to a list printed in block letters. "I have contacted the Augusta Morticians Association for a list of 'credited mortuary science schools," he read haltingly. "And I have called up the school close to my home. Miss Hannah Brice will send me a brochure and a form." He slapped the tablet shut. "My name is Lavender Howell."

"Sounds good." Ellis suspected Lavender's girlfriend, an ambitious kindergarten teacher, had conceived of, written, and executed the first steps of the plan—too bad she had to teach and couldn't attend the classes in mortuary science for him, as well.

"Touching the dead." Ayo shuddered. "Why would you want to do such work?"

Lavender shrugged, but Buck, eyes wandering wildly, said, "Hell, it's honest work, even creative, am I right, partner?" It wasn't clear to whom he was speaking, but Caridad nodded. Inexplicably, women responded with warmth to the runty truck driver, despite his crazy eyes, thinning thatch of pale hair, and large freckled forehead.

"Tell us your plan, will you, Buck?" Ellis asked.

Buck didn't even bother to open his burnt tablet, but he

stood up and smoothed his denim jacket before crossing his arms over his chest. "My name is Buck Rhodes, ma'am, pleased to make your acquaintance." He winked at Caridad before addressing the group. "Well, I called up my brother. The one I had that fight with over Christmas, the one stabbed me in the hip. I called him up, and I says, I forgive you, my brother."

"That's good," Ellis said. "But how does that relate to your action plan?"

"Well, I had to borrow some money from him to replace the battery on my truck, so I can work next week, but we talked, my brother and me. We talked about starting up a business together." He fished in the breast pocket of his Levi jacket and pulled out a nut in a smooth dark shell shaped like a fat teardrop. "This here's a buckeye. I got a tree full of them in my backyard. My brother and me, we can punch these teeny, tiny little holes in them and string them on chains, like jewelry or souvenirs. They're for good luck, you see, lucky charms. And it goes with my name—Buck and Big Brother's Buckeyes." He handed the drop-shaped pod to Caridad and sat down. "It's for you."

Lucky Charms, Ellis couldn't help thinking of the breakfast cereal. He resisted pointing out that a tree full of these hadn't exactly been spelling out good fortune for Buck lately. Ayo let out a sound like a teakettle emitting steam, and Lavender stared at the table top while P.J. munched another cracker. Caridad slipped the nut into her purse.

"O-*kay*," Ellis said, after a quick glance at his wristwatch. "As I said, we'll get to Ayo and the next assignment at the end of the session. Now, I'd like to introduce our guest today. This is Ms. Caridad Bausch, she's a coworker of mine at the substance-abuse prevention center over in Gainesville, and she's going to bring us a perspective on domestic violence we haven't heard yet."

Caridad smiled at the men, one after another. Buck and P.J. grinned back. "Thank you for inviting me here. I don't know what you expect, and this might sound strange, but I have wanted to say what I have to say today for a long time. It is a story, really, about my experience with this problem." Then she told how she drove across an intersection with a green light and was hit by a woman turning left illegally. No one had been injured in the accident, Caridad explained, except that she'd been bruised on her calf, pelted by a plastic bottle of window cleaner that shot out from under the driver's seat with the impact. And everyone agreed—the other driver, the police who arrived on the scene, and later both insurance companies—that the accident had not been Caridad's fault. Everyone, that is, but her husband.

Though her husband had been sympathetic on the telephone when Caridad called about the wreck, he'd exploded with fury when she picked him up from work that evening. "He was very angry." She paused, compressed her lips. "With my children in the car, he called me terrible, terrible names," she said, surveying the group. "Right then I thought this man is going to jail tonight."

Buck scratched his neck, inclined his head, and Ayo's eyes were wide, unblinking. P.J. stopped chewing, and even Lavender leaned forward.

"When I made that choice," Caridad said, her face relaxed, eyelids lowered, recounting this, "it felt so nice, I started to hum with a song on the radio. He did not like that and turned it off, but I kept humming, all the way home."

"What happened?" Ayo asked. "What happened after that?"

"Of course, I *knew* what would happen, so first I sent the children over to the neighbor's house. I don't like them to see such things. I had an action plan, as you call it, and not too many more steps to make."

"She's right." Buck scratched his scalp producing a sandpapery sound. "This is how it is—we get worked up, just like blisters ready to be popped. I know it's true."

"When the children were gone, he hit my head into the wall, and then he tried to strangle me, but I collapsed, pretended to faint, and he stopped. He did not want to go to jail, but it was too late," Caridad said. "I had already decided."

"Um," Ellis said, worrying that she might be misunderstood by these men who were only too eager to shirk the blame for their acts. "What Ms. Bausch means is that her *husband* made a poor choice. He made the decision."

"No, it was *my* choice. I wanted him to go to jail."

"This is how it is, how it really is," Buck said. "I know it. Right before Christmas when my brother stabbed me, my wife drove over to the Golden Pantry and bought me a case of beer. Now, she's been riding my ass since we first met, some thirty-odd years ago, for me to stop my drinking, but she *buys* me this case of beer. See, I was like a blister, ready to pop, so she did what she had to do to pus the demons out before the family dinner. Only thing—she didn't get them all."

"Tell the rest of it," Ayo said to Caridad.

"I got away, called the police from the manager's apartment, and they arrested him. He went first to jail, and then to the prison. This was not the first time, you see. When he got out, we were gone, the apartment empty." Caridad examined her hands, the long fingers tapered into well-shaped nails. "We were divorced, and I moved over a thousand miles away, with my children."

"I am not an abuser of substances, including women," Ayo said.

"It doesn't matter what *you* are," Buck told him. "It's not up to you."

"But it *is* up to him. It's up to all of us," Ellis insisted. The most difficult thing the group had done in the early weeks was to acknowledge their responsibility, to recognize—in the manner of alcoholics in AA—the problem. The first few weeks, they had opened each meeting introducing themselves and citing the act that consigned them to this training: they were batterers. Now, in a matter of minutes, this was coming undone. Ellis shot Caridad a sharp look. She seemed calm, even pleased, examining the fingernails of one hand and then the other, and now pinching at a cuticle. Who was she to take this hard-won agency from these men, whose excuses—*she made me so mad, I had no choice*—Ellis struggled again and again to dismantle?

"*We* are the abused ones," Ayo said. "I am the victim."

Buck ran a palm over his sparse hair. "I'm really more of an entrepreneur myself, but I see where she's coming from."

"What else I have to do to finish the program?" Lavender asked Ellis. "I done everything, haven't I?"

P.J. stuffed the pockets of his oversized pants with the remaining graham crackers.

Just over half an hour had passed, and Ellis wondered if he ought to let Ayo speak. Undecided, he said, "Next week, the assignment is to write *why* you are here in this program, what *you* had to do with being here. Now, come on, men, don't be blind. We did this the first week, and you can look back in your notes, if you have trouble remembering."

"I have only told what you must know," Caridad said.

Ellis lowered his voice. "Do you have *any* idea what you're doing?"

She cleared her throat and gazed at the men seated around the table. "You live with people who know you. They know what you are likely to do. Believe me, a woman who has been hit by a man often can tell what is coming next." She dropped her eyes to the scarred table top. "You think that will not be used against you? If you think that, then you must believe we are like gods or angels, or else you must be a little stupid," she said. "I do not think that you are stupid."

As she spoke, sirens droned in the background, growing louder and louder, until the piercing wail silenced her. Ellis wondered if the nearby picture frame factory had caught fire again; it sounded as though two county stations were responding, there was such clamor as the sirens drew nearer.

Lavender stood and seized Ellis's wrist. "Tell me what I got to do, you hear?"

Tires sputtered onto the gravel lot and still the sirens blared. Was the church itself on fire? The blinds in the meeting room were drawn to keep out the heat. "What the devil?" Buck rose and cracked open the door. Two squad cars had pulled onto the lot, and a few more were cruising up the drive. The sirens cut off, and car doors swung open. An amplified voice rang out: *Lavender, Lavender Howell!*

"Good lord, man." Buck kicked the door shut. "What you done?"

Lavender squeezed Ellis's arm so tightly it throbbed. Ellis willed himself into an artificial calm, a deliberate slowing of his heart rate, the drawing of deep, easy breath—the artificial relaxation he achieved when mugged by machete-wielding thugs near the Haitian border.

Lavender turned to the others. "He didn't tell me what else I got to do." Perspiration beaded on his pale brow, one drop trickled to the tip of his nose and plopped to the linoleum floor. He looked at Ellis. "You're supposed to tell me what to do."

"You've got to go out there, man." Ellis shrugged, pretending it didn't matter to him what Lavender did. "That's what you have to do. There's nothing left."

Lavender dropped Ellis's wrist. He looked shy, even embarrassed, his dark eyes blinking back tears. "I thought it would end different than this."

After Lavender surrendered himself, a tall, stringy sheriff's deputy with a ragged moustache took statements from Ellis and Caridad, while his hefty female partner wrote down what Ayo and P.J. had to say.

"It was his girlfriend," the deputy told him when Ellis asked what Lavender had done. "Her mother found the body in the house they rented over by the trailer park. A shame 'cause she was a nice woman, taught my Candace at the elementary school."

Ellis remembered Lavender's carefully printed plan. He felt Caridad shiver beside him, and he touched her elbow. Then she waited in the kitchenette while Ellis gave his statement, and he loaded up the car during her interview. The sky deepened and shadows spread, welling like spilled ink. They would be lucky to get back to Athens by ten. He would have to forget about dinner in Augusta, forget about it altogether. Besides, he no longer knew what he felt about Caridad after what she'd told the group. In the confusion of Lavender's arrest, Ellis unreasonably blamed her for what Lavender had done. As he told himself this was wrong and slammed the trunk shut, he again spied Ayo, standing at the far side of the parking lot near the street, still waiting for his wife. He trudged toward the Nigerian, who stared as though transfixed by the faded willow under which Buck had parked his truck's cab.

"Pretty strange stuff, huh?" Ellis said, remembering that Ayo had never had a chance to have his say. "You never talked about your action plan. What is it?"

"It's in here." Ayo pointed to his forehead dully. "And in here." He held out the tablet. "You can read about it."

Ellis took the notebook. "Your wife, then, you had something to say—"

"Ah, my wife, my wife is behaving so foolishly." His face shone and eyes flashed. "You would not believe what I must put up with." Ayo embarked upon a masterwork of accusation, indignation, and outrage, a litany to which Ellis hadn't the heart to do more than intersperse the occasional "really?" and "is that right?"

According to Ayo, the woman had overfed the cat causing it to vomit in Ayo's new shoes, she'd bought several cases of diapers on sale only to give them away to friends, she'd spiked his herbal tea with Dramamine so she could go out late at night, and she had accidentally flushed a set of keys down the toilet. Ellis couldn't recall the man's line of work, but Ayo's genius lay in weaving these extraordinary tapestries of lament and invective, each more complex and richly detailed than the last. Even Ellis had to admire the eloquent beauty of this man's song of spousal reproach. And as long as Ellis listened to Ayo, he didn't have to think but fleetingly of Lavender, who would have been the first to complete the program, how he'd failed him, and cost a woman her life.

"I came here to escape war," Ayo told him as he wound to a close.

"Yeah?"

"But in this country, there is also war."

"I suppose there's war," Ellis said, "wherever you want it to be."

"The women are winning, even when they die, like Lavender's woman, they win, again and again. They cannot lose. Here, the women always win."

Caridad appeared in the threshold of the church meeting room with Buck.

"Is that so bad?" Ellis asked, but he didn't wait for an answer. He turned away and hurried to meet Caridad and Buck near the car. "Can we go?" he asked.

Buck nodded. "My wife's probably having fits by now."

"Do you want to call her?" Ellis reached for the phone holstered on his belt.

"No phone, buddy. Got disconnected yesterday, right after I called my brother." Buck laughed, and he bolted for the semi cab parked on the lawn.

"That was something." Caridad's eyes were wide with excitement, glimmering in the dark like deep water. "I didn't know you had such meetings."

"There's a lot you don't know about me." Ellis, who'd remained calm until this time, felt a sudden chill and clenched his jaw to keep his teeth from chattering.

"How are you?" Caridad clutched his arm, her touch radiating cozy heat.

"Why did you say that stuff to my group, Caridad?" he asked pointblank. "I talk and talk to them about taking responsibility and owning up—"

"I thought you would want me to tell what is true, what I know."

What a mistake this had been, what a disaster. "I guess it's too late for dinner in Augusta," he said.

"If you say so."

Ayo's plump wife bumped their old boat of a car up the drive and steered it into the lot. She had loaded the passenger seats with her girlfriends, and their bangled arms hung from the opened windows. Throbbing rap music and laughter poured from these. Ayo's wife was much too young for him, Ellis thought, as he watched the man take stiff-legged steps toward the car. Talk about mistakes and disasters. But, when the headlights lit on the spare man, Ayo's wife squealed with joy. The front door was flung open, a girlfriend hopped out to scoot into the backseat, and as for Ayo, he was grinning, his cheeks bunched with pleasure.

Ellis dropped the keys. But instead of stooping to pick them up, he reached for Caridad's bare arm—brown as a mouthful of warm honey—and pulled her close, as Ayo slid into the seat beside the unsuitable woman who finally had arrived to claim him.

Human Services

In his excitement over the Monday night football game that brought the Green Bay Packers to Southern California, Rita's ex-husband Beto managed to forget—if he'd ever comprehended this—that she could barely stand the sight of him. Why else would he linger at her threshold, grinning and trying to engage her in discussion of statistics and player injuries, as though she were one of his buddies? Why couldn't he wait in the car? He usually did when he took their children out for what he called their "visitations," as if he were on the level of the Virgin Mother, given to manifesting before them in some grotto. Though he lived in the same duplex as Rita, he'd usually climb into his dusty Honda hatchback (the filth-mobile, she privately called it) parked in their shared driveway, honking obnoxiously, in an effort to speed up their departure, or else he waited next door, on his side of the house, his television set booming with explosions and gunfire, rattling the framed school portraits of their children on Rita's mantel.

"Hurry up, Sammy," Rita called over her shoulder. "Your father's here." She was tempted to close the door on him and return to her laptop on the kitchen table where she was drafting a grant proposal. Though she'd worked on it all day at the office, it still wasn't complete, and she'd brought it home to finish. Rita had less than twenty-four hours to meet the deadline for electronic submission, so she had reason to nudge the door partly closed. But what if he followed her inside? Rita remained rooted at the threshold, her arms folded over her chest.

"That boy needs to hurry." Beto's brown eyes shone under thick lashes that were dewy with excitement. Rita knew her ex-husband's enthusiasms quite well. There'd been a time when she—though a plain-looking woman who could never be called sexy or alluring except maybe in an ironic way—was the focus of his intense and thrilling attention. But apart from his devotion to the Packers, Beto's passions never lasted. The ardor that carried Rita away, like a truck without brakes, chugged out of fuel after the first decade of their marriage.

"We need to get there before the players' bus arrives," Beto said, "so we can get some autographs."

"I see." Rita controlled the urge to roll her eyes. She remembered a family trip from Southern California to Tempe, Arizona, years ago for a preseason game between the Green Bay Packers and the Phoenix Whatevers. They had all stood in the bludgeoning heat while Beto pestered arriving players to sign his program. Alongside the towering athletes, Beto resembled a husky child. The few who stopped had to stoop to shake his hand. Many just brushed him away like an insect. How tender and protective of him she'd felt then, as he pursued his humiliating quest. Now, she thought this autograph-seeking every bit as contemptible as it seemed to the impatient players.

"I told Keran we'd pick her up in ten minutes." Beto glanced at his watch, an impatient gesture that suggested Rita somehow was the one detaining him.

Rita gripped the doorknob. "Maybe if you wait in the car and honk a bit, he'll step up the pace." She pushed the door and clicked it shut, gently, always gently.

On her way back to the kitchen, she passed Sammy in the living room with her seventeen-year-old daughter, Darla, who was sprawled on the carpet before the television set watching music videos, a grim expression on her face. Sammy slumped on the couch, his jacket wadded up in one hand, which he punched like a baseball mitt. "I hate the Green Bay Packers," he said. "I hate football games."

The Honda bleated in the drive.

Rita gave him a sympathetic smile. "That's your father."

"I hate being nine," Sammy said.

The horn tooted again.

"You are *so* lucky you're a girl," Sammy told Darla, who glanced at him over her shoulder and nodded.

Sunlight poured through the bay windows in the kitchen, where Rita kept her many houseplants. Fern tendrils dripped from terra-cotta pots arrayed on neat shelves, spider-plant shoots crawled over the shiny counter tiles, and a row of miniature cacti squatted on the window sill. Before Rita sat down to work at the drop-leaf table where she and her children took their meals, she remembered she needed the nonprofit identification number for Catholic Social Services from her briefcase.

When she returned to the living room for it, her daughter muted the television, sat up, and yawned. "Keran," Darla said. "What kind of name is Keran anyway?"

"Armenian, isn't it?" Rita said.

"I know, but still. I looked it up on the computer, and you know what it means?"

Rita shook her head.

"It means *wooden post.*' Who'd name a kid after a *wooden post?*" Darla said. "Fitting, though, isn't it?"

Rita shrugged. She often struggled against temptation to criticize Beto and Keran in front of the children. Rita lifted her briefcase onto the coffee table, flipped it open.

"Hey, Mom, do you think I could use the car?" Darla asked.

"Why? Where do you want to go?"

"I kind of want a doughnut. You feel like having one?"

Years ago, they all used to walk over to Foster's Family Donuts on Reseda Boulevard when it wasn't too smoggy. Rita liked the "olde fashioned" chocolate buttermilks, Sammy always ordered bear-claws, Darla had a weakness for anything jelly filled, and Beto favored maple crullers, though if these weren't available, he'd eat any kind of cruller. Rita had the idea he just liked the word, liked saying it—*cruller.* She'd once watched him eat one that was dipped in frosting the same shade of pink as the bottled antacid in their medicine chest. Rita shook her head. "No, but you go ahead. The keys are in my purse." She rifled through the files in her case. In the periphery, she glimpsed a dark shape on the couch. "That cat's not on the furniture again, is she?"

"That's Sammy's jacket." Darla stood, headed for the kitchen.

"He's going to freeze tonight," Rita said. Maybe they'd stopped at Beto's for something or another—he was always forgetting things and having to return for them—and she could catch them. She grabbed the jacket and dashed out. But the filth-mobile was absent from its oil-stained slot in the driveway, and Rita turned to go back inside. As she glanced toward her ex-husband's half of the house, she noticed his door hadn't been shut completely. She reached for the faux-crystal doorknob to draw it closed.

Her own front door banged open, and Rita lunged away from the knob, her face hot. Darla appeared on the porch, a baggy oatmeal-colored sweater thrown over her shoulders. "You sure you don't want a doughnut? Last call."

Rita patted her stomach. After months of body-sculpting classes, it was still wobbly, the skin curdy and loose, even under her control-top pantyhose. "Maybe just one, a chocolate buttermilk." She'd eat only half or save the whole thing for Sammy.

"Got it." Darla leapt down the porch steps and slipped into Rita's compact car. The car glided in reverse, knifing through the lace of gnats hovering over the drive and rolling onto the quiet street. It disappeared around the corner, heading for Reseda, while Rita still stood before her ex-husband's slightly opened front door. The glinting cut-glass knob—refracting amber luminescence from the sun's last fiery streaks—mesmerized her like a magical gemstone.

Rita draped Sammy's jacket on the porch railing, in case they returned for it. It's never a good idea, she told herself, for ex-spouses to share the same roof. She'd repeated this to herself many times, but especially in the beginning, when Beto failed in his attempt to gain full custody of the children, so as to receive instead of pay child support, and then declared bankruptcy when he couldn't afford his legal fees, after which, he lost his condominium, and, according to the children, began living in his car.

In her work, Rita had often seen this downward spiral. People, even entire families, who—little by little—lost everything they owned and had to appeal to charities. At the time, Rita regretted she was not a better person, the kind who would have immediately offered Beto the newly vacated half of the duplex she'd purchased with her share of the property division. But she *had* hesitated, leaving the space empty after her tenants moved and consigning Beto to live in his car for weeks, while she anguished and even prayed over this decision that no one, not the children, or even Sister Janet, the kind-dearted director of Catholic Social Services, suggested she consider.

After offering Beto the rental portion of the duplex at a nominal rate, which he nevertheless grumbled about and was usually late in paying, Rita felt blessed by virtue only briefly before being visited by sharp, persistent headaches that reminded her of her namesake, Santa Rita of Cascia. After years of marriage to a brutal lout, the widowed saint was afflicted with agonizing pain when a thorn from Christ's crucifixion crown mysteriously imbedded itself in her temple, a wound so offensive that she went into seclusion for the remainder of her days. Still, Rita insisted to herself that Beto was family and family should not live in automobiles. That's what she told her sister Imelda, who had gawked at her when she learned that Beto had moved into the duplex. "I'm family, too. You could have offered the place to me." Imelda, a single mother with a four-year-old son, paid inflated rent for an apartment in the worst part of Burbank.

"My children's father should not be homeless," Rita had said at the time.

"Ordinarily, no," Imelda agreed. "But Beto's such a fuck-up. I mean everything he touches turns to shit. What if he blows the place up?"

Remembering this conversation, and the time Beto accidentally set fire to an apartment they once rented when he left candles burning too close to the drapes, Rita hesitated before pulling the glass knob to shut his door. What if he was doing something dangerous or illegal in there, something that might destroy the entire house? In the same way she determined that Beto was family and family should not live in cars, she reminded herself that she was the landlady and entitled to inspect and protect her property, so she elbowed the door wide and covered her hand with her skirt to clasp the inner knob and close it behind her.

The mess! The absolute squalor! Had he no respect for anything? The convertible sofa, a donation from her work, was left open and tumbled with yellowed bedding that smelled as rank as wrappings from spoiled meat. Coffee cups with mold-splotched dregs, beer cans, clouded drinking glasses, fast-food wrappers, sports magazines, and newspapers covered nearly every surface in the front room. As Rita made her way through to the kitchen, she had to watch where she stepped, so as not to entangle herself in the heaps of clothing scattered on the carpet. At one point, she snagged her heel on a pair of silky boxer shorts.

The kitchen was worse than the living room. An opened ketchup bottle, a green fly wandering its neck, stood at the center of the littered dinette table, also contributed by her agency, and beside that sat a saucer with a molten cube of butter. The sink, *her* sink, was stained with rust streaks, the countertops lucent with grease. She almost couldn't bear to look at the stove, and when she did, she wished she hadn't. Flocculent streamers of grimy dust hung from the overhead vent, and the burners were crusted with a creosote crud. Maybe Beto really wasn't family. He wasn't a blood relative after all. Maybe he *should* live in a car, she thought as she stepped out of the kitchen and headed for the bathroom.

Water, at least a quarter-inch of it, covered the linoleum

and seeped out, welling on the carpet, when she opened the door. He didn't have a shower curtain! Beto was just showering and letting the water fly where it may. The flooring curled up in the corners of the bathroom and warped at the center. In the toilet floated a tremendous turd. Rita curled her lip in disgust, recalling Beto's aptitude for prodigious bowel movements and his reluctance to flush away his accomplishment. Unable to control herself, Rita pressed the handle on the tank. The water rushed and whirled, but the fecal torpedo remained intact, unfazed, as stubborn and noxious as Beto himself.

Rita peeked into the storage cabinet under the sink to be sure the drain wasn't leaking, and she found an opened cardboard box with the letters *EPT* written on it. What's this, she wondered, pulling it halfway out before it struck her what was inside—an early pregnancy test. A harsh, hot wave of anger nearly toppled Rita. She dropped the box and stepped back into a rack of mildewed towels to steady herself. The thorn in her head throbbed cruelly, nearly blinding her. How horrible it would be to faint here, she thought, with a glance at the slimy floor. She breathed deeply, forced herself upright, and thought of Sister Janet, her splendid posture, her serene smile. Of course, Sister Janet had never married. She'd never stood in the damaged bathroom of an ex-husband, trying unsuccessfully to flush his shit before discovering his girlfriend's pregnancy test.

Rita grabbed the box with shaking hands. *A plus appears on the stick if the test is positive and a minus if the results are negative.* She shoved the box into the cabinet and kicked it closed, and then she crouched over the waste basket to rummage through the trash. Rita sifted through the wadded tissues, empty toilet-paper rolls, and hairballs to find the stick, on which a minus was clearly displayed. Relief whooshed out of her like air from a punctured tire.

If Beto was family, then his child would be, too. Would he expect her to house him, Keran the Post, and their offspring indefinitely? How would she ever be able to consign a newborn to begin life in the filth-mobile? She washed her hands, dried them on her skirt, and hurried out of the bathroom.

As she rushed through the front room, she caught sight of Beto's special shelf, the little shrine he'd kept in the home they'd shared, a devotional display of Green Bay Packer paraphernalia: the pennant, the toy helmet, the signed programs in frames, the neatly stacked issues of *The Packer Report*, the folded jersey, and his beloved bobble-head doll. Rita remembered how he'd raged when she'd taken it down once for her nephew to play with. He'd bloodied her nose that time. Of course, he'd been so sorry afterward that he wept with remorse. She glanced about the room—no pictures of Sammy or Darla anywhere to be seen. But the bobble-head grinned insipidly from the center of Beto's shrine. The wave of heat crashed over her once more, and the thorn twisted into her scalp. Rita snatched the head off the doll and marched into the bathroom where she plopped it into the toilet. Immediately, she regretted this, but no way would she fish it out. Maybe he'd assume the Post had done it, she thought, as she bolted out the door before Darla returned.

She would have made a clean getaway, too, if Raúl and Hector, her neighbors, hadn't been sitting in their car in the driveway next door. They waved her over the moment she emerged from Beto's place. For the first time, Rita regretted moving into this close-knit cul-de-sac, where health-conscious residents much enjoyed bearing mild gossip to one another on their regular evening walks. In no time, these two would tell Beto they'd seen Rita exiting from his half of the house. She took a deep breath and forced a wide smile as she crossed her small yard, the dense growth of Saint Augustine crunching beneath her shoes, to their drive. "I was just checking the—"

But Hector put a finger to his lips, and Raúl, in the passenger's seat, held a fluffy coral-colored bundle to his chest. "We got the baby," Hector whispered. The couple had been working on an adoption for over a year now. Rita recently had put them in contact with an organization that handled surrendered terminal-case infants.

Raúl lifted a fuzzy pink flap to reveal a tiny, wizened face, as white and tightly furled as a frosted rosebud.

Rita had never seen a baby this small. "A premie?"

"Dwarfism," Raúl said in a low voice.

"And she has a hole in her heart," Hector added. "We're going to call her Veronica. Isn't that pretty?"

"It means true image." Raúl tucked the blanket under the baby's chin. "She had a rough time at the doctor's office this afternoon. We're trying to figure out how to get out of the car without disturbing her."

This made Rita want to weep with shame.

"Any ideas?" Hector asked.

"Gently," she said, "very, very gently."

The next day, in the double-wide trailer that temporarily housed Catholic Social Services while the permanent office was being renovated, Rita sat in her wood-paneled cubicle proofreading the grant narrative she'd composed. She glanced at the clock on the file cabinet across from her desk. If she could get Sister Janet to approve the final draft by three, they'd easily meet the deadline. Rereading her work, Rita felt a glow of pride: the sentences flowed smoothly, one into another, and from these the rationale emerged with convincing weight and clarity, as undeniable as a smooth stone at the base of a crystalline pond. Sister Janet would be pleased with the work.

The phone jangled at her elbow, and Rita was tempted to ignore it, but then Carly, the receptionist, would have to pick up and heave herself away from her desk to let Rita know that she had a call, so she lifted the receiver. "Catholic Social Services," she said, adopting a brisk tone intended to inspire the caller likewise to be brief. "Rita Portillo."

"Mom, thank God." Darla's voice was breathless, strained. "You've got to come home. There's water all over the place."

"What?"

"The house is flooded, Mom, and I don't know what to do!"

"Where's the water coming from?"

"The kitchen, I think," Darla said. "That's where most of the water is."

"Okay, okay, don't panic. Go over and get Hector or Raúl," Rita said.

"I already went over there. They've got a *Baby Sleeping* sign on the door."

Rita rolled her eyes. "I think you can go ahead and knock."

"No, Mom, *no* way."

"Listen, I'll be right there. In the meantime, look under the sink, see if a pipe's leaking, and try to stop it, if you can. Tie some rags around it or something. I'll be there in fifteen minutes, so just hold on." Rita hung up, clicked the print icon, and grabbed her purse on the way out. Then she rapped on the door to Sister Janet's office.

"She's meeting with Father Gillespie," Carly called from the reception area.

Rita strode through the hall to Carly's desk, the trailer vibrating with each footfall. "Did she say when she'd be back?"

"Any time now." Carly squinted at her screen, biting her

lip, so that facing her one would think she was working with profound, even anguished concentration.

Rita stepped around the desk to watch the receptionist drag the queen of spades and click it over a king of diamonds. "Listen, Carly, this is important."

Carly raised one eyebrow, but didn't lift her gaze from the monitor.

"There's an emergency at home. The house is flooding."

"Damn," Carly said. "This always happens. I get just so close and—"

"Carly, please, listen, this is an *emergency*. Tell Sister Janet I had to leave and remind her about the grant. It's due today at four. Have you got that?"

"Today at four," echoed Carly, who continued clicking on draw cards.

"It's printing in my office now, so please get it to Janet to read over and have her send it electronically. The file is open on my computer, and it's also on the disk in the A drive." Rita wanted to shake Carly's shoulders. "Maybe I should write this down."

"I've got it. I've got it," Carly said, a glazed look on her heavy face. "What do you think I am? Stupid?"

Rita wrung the rope mop out on the porch, the filmy water splashing onto the dark ivy woven through the latticework below. As she twisted the warm sodden strands at the end of the splintery stick, Rita thought of Keran and wondered what she saw in Beto. True, the girl had flunked out of community college before taking a receptionist job at the R.V. dealership where Beto worked as a salesman, so she wasn't exactly think-tank material. And she wasn't very pretty, but she was young, nearly as young as Darla.

Beto always had an eye for the girlish receptionists. Rita remembered the time he "borrowed" an R.V. to take a former receptionist for a weekend in Las Vegas after work one Saturday. She and Beto were still married at the time, at the beginning of his so-called midlife crisis. He'd phoned Rita from the Stardust Hotel just after she'd returned from Mass on Sunday. He was having an anxiety attack, he'd said, and the upshot of it was that he couldn't bring himself to drive the oversized vehicle back to the Valley. "It's too big, too high up. I just can't handle the thing."

"I see," Rita had said. Only thoughts of Sister Janet, and what she would do in her place, kept Rita from slamming down the phone. In the end, she agreed to drive to Vegas to pick up the R.V. and return it to the lot before it was discovered missing and Beto discharged by the company, maybe even prosecuted for grand theft. *Family should not have to live in penitentiaries.* Beto and the girl followed in Rita's car back to the lot. Unlike Beto, Rita had enjoyed riding high above the other travelers on the highway, threading the bulky bus through the narrow lanes with ease and authority. Her initial fury had metastasized into a cool calm. When the bewildered girl dashed for her car in the employee lot, Rita even had the composure to call after her, "You take care now."

But what had they seen in him, first that earlier receptionist and now Keran? Despite his slovenly habits, he always managed somehow to appear well-groomed. He was like the sepulcher that gleams on the outside, yet teems with maggots within. What had drawn Rita to him? They had both been young, when they'd met in college, and he was quite handsome then, if squat and thick bodied. True, she'd succumbed to his intense attention to her, his convincing declarations of love and desire, but it had also been sexual attraction for Rita, an inexplicable force she had been helpless to withstand. He had been her first lover, her only lover, and she'd believed they'd be lifelong mates. But after Sammy's birth, Beto said he no longer enjoyed making love to her. According to him, she was too big down there, too stretchy, and he complained that he couldn't get aroused at the thought of having intercourse with "the mother of a couple of kids."

She banged the mop back into the kitchen for another swipe at the floor. Darla squatted near the water heater closet, replacing sodden towels with dry ones. "Who'd have thought that thing could hold so much?"

"Not me," Rita said, swishing the mop over the linoleum.

Sammy had arranged a box fan and two rotating fans systematically to dry the carpet, section by section. At intervals, he'd test for dampness and rearrange them accordingly. "Don't electrocute yourself, son," Rita called to him from time to time.

The plumber she called told her that the water heater was so old and rusted it should have given out long ago. He appeared to consider himself something of an expert on the subject. "See, your soft water—sounds all nice and gentle, huh?—but it contains these caustic substances. This creates corrosion, and that just eats away at the tank from the inside." Rita nodded, smiling in an appreciative way. She couldn't stand him one whit. He smelled of sweat and cigarettes, and he acted as though she should be grateful it held out this long, but if the tank had leaked on schedule, then the previous owners would have had to replace it. So that wasn't lucky. And he treated her like she was paranoid when she asked a second time if he was sure there had been no foul play.

After the kitchen floor was reasonably dry and she'd ordered the new water heater to be delivered by the weekend, Rita's lower back ached as though she'd been mule-kicked at the base of her spine, and the imaginary thorn seemed to dig its way through her cranial wall. She told Darla to order a pizza and slipped into her bedroom to lie down until it arrived. Just the sight of the pale apricot walls and the spare wooden furniture—mission bed table, dresser, bookshelf that she'd lacquered black herself—unclenched her back muscles and loosened the thorn in her head. Rita stretched out on the bed, gratitude constricting her throat, filling her eyes, and she sank into a deep sleep from which she didn't wake until just before dawn.

That night Rita dreamed she was talking to God, but even in her dreams, Rita was rational, so of course, God didn't answer her. She'd just struck up the conversation on her own. "If you exist," she told God, "you must let me know." Though she attended Mass on holy days of obligation, though she'd received all her sacraments and made sure her children received them, too, though she was active on the parish council, and though she never failed to pay her tithe, Rita wasn't really sure God existed. She lacked faith the way some cannot carry a tune or draw a straight line. It was a skill she'd never developed, and so she'd become what she considered a fairly cunning mimic.

"Here's what you do," Rita said to God in the dream. "If you exist, place an eyelash in that glass of drinking water on my bed table, and when I wake up and see it, I will know you are real, and I swear I will believe."

The simplicity of the plan pleased her. "It's such a small thing," she told God.

She then dreamed she woke up and examined the water glass on her bed table. Unmistakably, a curved black eyelash floated at the surface. Rita tumbled back as though shot in the face at point-blank range. The force of this blow paralyzed her as surely as sudden death. But soon, reason reasserted itself. Just a dream, she thought as she roused herself, blinking open her eyes in the predawn bleakness of her room. She flicked on her reading lamp, knowing she'd not be able to fall back to sleep. Of course, there was no eyelash to be found. She had been so exhausted that evening, she had neglected her nightly ritual. There was not even a glass of drinking water on the bed table.

That day was the anniversary of Rita's father's death. She'd scheduled a 7:00 A.M. Mass for him, so it was fortunate she was up early. Rita prepared a pancake breakfast for the children to compensate them for their cold showers and the early trip to church. She woke them at six, and they had plenty of time to eat, dress, and drive to Mass. By five minutes of seven, the three of them knelt in a front pew waiting for the service to begin. At exactly seven, Sister Janet appeared at the side entrance. She dipped her fingers in holy water, genuflected, and joined them, taking her place beside Sammy. Minutes after the priest had begun Mass, her sister showed up, looking puffy in the face and irritated, as she slipped into the pew alongside Rita. Imelda didn't return Rita's welcoming smile, and she cut her a hard look when she caught Rita peeking over her shoulder to see if Beto had turned up. Last year, he had surprised Rita by attending her father's Mass and taking Sammy and Darla out for waffles afterward, so Rita could drive directly to work. She'd been pleased to see he was still capable of the spontaneous kindness that had punctuated their early years together. This year, though, he didn't make the morning service.

Padre Piedra, the youngest priest in the rectory who'd just arrived from Honduras, said Mass, so it was in Spanish, which the children and Sister Janet couldn't understand. The service was so predictable that it didn't matter much. His sermon was a variation on one Rita had heard him give before. The gist of it was to do unto others as you would have them do unto you. *Puh-leeze,* thought Rita, does he think this is the First Communion class? Padre Piedra was vapid, but in the context of the rectory, he wasn't half bad. She and Sister Janet tolerated the priests as best they could, and they spent many pleasurable moments discussing their shortcomings. Sister Janet had the habit of clicking her tongue against her teeth when most disgusted by the priests' behavior and then releasing a sigh of disbelief and resignation that was just tinged with contempt. Rita loved that clicking sound, that sigh. She felt closest to Sister Janet at those times, the real Janet, a woman like herself, who was on her side, equally exasperated by insufferably arrogant priests. The garrulous Father Gillespie was the worst of the lot. Rita shot Sister Janet a sympathetic look, remembering her session with the old bore yesterday. Trim and immaculate in her black business suit habit, Janet smiled back. Rita looked forward to asking her how she'd like the grant proposal as soon as the service ended.

But Sister Janet had to rush. She was meeting the architect in his office at 8:00 and the contractor for coffee at the agency afterward. Darla had the car to take Sammy and then drive herself to school, while Rita would catch a ride to work from Imelda, who yawned as they left the church and said, "Can't you get a later Mass for these things?"

"This is the only Mass available on a weekday," Rita told her sister. "It's not my fault the anniversaries fell on Wednesdays this year." Their mother and father had died exactly one week apart. "Don't forget Mom's Mass is next Wednesday."

"Great," Imelda said. "We get to do this all over again in a week."

"It's worth it," Rita told her, as they trudged through the parking lot. "It's a good time to remember them, to reflect and pray. I miss them. I miss Dad." Rita's father had been good in the way Sister Janet was, in the way Rita could never hope to be. Like Sister Janet, he had a cleansing, even purifying effect on people around him that inspired them to be better than they usually were. He'd spent his weekends working for the St. Vincent de Paul Society, collecting secondhand furniture from well-off parishioners to haul it to the poorer ones. "Remember he used to say, 'No one is too poor to give'?"

Imelda shook her head. "No, but I remember Mom telling him that 'charity begins at home, you know.' It sure pissed her off that he was gone all the time."

"He was so good to those boat people." Rita's father had more or less adopted a refugee family from Vietnam, finding them an apartment, furnishing it, and collecting donated groceries and cast-off clothing for them. He had even bought toys for the children out of his own pocket. "They named that baby after him, remember? A little girl, but they called her Pablo." Rita laughed.

"I remember wondering why he liked *that* family better than ours."

"He had such inspiring little sayings. I should've written them down." Rita could almost see his face—warm hazel eyes, wiry eyebrows, his generous mouth—but what were those quotes he liked so much? "What else did he use to say about charity?"

Imelda gave her a sharp look. "I would think you'd remember him saying, 'Keep your friends close, but your enemies closer.' He used to say it a lot."

"Funny, I don't remember that."

"That's really weird, Rita, because he said it *all* the time."

Not long after the contractor, scrolled plans tucked under one arm, departed from Sister Janet's office, Rita tapped at her door. "Have you got a minute, Sister?"

"Sure, Rita, come in." Sister Janet was writing something on her desk calendar, a steaming mug at her elbow. "Would you like some coffee?"

"No, thanks." Rita sank into the chair facing Janet's desk. It was still disturbingly warm from the contractor's bottom. "I was wondering what you thought of the grant application."

"I haven't seen it. Did you get it off in time?"

"Didn't Carly tell you? The house flooded. I had to leave," Rita said. "I printed it and left it on disk on my computer. I told her—"

"Oh, dear," Sister Janet said with a frown.

Rita cringed. Sister Janet's soft-spoken "oh, dear" stung more bitterly than Beto's curses, shoves, punches, slaps, and spit full in her face—all put together. "I thought you had seen it because it's not in my printer tray."

"Oh, dear," Sister Janet said again.

A scorching lump constricted Rita's throat, and she thought of what the plumber said about corrosion. She swallowed it back and rose from the chair. "I'll check again." Carly was out sick, so there'd be no way of asking her about the draft. Rita hurried into her office. And then she saw it—the blinking red light: the paper drawer was empty.

A sob nearly escaped Rita, but she sensed a cool shadowy presence in the doorway, and she controlled her voice. "No paper in the printer. It never printed."

"Please," Janet said in her gentle way, "please don't take this so hard, Rita."

Rita wished Sister Janet would yell at her, kick the desk, or simply ask her how she could be so stupid, but instead, the nun placed a warm palm on Rita's shoulder. "Maybe we can still send it."

But Rita knew the agency to which they'd planned to appeal for funds was stricter than the church itself before Vatican II. No way would they accept a late application. She nodded, though, not wanting to disappoint Sister Janet. "I can call and ask."

Rita, as usual, had to perform Carly's duties when she was out, so she brought her work—another grant application—out to the front desk where she could deal with walk-ins and answer all the phones. Something about sitting in the sullen receptionist's swivel chair cast a heavy mantel of lethargy over Rita's shoulders, and just before ten, when Sister Janet departed for yet another meeting, she found herself clicking on Carly's solitaire game and electronically shuffling the cards. After half an hour, Rita still hadn't won a game, though she'd come tantalizingly close a few times, and when the first walk-in appeared, Rita glanced up from the screen with deep annoyance.

She was a woman about Rita's age, though at first glance she seemed much older because of the dark circles around her eyes and the black scarf binding her hair. "I am not sure I am in the right place," she said in an accented voice.

"What is it you need?" Rita fought the temptation to draw one more card and minimized the game screen to face the woman fully.

"It is so embarrassing. I need help, I suppose." The woman went on to explain how her son had fallen in with bad people (criminals, Rita presumed) and gotten himself in trouble (arrested, no doubt), and before doing so had argued with family and friends (then ostracized) who ordinarily would have helped him out, so now she had to turn to the church, and Father Gillespie (of course) suggested she try Catholic Social Services as a resource in finding assistance for her son.

Rita pulled out her list of phone numbers for legal aid and local attorneys willing to provide pro bono services and photocopied these for the woman. "Your accent," she said, "is so interesting. Where are you from?"

"I am from Armenia," the woman said.

"Armenia," Rita repeated, nearly adding conversationally that her ex-husband's girlfriend was also Armenian. Instead, she said, "I know a man who is dating a nice Armenian girl. Her name is Keran, I think."

"I know Keran. She works at the R.V. lot on Sepulveda, no? I know her family."

"Yes, yes," Rita said with a smile. "That's her."

"But I didn't know she had a boyfriend."

Even if her family named her for a wooden post, they'd no doubt have an interest in this information, so Rita said, "Well, he's not exactly Armenian. He works at the lot."

The woman lifted a dark eyebrow, a hungry look on her face.

"He's Latino, an older man." Though they were alone in the office, Rita leaned forward, cupped her hand around her mouth and whispered: "He's *divorced.*"

The day dragged on. Sister Janet returned around one o'clock bearing a french-dipped sandwich for Rita from Felipe's, with a little card that exhorted her to cheer up. *Because God loves you*, she had written in beautiful script on the inside. With Sister Janet back in the office, Rita could return to solitaire only intermittently as she listened for the nun's soft footfalls. The minutes crawled past, and Rita was relieved when her line rang at half-past four.

"Catholic Social Services—"

"Mom, listen, something terrible happened." It was Darla again, her voice once more panicky. "It's Dad."

"What's he done this time?" Rita said, bearing up for a cruel twist of the thorn. "Is the house okay?"

"The *house?*" Darla asked. "It's Dad, something happened

to him at work. He had like a stroke or heart attack. They don't know for sure. They had to call an ambulance to take him to the Van Nuys Medical Center."

"Are you sure?" Rita wouldn't put it past Beto to pull some stunt—

"Of course, I'm sure. Mr. Miller called from the showroom," Darla told her. Mr. Miller owned the lot. He was president of the parish council and an officer in the Knights of Columbus. And according to rumors, he was also at the end of his patience with Beto's weakness for receptionists. He'd have no part of her ex-husband's shenanigans.

"Oh, my God," Rita said. "Is he going to be okay?"

"I don't know. We have to get to the hospital," she said. "Listen, I'm in the car, on the cell. I'm coming to pick you up, okay? I'm like five minutes away."

"Where's Sammy?"

"He's over at Hector and Raúl's having a hot shower. I already called over there, and told them to keep him until we get back."

Poor Darla, thought Rita, remembering how hard it had been to lose her own father, though, of course, *he* had been a decent human being… "I'll meet you in the parking lot," she said. "Drive carefully, and don't worry. He's still young and strong. He'll probably be just fine."

Rita clicked off the solitaire game, tidied the desk, and rose to make her way to Janet's office. "Sister, something's come up."

Sister Janet looked up from an opened file on her desk, her gray eyes wide with concern. "Oh, dear, what is it?"

"It's Beto. He's had some kind of collapse at work. Darla's picking me up in a few minutes. We have to go to him at the hospital."

Sister Janet nodded. "Of course, you must go. Take

tomorrow off if you need it. I'm so sorry." Sister Janet's phone rang, and she glanced at the caller identification display. "It's my mother. I'd better take it." She lifted the receiver and covered the mouthpiece. "Please call me tonight, Rita. Let me know if you need anything."

Rita backed out of Janet's office, wanting to ask her to give her regards to her mother, whom she also admired, but not knowing how under the circumstances. Oh, well. She rushed back through the hall, listening to the lilting music of Sister Janet's voice as she spoke to her mother. Rita stepped out of the trailer, shutting the door more firmly than she'd intended. She was down the rickety wooden steps before she realized she'd left her purse in Carly's desk. How absentminded and dithering. She trod softly back up the steps and opened the door without a sound. As she rounded the corner of the desk to pull open the drawer, she distinctly heard Janet's voice from the other room: "You know you're right, Mother. I'm afraid our Rita *is* a bit of a masochist." And then, through the thin partition, Rita heard it: the click of Janet's tongue against her teeth followed by the sigh, but this time the contempt was as pronounced as an exclamation point. Rita's eyes burned with thick hot tears as she tiptoed away from the desk and out of the trailer.

At the hospital, Rita and Darla met Mr. Miller in the E.R. waiting area. The tall, bearded man greeted Rita with a stiff embrace and shook Darla's hand.

"How is he?" Rita asked him, as though he were a doctor instead of the owner of a recreational vehicle lot.

"Well, we don't know yet. He's in observation."

Darla wrung her hands. "What happened?"

"There was a fracas right in the showroom this afternoon. It was Keran's family, I guess, and their friends, too, because this whole group of Armenians just stormed in, filled the sales area. I heard shouting and came out of my office to see what was going on, and Beto just collapsed. The other salesmen and I cleared away the crowd—they were leaving anyway, taking Keran with them—and one of the mechanics called 9-1-1." Mr. Miller compressed his lips, shook his head.

"Oh, my," Rita said, thinking of the scarf-wearing woman who'd come to the office that morning. Her cheeks flamed. "But I had no idea—"

"What if it's a heart attack?" Darla asked. "What if it's a stroke? He could be in there dying, and we'd never see him alive again."

Rita doubted this. "Hush, honey. There's no point in worrying until we hear what the doctor has to say." She moved to the reception desk, where she gave the nurse her name and asked to see his doctor. Then, they all sat on an orange vinyl couch in the waiting room. An impossibly overweight woman with a howling red-faced infant occupied the seat across from them, and a young cholo with a bloodied rag on his wrist leaned against the wall near the door. Mr. Miller and Darla watched a game show on the wall-mounted television, while Rita thumbed through a back issue of *Cat Fancy*, looking for pictures of cats that resembled theirs. She nudged her daughter when she thought she found one. "Doesn't this look like Matilda?" But Darla drew a ragged breath, her shoulders quaked, and she sobbed. Rita dropped the magazine in her lap and drew her daughter close. "Oh, honey," she said. "He's going to be fine. I know he is."

After half an hour, the doctor finally appeared. "Rita, Rita Portillo."

"Yes," Rita said, raising her hand as though a student in

class. "I'm here." Rita stood to follow him into a corridor. She gestured at Darla to come with her.

"Your husband is doing well, now. He's resting," the doctor, who looked no older than Darla, told her. "Physically, he's fine. His EKG and CAT scan indicate no problems. I think he's suffered a very severe anxiety attack."

Darla narrowed her eyes. "*Anxiety* attack?"

"Stress-induced." The young doctor scribbled on a pad he produced from his pocket. "Here are a few agencies, a few mental health resources that might be—"

"I'm in human services, Doctor," Rita told him. "I have all those numbers."

"We're going to keep him overnight, but your husband seems a healthy man."

Rita shook her head. "He's not my husband. We're divorced."

"Oh." The doctor paused a moment. "Well, what I was going to say is with therapy and, possibly, medication, he should be fine."

"Doctor, can I see him?" she said.

"Sure." He gave her directions to Beto's room.

Rita turned to Darla. "Honey, wait with Mr. Miller, would you? I want to talk to your father alone first, and then you can visit with him."

Darla's jaw tightened. "Mom, *don't*," she said through clenched teeth. "Don't *ever* let him do this to us again." She wheeled around, headed for the waiting room.

Rita took the elevator up several floors and then made her way through the maze-like hospital corridors to find his room. In it, Beto rested on a narrow bed, wearing an aqua smock. Beside the bed was a plastic wastebasket, similar to the one Rita had fished the pregnancy test stick from, and like it, this receptacle brimmed with wadded tissues. Had he been weeping? Waste, Rita thought, what waste, and her

gaze traced the shiny linoleum to the bathroom door, which
was open. In it, she saw a spotless vinyl shower curtain the
color of vanilla cream. See there, she wanted to say. That's
what you need.

But Beto looked too pathetic to reproach. His face was
pale, but his stubble-shadowed jowls and the nests of black-
heads outlining his nostrils gave his face a pocked and grimy
look. Ashamed by her exhilaration at this sight, Rita wondered
if turning from masochism to sadism would in any way be a
promotion for her, or just a lateral move, like Sister Janet's
transfer from Mother Superior at the convent to Director of
Catholic Social Services, right after she'd taken a busload of
nuns to a rally for the Democratic candidate who supported a
pro-choice position. Janet had gotten her own apartment out
of it, to limit her influence on the other sisters, but otherwise
no benefits attached.

"How are you?" Rita asked.

Beto shrugged. "I lived."

"You gave Darla a scare. She's worried sick about you."

Of course, this didn't interest him. "They took Keran
away. They're sending her back to Armenia to live with her
grandmother," he said. "It was over between us anyway. She
desecrated Packy and then lied to me about it."

Packy? Rita was confused for a moment, before she
remembered the bobble-head doll.

"And Miller fired me," Beto told her.

Not surprised Mr. Miller had left *that* out of his version
of Beto's collapse, Rita nevertheless said, "But he's out there
in the waiting room. He's worried about you."

"He's covering his pious ass. He doesn't want to be the
reason I keel over."

"Well, at least, you'll be fine. It's not a heart attack or
stroke." Rita turned away from the bed to look out the

mid-sized window, wondering idly if Beto's body would fit through it, if she were able to lift it to toss him out. She'd have to raise the blinds first.

"Coming through this made me realize something." Beto reached for her arm, reeled her close. "You're the only one who's always cared for me." His breath on her face had the rotten stench of his sheets, a stink she remembered from when they were married. Weekends, he worked evenings, and he'd sleep until noon while she kept the children as quiet as possible. When she'd bring him coffee at twelve, the sweetish putrescence of his body had lofted her spirits with the surety that she would outlive him.

"My parents turned on me when we got divorced, Miller's cut me loose, and Keran's gone." Beto adopted his familiar drone of complaint. "You're all I have left."

Rita remembered that Jesus on the cross had said, "Father, forgive them, for they know not what they do," and surely he had gazed out upon faces more affixed with ignorance and stamped with greed than Beto's here before her, as he flicked his tongue over his cracked lips, already tasting Rita's next act of absolution, of charity. *And parting out his garments, they cast lots.*

Hector and Raúl, Sister Janet, her father, and even Imelda would never kick a broken man. But they hadn't lived as she had, as Rita of Cascia had, and now she had to choose: the thorn or the boot. California landlord/tenant law tipped perniciously in favor of the renter, but an owner may evict to provide shelter for a blood relation—say, a sister. Rita wrenched free and moved closer to the window, where she peered out at the insect-sized people scurrying on the sidewalks. She thought of driving the R.V. back from Vegas, how she'd sat high above the others, stitching the oversized vehicle through traffic with benevolent grace, but that was so long ago, it seemed to have happened to someone else.

Thirty days, she would tell him, *you have thirty days to move.* Her stomach fluttered as though quickening with new life. She felt nervy, electric with energy, her heart thrashing, as if she'd finally been summoned on stage to recite what she had been rehearsing for almost two decades. She turned from the window to face him. Beto held out his arms to her as if he feared slipping away, falling into an abyss, and he was beseeching her to hold onto him. She straightened her back and cleared her throat. Rita flashed on an image of the Armenian woman with her eyebrow raised, and she pictured the sales floor where Beto had collapsed and envisioned Mr. Miller's curt dismissal.

Rita deeply doubted that her namesake had been capable of miracles such as this, and she opened her mouth to speak.

Women Speak

Lucinda Aragon swallowed a small yawn and glanced at the clock. She perched at a desk in the back of the classroom, her pencil poised over the grading sheet while Kayla Martin, a freckle-faced girl with a snout-like nose, stood up front before the dry-erase board demonstrating for the dozen girls in the class how to wrap a gift. Lucinda gazed at the ceiling. Of all the topics, in the entire world, *this* was what she had chosen—gift-wrapping. No doubt Kayla had fixated on the *present* component of *presentation*. The girl's lisping voice was amplified, clear despite her braces and the occasional spittle that sprayed from these. Her dirty-blond ponytail quivered and hazel eyes shone with fervor, as though she were rededicating her life to Jesus, instead of taping green and red holly paper to a shoebox.

"You take this little old thing off the bottom of the bow." Kayla pulled the waxy square from the adhesive tag. "See, like this, and stick it on just wherever you want." Beaming, she held up the wrapped box for all to see. The class clapped appreciatively, though, surely, most had known how to wrap gifts for years.

Lucinda gave her a high-average mark for delivery and an average score for organization but subtracted points for relevance. Kayla's limited comprehension was, after all, what had placed her in this remedial class that Bunting Women's College euphemistically called "Language Enrichment Laboratory!" (Yes, always the exclamation point, which made Lucinda feel she ought to shout when saying it.) This was a course designed to prepare students with low S.A.T. scores to meet minimum written and oral proficiency requirements before entering Freshman English. As she tallied the score, Lucinda remembered a paper in which Kayla compared a female character in a short story to Eve, who had been tempted "by satin," and she erased the minus sign beside the C grade.

On this first day of extemporaneous oral presentations, the class had already endured a stream-of-consciousness rant dealing with vampires that Lucinda had to cut short by clapping vigorously when the speaker finally paused to draw breath and after that, a speech on feng shui that consisted of the student reading haltingly from a magazine article on the subject. In this context, Lucinda judged Kayla's presentation to be the best, as she stepped to the front of the sun-filled classroom to lead the post-speech discussion.

Autumn afternoons in Gainesville, Georgia, had been no cooler than summer that year. Tornado weather, the girls explained, when Lucinda had commented on it. She'd moved to Georgia from the west coast only a few years earlier. Her natural disaster experience was limited to earthquakes, which were not precipitated by unseasonable weather. At Bunting, Lucinda kept the wall-length windows shut that fall, the venetian blinds slanted to shift the glare toward the ceiling, and the air-conditioning cranked to a constant throaty rumble.

"Any comments for Kayla?" she asked the class.

"I thought it was good," said Katie, another porcine-faced girl with freckles who so closely resembled Kayla that Lucinda had asked them the first day of class if they were sisters, managing to offend both girls. Even so, they always sat together, alongside another girl named Kelly, who, though slighter, also shared their coloring and upturned nose. When the three wore sorority baseball caps, Lucinda couldn't tell them apart.

"I liked that she *actually* wrapped the gift," Kelly said. "She really showed *how*."

"Nice speech," said Penny Dominguez, no mistaking her for Kayla, Katie, or Kelly. Captain of the soccer team, Penny was a sun-bronzed girl with a mass of coarse black hair knotted into a scrunchy that matched her gray sweats.

Meredith Knell, a former quadriplegic with brain injuries, lifted a palsied hand. "I have one question." Her voice quavered, her speech as garbled as that of the profoundly deaf. She would be the next and last speaker that day. "What's in the box?"

"Nothing." Kayla shook the demonstration gift soundlessly. "It's empty."

Exactly, Lucinda thought, but said, "Show of hands, please. How many of you knew how to wrap a gift before hearing Kayla's speech?"

Every hand, but Merry Knell's, shot up. "I can't wrap ... anything." She flashed a grin, exposing a good bit of gum and longish teeth that gleamed against her scar-mottled face. Merry Knell could barely hold a pencil. She had to be helped to her classes by her roommate, Nadezhda, an art major from Romania who was placed in the remedial class because Bunting offered no E.S.L. instruction.

"That's okay," Katie assured her. "Lots of stores will wrap for you."

"Keep your hands up," Lucinda said, "and look around." Eleven of the twelve students in the audience held hands in the air. "What does this suggest about relevance?"

A few blank looks met her gaze, but most of the girls looked away, suddenly transfixed by their desktops.

She rephrased: "How useful is a speech like this for an audience that knows how to wrap gifts?"

"Not so useful, I guess," Penny said. "But, damn, at least, I understood the girl—none of that Dracula or *fun-sway* stuff. I still don't know what all that's about."

Lucinda nodded. "Good point, Penny. The speech was clear. But did we *need* to hear it?"

Kayla's face crimsoned. She blinked several times.

"An exceptionally clear speech," Lucinda said, initiating another swift burst of applause. "High points for clarity. But let's remember relevance." She checked the wall clock—fifteen minutes of class remaining. "We have time for one more. Merry Knell, you're up next. Do you want to address us from your desk?"

"I want to go up front." She rose shakily from her seat. Nadezhda, her thick dark braid swinging, rushed to her roommate's side to guide her to the podium, which Merry Knell grasped like a walker with both forearms, her sparse hair spilling into her boiled-looking face like the fringe of a pale shawl.

"Hello, everybody," she said in her mangled way. "My name is Merry Knell." She leaned heavily on one side, freeing a hand to signal Nadezhda, who again bolted up front with a rolled poster.

"This is me now," Merry Knell said, pointing to herself, as Nadezhda unfurled the poster: an enlarged photograph of a curly-haired cheerleader doing the splits on a football field. "That was me before my accident." Merry Knell's trembling hand gestured at the poster Nadezhda held. Someone—possibly one of the K-girls—drew in a sharp breath, and Merry Knell said, "Yeah, I know. I was a lot different. Okay, so here's my speech."

Nadezhda grimly rolled up the poster and returned to her seat.

"Right after I graduated from high school, that exact same day, I was in my car with some friends over by the Rock. You guys know the Rock?"

Several students nodded. Even Lucinda, who lived in Athens, knew the Rock, an elephant-sized boulder with an odd shape that loomed near the park entrance. It was something of a Gainesville landmark, so familiar that no one, except Lucinda, seemed to notice or be embarrassed by its pronounced resemblance to the human pudenda. The Rock was painted chalky pink and scrawled over with sentimental graffiti: flowers, cupids, and curlicue-scripted names enclosed in plump hearts skewered by arrows.

"We were stopped at the red light. You guys know that light there by the Rock? We were stopped there, when this other car pulls up in the next lane, and this real good friend of mine, a really fine guy named Brady reaches over to honk at them. Turns out, he knows the guys in the next car, so he goes, 'Hey, let me drive, okay?' I was, like, 'fine,' and I hopped out of the car and ran around to the other side, got in, slammed the door shut, and honest to God, you guys, that's the last thing I remember."

The girls seated in front sat still, their necks elongated and heads inclined in rapt postures, and Lucinda hadn't yet lifted her pencil. Over several weeks, she'd grown so accustomed to Merry Knell's distorted speech that Lucinda could make out most of what she said. Now the focus of her attention rendered the girl's words crystalline, even irresistible in the way a hypnotist's suggestions compel entry into a twilight sleep.

"They say," Merry Knell continued, "I was in a coma for three months. Three whole months! When I woke up, there was only my mom and my brother there, and they told me it was a head-on collision. You know where the two westbound lanes go into one? Brady must have swung into the oncoming lane to pass those guys and crashed into this minivan. When I woke up, I couldn't talk because my brain wasn't working too good yet. My brother said no one died, and that was lucky. I couldn't say anything, but I was, like, wondering where my dad was. Turns out, he booked." She lowered her eyes.

Booked? Lucinda glanced about, but no one else seemed puzzled by the word.

"Just like that, he moved out and divorced my mom. Turns out, he couldn't take it: the accident, the hospital, all that." Merry Knell shook her head, biting her lower lip.

"I stayed in the hospital a super long time—months and months. Had all kinds of therapy. I had great therapists and nurses and real good doctors. At first, they said I couldn't walk anymore." Merry Knell grinned. "And, hey, look at me now. I got better. But when the hospital let me out, I couldn't do anything by myself. I'd stay alone in bed all day until my brother got home from high school, and he had to carry me to the tub and clean up all the poop and pee and wash the sheets."

Several girls tittered and a few glanced back at Lucinda to gauge her reaction to the scatological references. Lucinda ignored them, fixing her gaze on the podium, as she imagined Merry Knell's long lonely days spent swaddled in befouled bedclothes while she waited for her teenaged brother's ministrations.

"He didn't ever say anything bad to me," Merry Knell said. "When my mom got home, she'd clean me up some more, put this zinc cream on my bedsores, and fix up my hair.

My brother..." Merry cleared her throat. "He didn't know how to fix hair, but he was a really good brother."

Lucinda caught Katie trading a look with Kelly, who shrugged.

"Little by little, I got better and better. I still have accidents and sometimes I just kind of go blank, sort of pass out, you know. Nadezhda helps me at school. She helps me put my clothes on and get cleaned up. Thanks, Nadezhda."

Heads swiveled to behold the Romanian exchange student, whose sallow face remained impassive under a thick curtain of bangs.

"I was going to go to the University of Georgia. I even got accepted. I wanted to be an animal doctor, but with the brain thing, I couldn't go there. I still can't remember stuff or talk too good. So here I am. Now, I want to be a physical therapist and help out people with problems like mine. And that's it. That's my speech. Do you have any questions?"

Penny's arm shot up. "Hey, what happened to the dude who crashed your car?"

"Brady." Merry Knell licked her lips. "Man, he is *fine*. He goes to Notre Dame. We stay in touch, except he can't call me because he doesn't have long distance in his dorm. I tell him to call collect, but he's a *guy*, you know. He's kind of embarrassed to do that. So I call him, but he's always real busy. We're still super good friends. He is *totally* hot. You'd really like him." She smiled broadly.

"What happened to your brother?" Katie asked. "You said he was a good brother."

Merry Knell's grin vanished. "He *was*."

"What happened to him?"

"He stole my grandpa's gun and shot himself." Merry Knell took a deep breath, exhaled slowly, like she was cooling tea. "He's waiting for us now, for Mom and me. He's waiting for us in heaven."

The entire room whooshed silent.

"Hey, don't be sad," Merry Knell said. "I love this school. I love my life and my friends and my teachers, like Professor Aragon here." She nodded at Lucinda in a jaunty way. "I had a bad accident, so now here I am. And I'm really glad to be here."

The evaluation sheet before her still blank, Lucinda lunged from her desk as Nadezhda helped Merry Knell back to her seat. "Comments?" she said.

Some girls had pink-rimmed eyes and pinched expressions on their faces. But hands rushed over heads.

"Simeko." Lucinda called on a diminutive black girl in back, whom she considered one of the best students in the group. "What's your opinion?"

"Why, that speech deserves an 'A' plus, plus, plus."

"I don't give 'A' plus, plus, pluses." That was the exclusive province of Lucinda's idiotic colleague Dr. Caspar, a vapid, elfin man who dispensed superlative grades as indiscriminately as he'd hand out candy canes to children waiting in line to see Santa Claus. She shook her head to free herself of an image of him, wearing a leaf-green leotard and slippers that curled at the toe, randomly passing out red and white sticks at the mall. "There are no such things."

"Well," Simeko said, "it was just the best speech I ever heard in my whole life."

The others murmured assent and Lucinda asked, "What made that speech work so well? Why did it have such an impact on us?"

"It made me feel all emotional," Penny said, "like I wanted to cry or something." *Emotion?* Surely, this was something new for Penny, the plagiarist who copied the back of a book jacket for the introductory paragraph of her last essay and then coolly called Lucinda "an Uncle Tom," "a racist against

our own people," when she'd summoned the girl to her office
to compare the two passages word for word and ask what
Penny had to say for herself.

"What's the term for that?" Lucinda persisted. "When
something moves us emotionally?"

Simeko curled her upper lip in distaste, as though she'd
been handed a scalpel for the purpose of dissecting a live
kitten in order to find out what made it adorable. "It's that
pathos thing, isn't it?"

"That's right," and before the tower clock chimed, Lucinda
launched into a quick review of the Rhetorical Triangle, winding up with an appreciation for the efficacy of pathos in Merry
Knell's speech, which all agreed was going to be tough to top.

Just minutes after the last bell, Lucinda nosed her small car
out of the parking lot and toward Jesse Jewell Boulevard
before the rush of departing students, hoping to beat them
and the traffic generated by the cluster of poultry plants in
the center of town. Though the Women's College brochures
boasted that the campus was "nestled in the foothills of the
Blue Ridge Mountains," one of Lucinda's students more aptly
described the location as "nestled in the fowl (sic) wing-pit of
a plucked fryer," in reference to the inescapable brothy stench
emanating from the vats, aluminum cylinders clustered like
massive missiles at the heart of Gainesville, the chicken capi-
tal of Georgia. Because of the poultry plants, the town itself
was undergoing a metamorphosis. Young Hispanic workers,
immigrant laborers in the industry, replaced the aging white
residents and upwardly mobile African Americans, who
moved farther north or into Atlanta for better opportunities.
Meat-and-three Southern restaurants, Ace hardware stores,

and roadhouses were being supplanted by taquerias, ferret-
erias, and cantinas. Independent taxi companies had mush-
roomed *(se habla español* stenciled on their doors) to meet
the demand for transporting workers from their homes to
the plants and home again. At four, these cabs would throng
the boulevards, competing with the commuting students, and
with the trucks.

Late afternoons, refrigerated eighteen-wheelers, bearing
iced carcasses to vendors, labored along the narrow highway
Lucinda took to her home in Athens. She dreaded nothing
like being stuck behind a chicken truck, especially on the way
home, though morning trucks, with their live cargo emitting horizontal funnel clouds of fluff and effluvia were far
nastier things. Afternoons, the plodding refrigerated trucks
stalled Lucinda unbearably, as she rushed to the daycare in
Athens to pick up the baby, who was not really even her baby.
Seventeen-month-old Dulce was her daughter Anita's child,
Lucinda's grandchild, but Anita could no more collect Dulce
from daycare than she could care for her on her own, though
she stayed home all day. At the time, Anita wasn't capable
of much more than watching television talk shows, where
people, goaded by the host, flung accusations, and sometimes
even chairs, at one another. Since giving birth, being fired
from her job at a fast-food restaurant, and losing her boyfriend—the restaurant manager and the baby's father—to his
wife and four other children, Lucinda's only child had sunk
into depression.

Before Dulce was born, Anita had nattered on and on, almost
in a fever. Diego, the boyfriend, would leave his family, she'd said,
they'd take a two-bedroom apartment in the complex right
across the street from Cluckers, they'd work different shifts
and never need daycare, they would name the baby Diego, Jr.
(even though Diego's oldest son already had this name), and

after the divorce was final, they'd (somehow) get married in the Catholic Church, have a huge reception (chicken nuggets catered by the restaurant), and invite all their co-workers and friends, even Diego's wife and kids would attend (though this seemed particularly doubtful) because really there's no reason for hard feelings. Anita had priced reception hall rentals, visited party decoration stores, and even asked Lucinda to give her away since her father, busy with his second wife and their young children, declined, saying he didn't approve of her marrying a man who already had a wife and family. (Though tempted to point out the irony here, in the face of her daughter's disappointment, Lucinda didn't have the heart to as much as snort when she heard this.)

When the baby was born, and Diego stopped taking her calls, Anita gave up her wedding plans, her excited speeches. In fact, she said less and less, until these days, she rarely spoke, except in unilateral conversations with the television, especially during commercials. "*Right*," she'd say, "those breath mints will make him want to kiss you forever and ever." Or: "I don't think you can use the word *suffer* when you're talking about a freaking head cold." Just after Dulce was born, Lucinda would drive Anita to sessions at the mental health center downtown, but when she asked her daughter if these helped, Anita would just shrug, and after a while she refused to go.

Luckily, the baby was born in late May, and Lucinda had the summer off to care for her. She would get up in the night with the infant, change her diaper, and wake Anita to breastfeed her. Lucinda crammed her desk and bookshelves into her bedroom and turned the study into a nursery for Dulce. The baby was much like Anita—wavy black hair, rosebud lips, and honey-colored eyes, tilted like a cat's—but Dulce was somehow *easier* for Lucinda, or maybe she was better at things this time around, more patient, less anxious. She'd glance at Anita

on the couch in her wilted, sour-smelling pajamas, staring, as
if in a trance, at those angry, overweight, and tattooed people
on television and then turn back to the baby, who'd reward
her with a wet, gummy grin, and Lucinda would wonder how
she'd gotten this second chance, when she did not deserve it,
when she was not yet finished with her first chance.

Whatever the reason, Lucinda was determined not to
squander it, though she was far from satisfied with the daycare, a factory-like arrangement of rooms containing cribs,
playpens, and miniaturized tables and chairs. It was the best
she could afford, she reminded herself that afternoon, as she
entered the office leading to the gleaming white hive of box-
like classrooms, abuzz with fluorescent tube lighting and reeking of pine cleanser and over-salted foods. The platinum-blond
director flashed a nicotine-stained grin as Lucinda reached for
the sign-out clipboard. "Hey, Granny," Miss Missy said.

Glancing over the counter, Lucinda noticed the woman
wore leopard-print leggings and teetered on absurdly high
lamé stilettos. Lucinda smiled. "How are you?"

"Busy," said Miss Missy, widening her mascara-smudged
eyes for emphasis. "Real busy and tired. God, I'm tired." There
was something in her full face that called to mind the K-girls
for Lucinda. With her faded freckles and swooped-up nose,
the daycare center director could be their mother.

No, thought Lucinda with satisfaction, make that their
tarted-up, superannuated biker-chick … *granny*. "Well, you
don't show it," she said, as if to make up for the unkind
thought. "You look terrific. Love the shoes."

As she made her way down the hall to Dulce's room, Lucinda peeked in the windows of various classrooms, a wall-
mounted television flickering in each. All of the aides and
workers looked familiar to her, though they were rarely the
same people. There was "real crazy turnaround," Miss Missy

often complained, in the daycare business. But these women always reminded Lucinda of her students, or future glimpses of her students. The heavy woman changing diapers in the infant nursery would be Simeko, some twenty years later and fifty pounds heavier. The muscular Latina talking on her cell phone and cupping her ear against the crying toddlers in her care would be Penny, still trying to get away with not doing her work. And the anonymous hair-netted ladies she spied in the kitchen could be any of the others. Depressingly, she could easily picture all of her students—older, thicker, and duller— toiling here in the frighteningly near future, all but Nadezhda, and Merry Knell. She didn't see anyone like Merry Knell.

As always, Dulce's small face bloomed at the sight of Lucinda. She dropped the toy telephone she'd been holding with a clang and bustled through the knot of noisy toddlers in her playroom toward Lucinda with her arms outstretched, her eyes moist and her smile almost too broad for her plump cheeks. "Nana! Nana! Nana!" she cried. Lucinda, who rarely generated any discernible reaction by her appearance—excepting mild dismay in her students when she showed up on time to administer exams— was thrilled by her granddaughter's glee. Though these reunions repeated daily from Monday to Friday, Dulce's exhilaration at the sight of Lucinda never diminished, though the desperate look in her eyes had vanished.

The first time she'd left the baby at the daycare, Dulce, just three months, had howled as if Lucinda had chucked her down a flight of stairs. And Lucinda blubbered all the way to the county line. After a few weeks, Dulce had no longer bawled when dropped her off at daycare, though she never seemed pleased about it, and Lucinda's tears stayed clotted in her chest, rising to her throat only as she meandered behind a lumbering refrigerated truck on her way to claim the baby from the place, too chicken herself to swerve into the oncoming lane and pass the thing, even when the broken yellow line on her side of the highway allowed this.

That evening, as Lucinda fed Dulce dinner—mashed sweet potatoes, turnip greens, and flaky bits of trout— she held a forkful aloft and said, "Fish, fish. Does Dulce want fish?" The kitchen nook was steamy and smelled of smoke, as she'd accidentally left the burner under the pan on too long after removing the fillets. The setting sun glared through the bay window, imbuing the room with a warm, ocherous glow.

Dulce nodded, banging her heels on the high chair. "Fitz," she said. "Fitz, fitz. Gimme fitz." She opened her mouth and waggled her pointy, pink tongue. Though Dulce was old enough to feed herself finger foods, Lucinda used mealtimes as opportunities to teach her new words. These were just coming in for Dulce, and like teeth, the prominent ones emerged first: the nouns—"Nana" (for Lucinda), "Doolee" (for herself), "cack" (for the cat), then the verbs "go," "gimme," "eat,"; and the prepositions "up," "down," "out-*shide*." Soon, Lucinda expected the adjectives to arrive, picturing assorted aunts and uncles appearing at the door with suitcases to join the immediate family. These would be followed by the adverbs, the late-arriving cousins—all welcome on special occasions, but some more superfluous than others, especially on a daily basis. Lucinda considered a lesson on this family tree for her students, who padded their sentences with so many modifiers that they often lost track of their nouns and verbs.

Next Lucinda tried again to get Dulce to say *mama* by repeating the word and pointing into the living room, where Anita sat watching a countdown of the top 100 sexiest celebrities. But unlike "fitz," Dulce had no sense of the importance of that word or why she might need it. "Mama, mama, mama," Lucinda said, when an unfamiliar noise, or lack of noise, came from the living room. Her daughter had switched off the TV and stood in the door way facing them. Her lips moved, and words spilled out. Anita was speaking. To her!

"*What?*" Lucinda said. "What did you say?"

"I *said* I should get child support from that asshole."

"That's right." Lucinda had wanted to suggest this for months now.

"I *said* I should get a court order for a paternity test."

"You're absolutely right."

"Then we could afford to put Dulce in a better place, maybe even a preschool."

"We sure could."

Anita folded up her blanket and thrust it in the hall closet. "And I *said* that maybe you should adopt Dulce." Anita glanced at Dulce, who was poking orange bits of potato into her mouth, and then back to Lucinda, her tilted eyes clear, unblinking. "We both know I'm not taking such good care of her. You should adopt her."

Lucinda nodded—her heart tight with fear that her daughter would snatch back her words.

"Good," Anita said, "then that's settled."

Lucinda's next trip to campus, the car's air conditioner wheezed in a warning way. The unending summer weather had no doubt strained the thing, so she shut it off and scrolled down the windows. When chicken fuzz whirled into her car, Lucinda blew it away from her face as best she could, trying not to think of the birds in the truck ahead, though she could see they were packed so tightly in their cages that they could not change position or even stand upright. Their curdy droppings oozed through the mesh, plopping onto the backs of the hapless birds trapped below.

Lucinda's early classes passed quickly and without much incident, except that Leota Firth accused her of assigning her a low paper grade because of being a racist against white people, tempting Lucinda to suggest she compare notes with Penny Dominguez. In no time, it seemed, she was again settled at the back of Language Enrichment Laboratory! with her speech evaluation sheets. Katie, this time, stepped to the front of the class, bearing a bulky object enshrouded in a black garbage sack. This she unveiled and plunked atop the podium. It was a flesh-colored plastic shell, shaped something like half of a torso, with grimy straps dangling from its sides.

"I'm Katie, as you all know," she said, "and this here is my back brace. I have a birth defect—curvature of the spine, also called scoliosis. My spine is crooked, kind of shaped like an 'S.' I have to wear this brace at night, and I used to have to wear the thing all day, too. I don't have anybody to help me with it." Here, she sent a sharp look in Nadezhda's direction. Then she went on to describe how she'd endured her curved spine and her back brace and how her doctor had accused her of not wearing it when she was supposed to, though she had worn it, really she had, but he wouldn't believe her, and how her parents were always checking up on her, lifting her pajama top to see if she was wearing it, and how because of this she could never ever have a normal life.

Her eyes brimmed, and she swiped at her nose with her wrist. Merry Knell, she said, had given her the courage to talk about her suffering, and she hoped everyone learned something *relevant* from her speech, like she'd learned from Merry Knell's.

Kellie and Kayla led the applause that followed this presentation. They stomped their feet and one of the two emitted a piercing whistle. Again, Lucinda made her way to the front to lead the debriefing, but no one had much to say, despite her provoking questions. They were reluctant to criticize a girl who had shared something as intimate as a plastic back brace with grubby straps.

Simeko Tyler was up next. She approached the podium bearing a slate-colored jeweler's watch case. "My name is Simeko," she said, and she opened the box, tilting it for all to see its contents: a milky ball, the size of a jawbreaker, nested on a burgundy cushion. "This here is my grandmama's eye."

A few girls gasped.

Simeko lifted the ball out of the box and rotated it for all to see the dark pupil. "It's a fake eye, you see. An actual eye would dry up. But this thing is made out of porcelain, I think. Grandmama got it put in after she lost her eye in a fight with my granddaddy, except he wasn't my *real* granddaddy after all and he got very pissed off when he found out about *that*. The neighbors called the sheriff's deputies. They clapped his ass in jail. An ambulance came for my grandmamma, and she was gone a long time. When she came back, she was wearing this artificial eye."

Penny Dominguez raised her hand. "Doesn't she need it? That eye?"

"She's dead, dummy," Simeko said. "She left me this eye in her will, said I should always keep it and know she's watching on me, every minute, every day." Tough little Simeko's voice broke, and she squeezed out a few shiny tears. "I am the granddaughter of a dead one-eyed woman, who is always watching on me."

This opened a harrowing speech on domestic violence: husband and then second husband against grandmother, boyfriends against mother, Simeko's ex-fiancé's drunken attempt to extinguish a cigarette on her cheek. "I smacked that shit-grin off his face and jammed his nose with my elbow, and I am never talking to him no more. 'Cause my grandmama's watching on me." She held the eye aloft and strobed the class with its ceramic gaze. "And she's watching on you, too."

After Simeko's speech, Lucinda almost suspended the oral presentations to shift the focus to the much less disturbing topic of subject-verb agreement. But Lee Radcliff wandered into the classroom, reeking of cigarette smoke and beer. She'd missed the previous week of class, and Lucinda had been wondering when Lee would ever turn up again. It'd be helpful, she thought, to have a speech grade for the girl, whose email address began with "barwench" and who was repeating Language Enrichment Laboratory! for the third time. Besides, she told herself, it's best to catch students like Lee by surprise. Last year, the girl had latched on to Lucinda's instruction to make the speeches memorable and brought in a drinking glass containing a goldfish. During her speech, Lee had plucked the fish out by its tail, popped it into her mouth, and swallowed it whole, causing Alexi Shearer, a dance major (and vegan) seated in the front row, to tumble from her desk in a faint. Lucinda had no idea what Lee's speech had been about, but that goldfish was unforgettable. "Are you ready to give your presentation, Lee?" Lucinda asked before Lee could cradle her head in her arms, and commence snoring.

"Sure," Lee said gamely. She ambled up front to report on the previous evening's episode of *Law and Order*. The change of topic provided relief, and last night, Lucinda had fallen asleep on the recliner before the television drama ended, so she was glad to find out what had happened. This emboldened her to continue with the speeches. She called on Penny Dominguez, who popped her saliva-webbed retainer from her mouth and confessed herself of the agonies concomitant with a protuberant overbite.

When Lucinda returned home after collecting the baby from daycare, she found her daughter, fully dressed for once—even wearing blue eye shadow, lip gloss, and Lucinda's tri-amber earrings—but slumped on the couch, holding a pack of frozen peas and diced carrots to the left side of her face. The television was turned off; the dusty green-gray screen gaped, vacant as a hollow socket.

"What's going on?" Lucinda asked.

Anita lifted the frozen pack revealing an angry splotch. "She hit me."

"Who hit you?" Lucinda shifted her hip to turn the baby away from the sight. Dulce squirmed, trying to see.

"That bitch, that's who, Diego's wife." She rotated the peas and carrots and reapplied them to her cheekbone, hiding the swelling.

"Down!" Dulce cried, wriggling, and Lucinda had to set her on her own feet before she lost her grip and dropped her. Dulce tottered toward her mother, eyes wide and mouth open.

"How did she get into the house?" Lucinda imagined the enraged woman climbing through the bathroom window that was kept open to prevent mildew.

Anita shook her head. "She didn't come here. I went over to Cluckers to ask Diego to provide DNA for the paternity test, like Legal Aid told me to. I called up a paralegal over there, see, and he said I had to *ask* Diego first, said I could only get a court order if he refuses to cooperate."

"Honey, I could have gone over there, or we could have phoned him."

"Well, *I* called a cab, and *I* went, and there she was, big as life. She works there now—*assistant manager*," Anita said with bitterness. Before her pregnancy, Diego had promised her that position. "I didn't even ask about the paternity test. She just got one look at me and climbed over the counter and wham! She knocked me down." Anita shook her head, her chin wobbling. "I didn't get to say one word about the test."

Dulce stood at her mother's knees, staring at Anita's face in a solemn way.

"He's such a chicken-shit, Mama. He didn't even stop her. He just ran to the back office to hide. The cashier had to pull her off me, and I ran out of there. Guess that makes me a chicken-shit, too." She sucked in a ragged breath.

"No, sweetie, you did the right thing, the smart thing," Lucinda told her. "Let me see your face." Anita flinched as Lucinda fingered the chilly swollen flesh. Redness welled on her damp cheek like a wine stain, but the bone seemed intact. "Maybe we should go over to Athens Regional."

"No, Mom, nothing's broken. It's just going to be a bruise. All's they'll do is to give me another cold pack and charge like two hundred dollars for it."

"We need to call the police," Lucinda said. "That's assault. You can't just hit people. I'm sure there were lots of witnesses who—"

"*Mom*," Anita said, "just forget it, will you? Calling the police won't do any good. If you call, I won't talk to them. Just let it go." Holding the peas and carrots to her cheek, she buried her face in her hands. "I don't get it," she said, her voice muffled behind her fingers. "First Dad and then Diego—how come nobody loves me?"

(But that's not true, Lucinda thought as she sat beside her daughter, pulled her close, and stroked her hot quaking back.)

Dulce's fat-padded hands, like plush pink starfish, reached up, and she touched Anita's hair, petted it. "Mama," she said. "Mama, Mama, Mama."

Over the weekend, Anita wouldn't change her mind about calling the police. She did, though, phone Legal Aid after breakfast Monday morning. As Lucinda wiped oatmeal from Dulce's sticky cheeks, she overheard Anita giggling at something the paralegal said on the telephone. "He has a really cute voice," she told her mother after hanging up.

"But what did he say?"

Dulce bobbed and weaved, ducking the damp washcloth. "*No*, Nana, no!"

"They're drawing up a court order. He'll be served this week, and he has to comply or be held in contempt of the order."

"*They're* serving him, right?" Lucinda marveled at how quickly she had picked up this officious discourse. Her daughter had gone from playing an elective mute in some existentialist drama to sounding like the Assistant D.A. on *Law and Order* in less than four days.

"Yeah, they'll send a messenger out with the papers." She nodded, the wine-stain on her cheek darkened to an amber-rimmed blotch the color of eggplant. "I wonder what all you have to do to become a paralegal," she said, rubbing her chin.

Lucinda shrugged and unfastened the tray to free Dulce from her highchair. "Did you get a chance to ask about the other thing?"

"What other thing?"

"You know," she said, trying to sound casual, "the adoption."

"Oh," Anita said, "no, I forgot all about that."

As Lucinda drove to campus that day, behind yet another rig loaded with doomed chickens, she decided to give a speech herself before continuing with the oral presentations in Language Enrichment Laboratory! She planned to ask the class: Is this what you think public speaking is? Griping about back braces and retainers? Charting family histories of injury and abuse? Showing how to cover an empty box with decorative paper and ribbon? Is this how women speak? To say "he's such a fine guy," and "he has a really cute voice"? Is this what it amounts to? When we finally step up to the front and seize the podium, is *this* all that we have to say?

That afternoon, Nadezhda was scheduled to speak, and Lucinda dreaded hearing the atrocities she'd likely report from her home country. By her calculations, Nadezhda had spent her first eight or nine years under Nicolae Ceaușescu's infamous reign. Lucinda hoped the girl would limit herself to discussion of the food and fuel shortages. But she could easily veer into the outlawing of contraception and the rash of bloody "home" abortions that followed. From there, she might segue to the unwanted babies flooding orphanages, the epidemic of failure-to-thrive infants, and the warehousing of diseased and deformed children. Then she'd no doubt bring up "Systematization," Ceausecu's plan for razing the villages in a psychotic attempt to modernize the country. And what was that Lucinda had recently seen on television about the shooting of dogs for sport in the streets of Bucharest? She remembered the photo of a greyhound bitch with a gaping hole clear through her muzzle where someone had shot the poor creature. Perhaps, this, too, would come up during Nadezhda's speech, and Lucinda cringed at the thought.

The car's air conditioner cleared its throat decisively and coughed before shutting down with a sigh. Lucinda rolled down the window, her lips tightly closed to avoid catching tufts of down in her mouth, as she continued planning the short speech she would give.

Only half a dozen students arrived for Language Enrichment Laboratory! that afternoon. There had been rumors of an impending tornado warning at lunch, but nothing official yet. The president of the college exhorted everyone to continue with classes until they knew for certain which way the weather would turn. The sky had yellowed, grown metallic, the air pressurized, as Lucinda imagined the atmosphere would be inside a balloon inflated almost to the point of popping. She phoned the daycare center, and Miss Missy boasted that the facility, and the staff, was "tornado ready," whatever that meant. Lucinda also called home. A busy signal buzzed in her ear. She pictured Anita tying up the line with the cute-voiced paralegal, but more likely, her daughter had failed to cradle the receiver properly that morning.

With so few present, Lucinda wavered about giving her talk. She would only have to do it again when the other half of the class turned up. And Nadezhda was decked out in her native costume: bulky white leggings under thick shoes with rawhide strips that criss-crossed to her calves, a pleated red skirt, an embroidered cotton blouse, and a muslin shawl that trailed in back to the hem of her skirt. She beamed so when Lucinda complimented her blouse that there was no way she could curtail the girl's speech, which would doubtless be about her home country. Nadezhda had even brought a slide projector, which she set up on a desk near Lucinda's in back.

As she headed to her seat in back, Merry Knell caught her elbow. Lucinda willed herself not to shrink from the injured girl's touch. "Me and Nadezhda are going to Athens today," Merry told her. "My mom's driving us out to see Widespread Panic."

"Widespread Panic?" For a moment, Lucinda thought they'd planned to witness helter-skelter reactions to the storm before she remembered the successful hometown band that returned to Athens regularly to perform free concerts.

"It's my favorite band," Merry Knell told her. "Maybe we'll see you there."

Lucinda nodded, thinking, surely they would cancel the outdoor concert in this weather. But the eager look on Merry Knell's face prevented her from saying this. The girl released Lucinda's arm, and she continued to her desk where she brought out her grading sheets and called Nadezhda to the front for her presentation.

"My name is Nadezhda," the Romanian student said, as she stood before the podium, remote control in hand. "I am speaking to you today about my country, yes. And this is the traditional clothes we wear in Romania. So I'm speaking about my country, yes, but also about art. These things I care about. My country is my home and very beautiful, but for a long time was troubled. Is the inspiration for many artists, yes. Please, Penny, shut off the light."

The room darkened, and Nadezhda clicked an image onto the screen. An oil painting: a gray background with an intricate and elegant twist of silver in the foreground, a delicate flowing thing as lovely as a crystal stream. "Do you know of Hedda Sterne?" Nadezhda asked, without waiting for an answer. "This is her work. It is not titled, but they call it *USA*, like this country, yes." She clicked on another slide—a pastel and oil rendering of a denuded tree, also spare and exquisite. "And this one is called *Tree*." Nadezhda went on to explain Hedda Sterne was born in Romania, but migrated, and still lives, here in this country.

Then Nadezhda projected a photograph from the early 1950s—one Lucinda had seen before—of famous artists, including Rothko and Pollock. The group consists of about fifteen men, who are arrayed in chairs or standing before two tall windows, and towering over the men—standing on a stool, no doubt—is the sole woman in the group, a girlish figure in a bulky belted dress with unruly hair that flips up above her ears, creating a shadow behind her that looks as if it is cast by a spy, an interloper in hat and trench-coat. Lucinda had wondered who the only woman in the photograph was. "This is Hedda Sterne," Nadezhda said. "It is so funny. Many believed she disappeared after that picture, but she continued to paint. And she is still alive. She is the last of the Irascibles." Nadezhda smiled. "The last of these grumpy men, she is a woman, yes."

Lucinda's mouth dropped open. She leaned forward, squinting at the projected image. The fine hairs on her arms rose and her skin pimpled as if chilled, though it was so warm in the classroom that she'd debated turning up the air-conditioning before deciding against this, as the noise would drown out Nadezhda's soft-spoken voice.

"Hedda Sterne's retrospective is called *Uninterrupted Flux*. Is almost a hundred pieces of her work from galleries and museums all over this country, yes. The reason it is called this is that Hedda believes she was never famous like Jackson Pollock or Willem de Kooning because her art is not about identity, not about *her* identity. She says..." Nadezhda reached for an index card tucked into her waistband and read from it: "'I am only one small speck, hardly an atom, in the uninterrupted flux of the world around me.'"

Nadezhda replaced the card and clicked on another slide of a painting: an effusion of color—spilling out like a tumble of bright veils—that was as overtly sensual as the previous paintings were elegantly austere. The harem swirls in shades of aubergine, fuchsia, apricot, and cobalt were muscled as if molded by unseen gusts, but feminized by sinuous curves and seductive labial folds, layers within layers, both a deepening and a blossoming of tint and hue. Lucinda had never before in her life seen anything like this. She craned her neck, squinting to see it better, to see it more, while suppressing the unreasonable urge to rush up and touch the projection screen, to run her fingers over the image displayed on it.

"This is my painting," the Romanian girl said. "I came to America to follow in the feet prints of Hedda Sterne. As you see, my painting is about me, about my identity, yes. To me, art is the expression of what is inside a person, with passionate delicacy. So I am not like Hedda. But her art, it encourages me, gives me hope that if I get angry enough, maybe one day I, too, will become irascible." Nadezhda gave a wink.

"This is the conclusion of my speech. My country, Romania, is my home and where I am from, yes. This art shows me where I am going. So my speech, like my art, it is to express what is inside me. Thank you." She bowed and ducked back to her desk.

From the dryness in her throat, Lucinda realized her mouth had hung open during most of Nadezhda's speech, and her eyes burned from not blinking. She felt as though someone had grabbed her shoulders and given her a rough shake. Her fingers buzzed and her legs tingled as she strode to the front of the classroom. The girls seated before her seemed stunned, their faces frozen with wonder.

Before they could collect themselves to beat their hands together, the public address system squawked and the college president announced the path of the tornado had shifted, moving east in the direction of Gainesville towards Athens. Commuters were advised to vacate the premises, while dorm-dwellers were directed to the vast underground gymnasium before the storm hit in the next few hours. As everyone rushed out of the classroom, Lucinda hurried to catch up with Nadezhda, to tell her how her speech and her painting had—she didn't exactly know how to put this—but they had *hammered* her. By the time she'd collected her papers and headed down the hall, Nadezhda had disappeared into the elevator with Merry Knell. Lucinda repeated the girl's phrase to herself. While she had delicacy in spades, no one could ever accuse Lucinda of passion, let alone its expression. No wonder most of her students' speeches were such laughable things. Lucinda, their teacher, relegated the best of what she had to say to the parenthesis, the suppressed feeling, the unspoken thought.

She unlocked her car, tossed her briefcase in back, and scooted in. Lucinda could be at the daycare in half an hour, if she didn't get stuck behind a semi. This early, the streets were fairly clear, but soon they'd congest with drivers anxious to outrace the tornado. She'd made good time to the highway, when an eighteen-wheeler, exiting from the processing plant, plunged in front of her, braking to a crawl just before the county line. First opportunity, Lucinda would swoop past those martyred chickens. When she arrived home, she should hand Dulce over to Anita and tell her she must never give up her baby. Lucinda knew her daughter was gathering her strength now, rousing herself from a long and terrible sleep. Unlike her, Anita was already preparing to jump once more into the fire. *She* should show her daughter to be bold, to have passion.

The double yellow line gave way to a broken one on Lucinda's side of the highway. She held her breath and punched on the gas.

The storm's path diverged from its predicted destination, veering sharply south. Athens was as sunny and clear as it was when Lucinda left it that morning. Despite the band's name, the concert promoters had not quailed, and Lucinda hit traffic near downtown, as people arrived early to get good seats. Other than this, the city was unchanged. Lucinda felt this was something to celebrate, so when she returned home after collecting Dulce, she forestalled relinquishing her granddaughter and convinced Anita, who was again dressed and wearing makeup after a meeting with her paralegal, to go out to dinner.

They headed for Zoorrific, another fast-food chicken restaurant—a chain competitive with Cluckers—where they advertised chicken nuggets and tater tots shaped like animals. Anita thought Dulce might like these, and Lucinda, grateful that her daughter agreed to go out to dinner, could not refuse. Though it was only early November, the restaurant was already decorated for Christmas. A stiff artificial tree stood in one corner with an array of wrapped gifts displayed on its skirt. As she waited to order, Lucinda thought of Kayla, suspecting these presents were also empty. The restaurant was crowded with young parents and their toddlers. Many of the children stared longingly at the mock-presents, but Dulce, as if sensing their contents, had no interest in these. She was fascinated instead by her mother's attention. Once seated in her high chair, she helped Anita color in the zoo scene on the children's menu.

When Lucinda returned to the table with their food, Anita pointed toward the door at a help-wanted sign: *Assistant Manager Needed.*

"You interested?" Lucinda asked her daughter.

The restaurant door yawned wide and in walked Merry Knell, supported by her mother, a harassed-looking woman with flat iron-gray hair that Lucinda recognized from Parents' Weekend, on one side and Nadezhda on the other.

Anita shook her head. "I am *done* with chicken." She unwrapped Dulce's nuggets and arranged them atop her tray. "Right now, I'm leaning more toward the legal profession. Think I could be a lawyer, Mom?"

"Absolutely," Lucinda said to Anita. "Of course, you could be a lawyer." She glanced again at Nadezhda, hoping to catch her eye, so she could ask about her painting. But it was Merry Knell who claimed Lucinda's gaze. The damaged girl pushed away from her mother and roommate to take one choppy step after another, on her own, bypassing the holiday tree and the decorative display of gifts without notice, as she groped for the counter to order what she wanted.

This Gifting

Though Daisuke's parents remained in Osaka, thousands of miles away from Athens, Georgia—where he'd transferred to the university to complete his degree—this did not prevent their spirits from manifesting from time to time in his dormitory apartment to offer him advice. In fact, they appeared so often that he asked his biology lab partner, Naoko, also from Japan, if she were likewise visited by the unbidden spirits of her mother and father. "My parents?" The question had startled her. "My parents show up only on Internet. E-mail, you know, like that."

On the morning Daisuke planned to visit his teacher, he could hear his parents rustling in his narrow bedroom as soon as he stepped out of the shower. And while Daisuke toweled his short black hair before the mirror, his father's spirit stood at his elbow in the cramped and steamy bathroom cubicle. *You must take teacher some small gift,* the older man said, as he stroked his chin. Daisuke's father had a long horse-like face, similar to his own, and thick silvery eyebrows—bushy as caterpillars—nesting in his brow. Now these hunched, as if tensing to spring. *Or you will be obligated.*

Hai, called Daisuke's mother from the bedroom. Glancing out, Daisuke noticed her spirit had gained weight, but she was still a diminutive woman, sitting now on his bed, frowning while she sniffed at the wilted clothing he had piled upon it. *Your father is right. I have not packed so many gifts merely to stuff your suitcases.* With an upturned palm, she indicated the closet, which held his luggage.

Despite the shower, perspiration dripped from Daisuke's hairline. He wiped his face, hung the towel, and stepped around the bed to the closet. From a rolling, upright traveling case, he extracted a yellow bag decorated with a splash of bold red characters, the insignia of a popular gift shop in Osaka. Daisuke opened it, peered in at a square of silk patterned with bronze discs on a burgundy field bordered in navy. He curled the mouth of the bag closed.

That is not the custom here, he explained to both spirits. *Here they do not take gifts to teachers in university.*

Take, his mother insisted. *You will be obligated. You must take.*

Daisuke's father nodded again from the bathroom threshold. It was no use. His parents' spirits were no more reasonable than their corporeal selves. Daisuke sighed, stuffing the small yellow bag into his backpack. Then he dressed with speed and hurried out. He did not want to be late for being early.

Downstairs in the garage, Daisuke tossed his bag of books into the backseat of the used compact car he had just purchased with the money sent from his parents as an early graduation gift. (Though Daisuke swore there were no *pachinko* machines in the southeastern United States to tempt him to gamble, his father made a point of sending payment directly to the car dealership instead of wiring the money to Daisuke.) Before starting the ignition, Daisuke stroked the dashboard, pretending to wipe off dust in case anyone should see.

He loved the car, the rush of the engine, the power steering, automatic windows, even its pine scent emanating from an ornament shaped like a tree. Daisuke especially loved the freedom the car afforded him on Sunday afternoons, like this one, to zip over to the teacher's house to work on his essay, zip to the library until mealtime, and zip to the noodle shop in the mall. Before purchasing the car, Daisuke had to wait humbly at kiosks for the unpredictable university bus to deliver him to a few campus and downtown stops on its abbreviated route.

As he drove to his teacher's house, he noticed many people waiting humbly—as he had—for the city bus, which was even more unreliable than university transport. He noticed many of these people were black, and he sighed again. Daisuke had powerful feelings for black people. This teacher he was visiting would understand that. She would not laugh as his parents had when he mentioned his desire to dedicate his life to helping black people achieve equality. She would not ask if he shouldn't instead *get* help for his *pachinko* sickness before he returned to Japan. She would listen with seriousness and ask how he planned to help black people.

Driving away from campus, Daisuke considered the ways in which he could help black people. First of all, he would have to remain in the United States, as there were simply insufficient black people to help achieve equality in Japan. Then he thought he might become a teacher, a college professor, and encourage others like himself to dedicate their lives to ending the suffering of black people. Yes, he could do that. He could be a teacher like the one he was visiting, and he also would never laugh when students told him their dreams. He would never mention ugly problems with gambling or even smoking—Daisuke fumbled in the glove compartment for an overlooked cigarette, forgotten from the time before he quit, but found nothing—to spoil their dreams. Instead he would encourage them to give their lives over to making things better for black people, just as she would. Yes, he felt much better about bringing the gift.

Daisuke could not imagine going to a teacher's house in Japan. But this teacher had invited their small English-as-a-Second Language class over twice—once to see a video and again for an international potluck dinner. (Daisuke had brought a carton of noodles to-go from the shop in the mall and a six-pack of Asahi beer.) He had liked the teacher's house, a comfortable single-story brick home in a quiet neighborhood. It was much like his host family's residence, where he stayed the summer he arrived in the U.S.

In minutes, he pulled past the driveway to park a short distance from the house. Though there was plenty of room— the teacher had only one car and a two-car port—Daisuke considered it impolite to park in her drive or directly in front of her house. He grabbed his backpack and glanced at his wristwatch. Good, a little early.

The house had two entrances: a front door and a side door to the carport. Daisuke hesitated on the driveway. Which entrance had he and his classmates used on the previous occasions? The carport door, he thought. Yes, that's right. Besides the grass looked too tall and rangy in the yard for Daisuke, wearing khaki shorts, to hike the overgrown footpath to the front door. The weeds would certainly scratch his bare calves, and insects would hop up and bite him. The last time he had been to the house, the lawn had been shaved as close as velveteen and pink and purple flowers had been bloom-ing about the mailbox. Now the lawn was choked with weeds, dandelion stalks bending under heavy seed heads. The mailbox flowers had shriveled into bronze twists that drooped from the faded leaves like clusters of tiny, tarnished corkscrews.

If he hadn't brought the gift, Daisuke might have felt a pinch of obligation to offer help with the yard. But this idea held little appeal. This teacher had a husband. He recalled the large man who had boomed when he spoke like a politician denouncing a rival. Why didn't *he* tend the yard? As he stepped over a longish claw-like weed that thrust through a crack in the driveway, Daisuke felt an unfamiliar surge of gratitude to the spirits of his parents.

Daisuke knocked on the carport door. From the garage window, he could see a vague figure in the kitchen, someone pouring something from a pitcher. Then he heard footsteps, and the door opened. "I hope I am not late," he said and smiled at his teacher. He was almost always early, but he enjoyed saying, I hope I am not late.

The teacher tried a brief smile, but her eyes and nose were swollen, pink-tinged as though she had been sneezing. Perhaps she had allergies from the overgrown lawn.

"Are you ill?" Daisuke asked, alarmed. He had only one day to work on this paper.

"No, not at all," she said. "I was just pouring some iced tea. Would you like some?" The teacher was short for an American and seemed even shorter in bare feet. She was not what anyone in Japan or in the U.S., for that matter, would call a pretty woman, but Daisuke liked the way she looked, the way her brown hair was always neatly tied back, the way she smiled, revealing even teeth, and how her eyes behind her glasses showed that she thought hard about what people said to her.

"Yes, thank you," Daisuke said, though the tea they drank in this country disgusted him. It was as bitter as something that might drip out from under a car, and if served sweetened, it was as syrupy as cough medicine. But it would be a terrible rudeness to refuse and ruder still not to drink every drop and accept more if offered.

"I thought we could work in the office," she said, point-ing to a room off the kitchen. In his host family's house, they had a similar room, but they used it for dining. The teacher's family apparently ate in the kitchen, where Daisuke saw the teacher's tall husband, bare-chested and bent over a telephone on the table. What was his name? They had been introduced twice. Daisuke raked his memory. The husband seemed a friendly man, except for his crushing handshake grip. What *was* his name? Something to do with meat or gravy?

"You remember my husband Hammond," asked the teacher.

Daisuke averted his eyes from the man's large pale stomach—Hammond, of course, like ham, a thick slab of ham. He wouldn't forget again. Daisuke nodded. Hammond covered the mouthpiece and said, "Hiya," to Daisuke, who felt relieved not to be expected to shake hands.

The teacher liked everyone to call her by her first name. She had a theory about how that somehow made it easier for international students to learn English. But Daisuke felt awkward calling his teacher by her first name, Yolanda, so he compromised by calling her "Miss Yolanda." Hammond, though, would do for the big man, not even wearing a shirt to hide the white fur on his chest as he hunched over the phone.

Daisuke followed Miss Yolanda into the office/dining room and seated himself before a dismayingly large glass of iced tea.

"Do you like sugar?" Miss Yolanda asked.

Daisuke shook his head. "Thank you, no." He reached into his backpack for his notebook, Japanese/English diction-ary, and the paper he had written.

"Well, let's have a look at it." Miss Yolanda put on her glasses, reminding Daisuke of the doctor at the student health center who had said the same thing to him as he bent to examine a boil that had developed on Daisuke's left buttock.

They worked on the paper for an hour. Daisuke had been horrified when Miss Yolanda found an agreement error and another problem with a plural form. But he was prepared for his mistakes with articles. They were so hard to get right that it was like trying to understand American football. Daisuke was also ready for her comments on developing his paragraphs. The topic sentences were good and the examples clear, but he had always been weak on synthesis and summary. As they worked to fortify his paragraphs, Daisuke sipped diligently at the tea. Miss Yolanda really did help him. He was wise to come, and by the time they finished, he *wanted* to present her with the gift.

"You know, Miss Yolanda," he began, "in Japan, when someone does a favor for another, then that favor must be returned. It is an obligation that—"

"But I'm happy to help." The skin under her eyes pleated when she smiled.

"Still," said Daisuke, rummaging in his backpack for the yellow bag.

"Come on, hon, it's time to get going." Hammond poked his head in the doorway.

"In a minute, Hammond." She raised her eyebrows the way she did when trying to be patient with argumentative students. "Just give me a minute."

"Let's shake a leg." The tall man stepped into the office, buttoning a riotous Hawai`ian shirt.

"I told you to wait," she said, enunciating each word crisply. "Now go start the car. I'll be out in a minute." Turning to Daisuke, Miss Yolanda smiled again, but her eyes looked sad. "I'm sorry Daisuke, but I've got to be somewhere in a few minutes."

Daisuke pawed through his papers and books. How could such a bright bag disappear? Why so many zippers and compartments? "Before I go—"

"Get a move on!" Hammond jangled the keys and walked with heavy steps toward the back door. Daisuke heard a car door chunk shut, and he listened for the click of the ignition, the rush of the engine. Soon he heard the click, but no roar. Then he heard another click. Click, click, click.

"This has the makings of a fine paper." Miss Yolanda stepped into a pair of sandals.

The car door opened, and the back door slammed again. Hammond appeared again in the doorway. "Battery's dead! Goddamn it, Elaine, you must've left the headlights on again."

"*Me?* You were the one to go out last for ice cream. Remember?" Her voice was harsh and the corners of Miss Yolanda's mouth quirked downward, but when she spoke again to Daisuke her tone was warm, gentle. "Would you mind doing me a favor, Daisuke? I hate to ask."

Daisuke fought a heavy feeling in his chest, as though she had passed him a boulder to hold. "What is it?"

"The thing is we need a ride," said Miss Yolanda.

"Do you have battery cables?" Though he only had his car a short while, Daisuke knew about jumping dead batteries, and he planned to buy cables as soon as he determined the best kind. "If you have cables, I can start your battery with my car."

"We don't have cables."

"*She* lost them." Hammond jutted his chin at his wife.

"I never in my life saw them," she shot back. "I doubt we ever had any."

"Oh, we *had* some. I know we did."

"I can take you to buy some. I will buy them as a gift."

The tension between Miss Yolanda and her husband chilled Daisuke's fingertips, made them tingle with numbness.

"No, no, you see, there isn't time. There's only one more hour of visiting. We have to see our daughter during visiting hours."

"Your daughter is ill? In the hospital?"

"No, not exactly. Would you take us, Daisuke? Of course, I understand if you have something else to do." She cast her eyes downward as she said this.

"I will drive you," said Daisuke. "You must tell me where to drive."

"I can tell you how to get there," Hammond said. They filed through the kitchen toward the carport. Daisuke caught a whiff of Hammond—cheese and soap. He was grateful for the pine-scented rearview mirror ornament. Nevertheless, he hoped the large man would take the back seat and roll the window down.

But Miss Yolanda took the back seat, and because of the length of his thick legs, Hammond sat in the front. The entire car dipped with the tall man's weight. Large *and* dense, thought Daisuke.

"Just take a left at the street up ahead," said Hammond, "and head toward the campus. It's not too far from the university."

Daisuke nodded, steering the car away from the curb.

"So, Daisuke," Miss Yolanda said, after they had driven a few minutes in silence, "what literature classes are you taking in the spring?"

"No, no more literature," Daisuke said in a low voice.

"What?"

"No literature."

"But you love American literature. Wasn't that why you came here to study?"

"Well, it's a long story." Daisuke did not like to mention the *pachinko*, the dimpled nurse from a local hospital that he had followed until she complained to officials, the gray Osaka mornings when he wished he could take his brain out of his head and rinse it in cool, clear water. "Basically, now, I have lost my love of literature."

Hammond snorted.

"But how?" Elaine leaned forward, her breath warm tickling his right ear.

"Is your seat belt not working?" Daisuke tensed. He'd heard the jingle often on the radio and didn't want a ticket because she wouldn't "click it." "I can fix it for you."

Miss Yolanda drew back, clicked the clasp. "It works."

"Ah, I'm so glad."

"Tell me, how did you lose your love of literature?"

"It was in your class," admitted Daisuke.

Hammond let out a hoot.

"During *my* class? Was it something I did? Something I said?" Miss Yolanda's voice rose higher and higher with each question.

"It was the black people," he tried to explain. "You remember?"

"The *black* people?"

"The poems, the play. Gwendolyn Brooks. *Langston Hughes*."

"Langston Hughes?"

"Sure, honey," Hammond put in, "you remember old Langston."

"Shut up, Hammond, will you?" Miss Yolanda said before asking Daisuke, "But what happened? And what did it have to do with the black writers we studied."

Daisuke shrugged. "I discovered there are things more important than literature."

"See." Hammond wagged a thick finger. "That's what I've been saying all along."

"What's more important than literature?" asked Miss Yolanda.

"You know, the black people, their suffering."

Hammond's laughter reminded Daisuke of the honking from the great-bellied geese in the park who had snapped up the crumbs he'd offered them as a little boy and then pinched his fingers with their hard beaks before chasing him from their pond.

"Please pull over, Daisuke," said Miss Yolanda.

"You want the restroom?" Daisuke asked. "I can find the gas station."

"No, just pull over to the curb."

"Come on, Yolanda. Not again."

"You want me to stop here?" Daisuke pointed to a space alongside a vacant lot.

"Yes, please."

"Oh, for the sweet love of Jesus," Hammond cried.

"Get out," Miss Yolanda said when Daisuke parked the car. "Go on, get out!"

Startled, Daisuke reached for the handle. His stomach lurched, twisting as though filled with slippery eels. How losing his love of literature had angered her!

"No, not you, Daisuke. I'm talking to my husband."

"She does this all the time." Hammond pursed his lips, nodded. "She thinks that's the way people do things." The big man wore a knowing look that made Daisuke think of his first English teacher in Japan, a blond man from New Zealand, who behaved as though he could regard all the bloody history caused by imperialism and racism from some lookout high on a mountain, cool wind blowing through his long hair and caressing his calm white face, which wore the expression of an angelic toad.

Nevertheless, he tried to reason with his teacher, "Miss Yolanda, I think maybe—"

"I have to put him out, Daisuke. I'm sorry if it embarrasses you."

"There's nothing here, not even a pay phone. What am I supposed to do?"

Daisuke thought to mention the bus but tucked his tongue behind his teeth.

"You should have thought of that before. You act up, and you have to get out."

Hammond hefted himself out of the car and slammed the door. "Some day you'll take this too far, Yolanda, and then where will we be?"

"I really am sorry, Daisuke." Miss Yolanda climbed into the front seat beside him. "Sometimes I just can't stand the way he acts. Haven't you ever felt like that?"

Though he never thought to put anyone out of a car, Daisuke nodded. Pushing a lever, he scrolled down the windows to clear out the thick Hammond stench.

"Where do I turn?" Daisuke asked at an intersection just past the campus.

"Go right. See that police car? Just follow it. You can probably follow it the whole way." Miss Yolanda arched her back, stretching, as though throwing her husband out of the car released the strain in her shoulders and neck. "I may as well tell you, Daisuke. My daughter's been arrested. She's in the county jail."

"That is terrible. The police made mistake?"

"I *wish*, but it's no mistake."

Daisuke shot a glance at Miss Yolanda. She seemed composed, even purposefully engaged, digging in her purse. It would be too impolite to ask what crime her daughter had committed.

"You're going to turn left at that light ahead. Keep following that police car."

The squad car turned into a drive near the building where Daisuke had registered his car. Perhaps the girl had been arrested for traffic violations or having no car insurance. They were strict about such things here.

"Now stay on this road. Follow those signs to the jail. It's not too far. See, there it is. Try to park under some shade." Miss Yolanda extracted something from her handbag, which she then stuffed under the front seat. "I'm going to leave this here, if that's okay. I just need my license. Have you got identification?"

Daisuke nodded. His ears burned. No longer preoccupied with driving, he felt such terrible shame for his teacher he could barely speak. "I have a shield to put in the window. Keep the car cool." He unfolded the accordion flaps of aluminum-covered cardboard and secured the shade behind the dashboard. "I can wait by that tree."

"Oh, no, you'll melt in this heat," Miss Yolanda said. "You have to come in."

"I prefer to wait here."

"I wish you would come inside with me." She tugged his elbow. "I really don't want to go in there alone. *Please*, will you come with me?"

Daisuke could not refuse. He followed Miss Yolanda into the squat concrete building, which shimmered like an immense cinderblock baking in the afternoon sun. The first gust of cooled air raised the fine hairs on Daisuke's arms and legs.

"We have to go through the metal detector," she whispered.

"What?"

"This thing, like at the airport." She put her glasses in a plastic tray and stepped under the frame. Daisuke placed his keys in another tray and crossed the threshold after her. He glanced around the waiting area at rows of white plastic chairs in the center and a bank of gray metal lockers across from a horse-shoe shaped desk. Several people stood at the desk in a line, more sat in the plastic scoop chairs. Black, all of them black people. This confirmed something very sad for Daisuke, and privately, he renewed his conviction to fight to end their suffering.

He and Miss Yolanda took their places at the end of the line curving around the desk. The lady in a uniform on the other side of the desk was also black, so Daisuke gave her a sympathetic smile when he caught her eye.

"What you want?" she barked, causing Daisuke to jump back a step.

"He's with me," Miss Yolanda said. "We're visiting my daughter."

"Fill out those forms and get your I.D. ready. Nobody holds up this line."

"Yes." Daisuke took a slip and a pencil stub from a jar nearby. "Sorry."

After he filled the form, Miss Yolanda took it and his license from him. She scribbled her daughter's name in the blank under "detainee." "Go sit down," she said, quietly.

Daisuke found two vacant seats near an elderly woman wearing a blue cotton dress printed with white checks, a pair of thick glasses low on her round nose. Though she sat upright, she slept soundly in her chair, soft snores rumbling from her parted lips. Seated in front of Daisuke, a boy, in a dress shirt and navy suit pants, turned around, rotating his head impossibly to stare at Daisuke, as though he were a lizard in the zoo. The boy had unblinking, intelligent-looking eyes, coffee-colored pupils in wide, milky-blue saucers. The poor youngster dragged to this terrible place to visit a father or brother who was probably unfairly imprisoned. Daisuke had read much about this treatment of black people. Daisuke gave the child a sympathetic smile. The boy rubbed his nose, and then extended his middle finger alongside one brown nostril, cupping the other fingers under his palm, his laughter spilling out like a handful of coins.

"Here, Daisuke, put your license in your wallet. You can keep that in your pocket. Everything else has to go in a locker." Miss Yolanda scooted into the seat next to his.

"I have nothing more. Just the wallet."

"You have to put your keys in a locker. Here, I'll put them with my sunglasses."

Daisuke shot a suspicious glance at the lock-less lockers. What if someone should take his keys? Steal his car? His eyes swept over the dark faces filling the waiting area. He handed the keys to Miss Yolanda and silently rebuked himself. She stowed the keys and her glasses in a locker and shut the door. As she walked back to her seat, the locker she had chosen creaked open. Daisuke fought the impulse to leap up and shut it more firmly.

Miss Yolanda sat beside him in silence for a moment before sniffling. Daisuke prepared to bless her should she sneeze, but she didn't sneeze. She sniffled again and again, and then she drew in a deep, ragged breath. Daisuke felt the heat from her body alongside his own. Soon she was quaking and sobbing.

At first, Daisuke looked around, pretending he could not see or hear his teacher. People shifted in their seats, turning to see Miss Yolanda cry. Next, he tried to shield her from view by leaning across her chair, as though to reach something in the next seat over. But he could feel more and more eyes upon them. "Shh, please, shh," he said softly in Miss Yolanda's ear. "People are looking." He patted the air above her shoulder.

He didn't like to touch his teacher, but he wanted to give comfort. So he patted the air tenderly, repeating, "Shh, please, shh." The sleeping woman nearby jerked and woke with a snort. She pulled a tissue from her dress pocket and handed it to Miss Yolanda without a word. Miss Yolanda blotted her eyes. She blew her nose with such force it startled Daisuke, and again everyone turned to stare.

After this, Miss Yolanda stopped crying, and she straightened in her chair. "Thank you," she said to the woman. She removed her glasses to wipe the lenses with the tissue.

The officer behind the desk shouted something Daisuke couldn't understand, and Miss Yolanda stood, replacing her glasses and pulling on Daisuke's arm. The boy who had given Daisuke the obscene gesture also rose and hurried to one of the glass doors. Two more officers—a man and a woman—emerged from the door and lined people against the wall to pat their clothing. It tore at Daisuke to see the boy prodded like this, though the youngster giggled as the officer ran his hands over his thin limbs. Next the officer pawed Daisuke's pockets, sleeves, sides, and even his crotch. Daisuke's cheeks flamed and he latched his gaze on his shoes while the female officer told Miss Yolanda to lean against the wall with her legs apart.

When all the visitors were searched, the officers led them through a series of buzzing doors and down a long corridor, which was marked with large orange arrows pointing straight ahead.

"It sure is warm in this hall." Miss Yolanda's voice was flat.

"Sure is," agreed a large black woman wearing a tight T-shirt, pink stretch shorts, and clear plastic sandals.

"They should put in air-conditioning here," Daisuke suggested, thinking guiltily of the cool jets from the vents on his dashboard. He turned to the black woman. "It's so unfair, so many of your people in this place. They cannot all be criminals."

"You Chinese?" the black woman asked, slapping her sandals along beside him.

"I am from Japan."

"See, I knew that." She smiled. "I knew you wasn't from around here."

"Come on," the officer, an older white man, said. "We don't got all day."

The visitors filed into a hall which led to a series of small rooms radiating from a central watch area, where several other officers were seated before a panel of switches, buttons, and video monitors, talking and eating hamburgers and French fries.

"We're going this way, Daisuke," Miss Yolanda said. Again, Daisuke felt the awkward pressure of her fingers on his elbow. She led him into one of the rooms, which had a long window looking in on a stall-sized compartment. Before the window was a circular metal stool that faced a shelf below the thick-paned window. A black telephone was mounted on a receiver on the right side of the wall. "You sit down," said Miss Yolanda, urging Daisuke onto the stool. "I'm too nervous." She lifted the phone and handed it to him. "I know I'll just fall apart again if I talk to her."

Daisuke took the phone and sat. In a few moments, a girl with matted, ropy-looking black hair and dark eyes shuffled in from an adjacent room and took the seat across the glass from Daisuke. Her thick, unruly hair and large, staring eyes reminded Daisuke of a story he had once read about a woman who had been raised among wolves. She had grown up without hearing human language and could only bark, snarl, and howl when people first came upon her. But this girl lifted her phone and said "Who the hell are you?" in a clear loud voice.

"Daisuke," he said, speaking carefully into the mouthpiece.

"This is my daughter, Felicia, and Felicia, this is Daisuke." Miss Yolanda crowded behind him, introducing them as though they were meeting for the first time at a party.

"What's she saying?" asked Felicia.

"I am pleased to meet you." Daisuke smiled.

"What's he doing here?" Felicia demanded of her mother in an even louder voice.

"What did she say?"

"Here you must sit down." Daisuke half-rose from the seat and tried to hand her the receiver, but Miss Yolanda pushed his shoulders down.

"No, it's better if you sit down. I'm too upset." Here, Miss Yolanda's voice cracked.

"She wants to know why I am here," Daisuke told Miss Yolanda, wondering himself.

"Tell her about the car battery and all that."

"It's not bad enough I'm in here," Felicia complained, "that she's got to bring strangers to see me."

"What's she saying?" Miss Yolanda asked. "I can't hear her."

"She's surprised that I am here," Daisuke translated with diplomacy.

"What I want to know is when I'm getting out of here. When are you going to get me out of here, huh?" she shouted at her mother.

"What?" Miss Yolanda shot Daisuke a puzzled look.

"Tell her to goddamn pay the bail and get my ass out of here," the girl said in a deliberate voice. Her tone reminded Daisuke of Hammond, and he felt anger rise in him, a heat that started in his stomach and bloomed on his cheeks.

"She is unhappy in the jail." He paused to slow his

breathing. "She is sorry for her crime, and she wishes she could be released to start making up for the mistake."

"Oh, honey," said Miss Yolanda, tears streaming once more from behind her clouded glasses. "I wish I could get you out, but there's no bail because you violated your probation this time. They have to have a hearing first. I'm so sorry, baby."

"What? What's she saying? I can't hear unless she talks on the phone, damn it."

"She says." Daisuke hunched in, cupping the mouthpiece, so his words would not carry back to his teacher. "She says you have done a terrible thing and brought shame on your family. Think about this while you are here. Your mother is not getting you out."

"Shit!" The girl frowned. "Well, then she needs to get my stuff out of the apartment. She's got to do it today, or he's going to throw it all away. He's kicking me out, Mama!" She turned her eyes to her mother. "Can you believe that? He won't even take my calls any more."

Daisuke turned to Miss Yolanda. "She asks if you will please help her. She has been asked to move. She fears she will lose her belongings."

"Of course, I will. Ask her if she needs anything else? Anything at all."

Daisuke spoke with quiet sternness into the telephone again. "This is a hardship for your mother. She will do it, but do not ask more. You must show gratitude for what your parents do for you, and you must not bring any more shame on them."

The girl stared at Daisuke, her eyes wider than ever. She smoothed her hair down, and for a moment, she did not look so wild. "What*ever*," she said, at last, before hanging up and rising out of her seat.

Miss Yolanda placed her palm flat on the glass divider

between her daughter and herself. Daisuke looked away in delicacy.

A guard poked his head in the room, calling, "Time's up!"

Daisuke and Miss Yolanda trod the steamy corridor once more, walking against the orange arrows this time. Again Daisuke wanted to broach the subject of the unfair imprisonment of black people with the friendly woman flapping her sandals beside him, but sadness had silenced her. Daisuke gazed around at the group, their downcast eyes and stooped shoulders, as he moved through the buzzing doors with Miss Yolanda.

While Daisuke refolded the accordion screen from the windshield, Miss Yolanda said, "I think she looks pretty good, don't you? I mean, for being in jail."

"Yes, she seems fine."

"Gosh, I hate to ask you." Miss Yolanda reached to place her cool fingers in the crook of Daisuke's elbow. "But could you take me to her place to get her things?"

"Where does she live?" Daisuke did not want to spend the remainder of the day driving long distances when he had his paper to revise. He should have given her the square of silk—dug until he'd found it—and he would be done with this gifting by now.

"Not too far. It was probably pretty convenient for the officers who arrested her."

"Tell me how to go."

Miss Yolanda directed him to an apartment complex a few long blocks from the jail. The building sat just across the street from a squat clapboard structure without windows bearing a roof billboard advertising package liquor. Beyond that were only vacant lots filled with kudzu-covered trees, weeds, and stray rubbish.

"Not a very good neighborhood, is it?" asked Miss Yolanda.

"Probably the rent is reasonable."

"If she'd paid it, I'm sure it would have been."

Miss Yolanda had Daisuke park his car in a slot near the rear of the building. "It's just up those stairs. We may as well park close. There might be a few boxes."

They climbed a dingy stairwell to a breezeway that was slick with rust-colored water streaming from the air conditioners protruding from low windows. Miss Yolanda deftly sidestepped these streams, advising Daisuke to "watch out."

She stopped to knock on a door in the middle of the walkway. A thin black man, wearing sunglasses and a blue velour warm up suit and smoking a cigarette in a long onyx holder, pulled the door open. "*You?* What do you want?"

"Felicia asked me to come for her things."

"That's one crazy girl, you got." The man laughed. "One wild bitch."

"Will you please let me in to get her things?" Miss Yolanda persisted.

Before coming to the United States, Daisuke considered becoming a corporate warrior like his father. As a child he liked hearing his father practice his resonant warrior voice in the bath—the deep tones reverberating against the paper walls throughout the house. These days, though, Daisuke did not like war of any kind, but he wondered what would happen if he used that warrior voice here.

"Ready to dump her crap in the trash." He puffed on the cigarette holder, releasing smoke from his nose like a dragon. "Should, too, way she left me with rent to pay."

Daisuke stepped in front of Miss Yolanda. "We will get the belongings and leave."

"What are you? Chinese?"

"I am from Japan."

"Kent," a sleepy female voice called from within. "Just let them take her shit."

"Would save me a trip to the garbage bins, I suppose," Kent said. "Already got most of it in trash bags for you all. Come on, then, hurry up and get it out of here."

The man stepped aside, allowing Daisuke and Miss Yolanda into the apartment. A young red-haired woman stretched out on the sofa and yawned. "It's over there by that table." She turned her back to them.

"There's more stuff in the bathroom." The man settled on the arm of the couch to watch the television set silently flickering in another corner of the room.

"Hush," said the woman on the couch, "trying to sleep here."

Daisuke followed Miss Yolanda from the living room to a bedroom recessed from the hallway. "This was her room." She gestured at the stripped mattress, a battered dressing table and a chest with gaping drawers. "I guess we ought to clear out the bathroom. Looks like everything's gone from in here." She opened the door to an empty closet.

Daisuke spotted a box of garbage bags on the floor near the bed. "We can use these, and there is a box."

Miss Yolanda pulled open the cabinets in the bathroom. "Look at all this, will you?"

Daisuke peered in the cabinets to see row upon row of bottles containing shampoo, conditioning rinse, hair sprays, tubes of toothpaste, jars of cold cream, stacks of soap bars—dozens and dozens of new, unopened bathroom and beauty products—crammed under the sink, behind the mirror and in a tall wicker cabinet near the bath. Outside of a supermarket's shelves, he had never seen so many cleansers, creams, and gels. The sight chilled him.

"What did she need all this for? What would a person want with all this? You can't think I don't love her enough." She turned to Daisuke and took a black garbage bag from the box he held. "I do. I love her more than anyone," she said, snapping the bag open for Daisuke to fill with bottles, tubes, and jars.

When they cleared out the bathroom, they loaded the bags they'd filled into the trunk of Daisuke's car. Then they returned for the four bags slumped near the table. Daisuke grabbed three, and Miss Yolanda hoisted the remaining one. Miss Yolanda set her bag on the railing. "Give me one of yours," she said. "I think this only has clothing in it. We can just toss it over."

Kent stood watching from the threshold. "Something's not right with her. You saw all that stuff—that's some crazy shit. I swear you can't do nothing with a girl like that."

"We do not wish to disturb you more," Daisuke said.

"You tell her I got me a new old lady. Tell her I don't want to see her no more."

"We will tell her." Daisuke again fought the temptation to use the warrior's voice.

They stuffed the last bag into the trunk before climbing into the car for the drive back to Miss Yolanda's house. Daisuke tried to think of something bright, something pleasant to say, while his teacher bit her lips and stared into her lap. "Do things like this happen in Japan?" she asked at last.

"I think everywhere bad things happen." Daisuke remembered a time after many promises, after swearing that he would never play again, he had glanced up from his *pachinko* game to see his father's face—white and twisted as a water-pocked linen—before him. A current of adrenaline shot through his body with the force of an electrical shock, so powerful it squeezed his heart. He knew then it would be madness ever to return to the machines again. Yet within a week, he was back, losing the money given for his textbooks.

Nearing Miss Yolanda's home, Daisuke noticed Hammond loping down the street. Miss Yolanda still stared at her lap, not seeing him, so again Daisuke tucked his tongue.

When he parked the car, Miss Yolanda said, "I want to thank you for everything, Daisuke. You were really wonderful to drive me all over. I will never forget this." They pulled the bags from the trunk, and Daisuke helped her lug them inside the house. After carrying the last bag in, Miss Yolanda untied its knot and reached in producing an unopened bottle. "Here," she said, handing it to Daisuke. "It's avocado conditioner. Take this from Felicia and from me—a little gift."

"No, no, please." Daisuke shook his head.

"I insist. Besides, it would be good for Felicia to pay something for your trouble."

Daisuke hesitated. "Thank you." He took the bottle to release her obligation.

"Thanks again, Daisuke. You've been great."

"Miss Yolanda, I almost forgot," said Daisuke. "I have something for you, too." He reached into the car and hauled out his backpack. Somehow his hand went directly to the yellow bag. "A gift from my mother and father." He handed it to her.

"What is it?"

"Silk. Silk from Japan."

Miss Yolanda unfurled the burgundy square, and the printed bronze coins glittered in the sunlight. "It's lovely. Thank you very much. Thank your parents, too. This is a treasure." She let the silk flow between her fingers, like water.

Driving home that afternoon, Daisuke could not understand something. Though he had received the gift of his teacher's help, had offered the gift of battery cables, had given the gift of his time and car, had received another gift of conditioning rinse, and finally had given the gift of silk,

Daisuke felt heavier somehow, more encumbered than ever, as if all the bottles, tubes, and jars in the girl's bathroom were piled on his chest. His lungs constricted from the pressure of all this gifting, and it was hard for him to draw a deep breath. Daisuke knew he must call his teacher in the morning. He would see the girl with wild hair in the jail again. He would still fight to relieve the suffering of black people, but that was for later, in the future. There were other people who suffered: those who could not help what they did. This he knew well.

He flipped on the car radio and tuned to a jazz station while he steered his car through the streets toward the university and his dormitory apartment. The station played a familiar bluesy piece that Daisuke always enjoyed. In his bucket seat and against the pressure of his shoulder strap, Daisuke bowed slightly toward the steering wheel. "*Arrigato*," he said aloud to the unseen disc jockey who had selected the tune.

Though he expected the spirits of his parents—conjured by the Japanese word of gratitude—they did not appear. Had they manifested, he would have told them that his teacher had thanked them for the gift, and he anticipated what they would say.

"Slow down," his mother would warn. "You are driving too fast."

"And look where you are going," would be his father's words to him.

The Landscape

They were about to cross under the highway when a goose plummeted out of the sky. It landed with a thud on the trunk of the car and bounced to the pavement. Lydia gasped. She tapped the brake pedal in reflex and glanced in the rearview mirror.

"Jesus," her husband Matt said. "What was that?"

Roxanne, strapped in her child's booster in the backseat, rotated her torso as far as it would go to peer out the back window.

"Looks like a goose." Lydia said. A chevron of geese, silhouetted against summer clouds thick as mattress ticking, had crested over the woods along the Harpeth River just before the bird's body struck. When Lydia pulled to a stop at the red light, she could make out, in the rearview, the reflection of its plump gray form from which the long dark neck curved like the top part of a question mark.

"Do you think it damaged the car?" Matt said.

Lydia shrugged. Her aging Toyota was so battered that another dent made no difference to her, as long as the trunk was staying shut, and it seemed to be.

"Go back!" Roxanne said. "We have to take it to the doctor."

Matt shook his head. "I'm afraid it's too late for a doctor."

"No way could it survive that," Lydia said.

"Turn around, turn around. The doctor can fix him." At five-and-a-half-years old, Roxanne seemed not to understand the finality of death. She turned so fully to stare after the bird that Lydia could see the part at the back of her head, her thick, wiry hair neatly cleaved into two tight braids.

"Oh, look," Lydia said, and she pressed the accelerator when the light turned green, "those people behind us are stopping." Sure enough, a jeep full of young men halted behind them. The passenger door opened, and a tattooed forearm reached out to grasp the goose's limp legs. "Maybe they're doctors."

Matt shot her a look.

Roxanne rolled down her window and shouted, "Make him better!" But there was no chance the boys could hear her over the rap music blasting from their stereo speakers, and besides, Lydia had pulled away, turning the car to climb the highway ramp. She raised the window with the driver's control and latched the child-lock.

"Wonder why it just fell like that," Matt said, twisting his wedding band, his habit—Lydia noticed—when perplexed.

"Something to do with the heart, I bet," Lydia said. "A coronary occlusion or clogged arteries, maybe. Heart trouble, birds have it, too." She merged the car onto Highway 40 East toward Nashville, neatly slipping between two semi trucks. Lydia turned to Matt, dropped her voice. "I don't understand why my cousin can't wait until she gets everything settled. I mean she's just out of that halfway house—"

Matt shook his head and put a finger to his lips. His thinning black hair, still damp from shampooing, clung to his smallish head in tight ringlets, and his sunglasses glinted, reflecting two miniaturized Lydias back at her. But behind these, she knew his eyes were narrowed, fixed with a stern, censorious gaze. They must never, he'd said, speak ill of Lydia's first cousin Shirley, who was Roxanne's mother. A child identifies with her parents—to insult the parent is to damage the child's sense of self. Matt was a sociologist, so he knew such things.

Lydia lowered her voice a bit more. "I mean, what's the rush? She doesn't even have a place to live yet."

"Silly goose," Roxanne said, "silly, silly goose." She rustled paper in the backseat and dropped something that fell with a muffled thunk onto the floorboard.

Matt swung around to see what she was up to. "Careful with that painting."

Lydia tightened her jaw, longing to complain about that as well, but it was too early in too long a trip—Nashville to Atlanta and back—to bring up how she felt about transporting the damn thing. Matt's uncle, an art dealer, had asked them as a favor to take the piece to his ex-wife, another dealer in the exclusive Buckhead suburb of Atlanta, for her appraisal. Ordinarily, Lydia would begrudge this uncle no favor. He was a thoughtful, gentle man she respected, but this time, he had asked too much. The trip, taken to return Roxanne to Shirley after over a year of raising the child, was difficult enough on its own, without the extra errand. Besides, Lydia's small car was crammed with Roxanne's clothes, books, and toys, and now the little girl had to share the backseat with the three-by-two-foot painting that Matt had wrapped in plastic bubble wrap and then blankets. He insisted it was highly valuable, warning it should not be touched, not even accidentally. For Roxanne, no doubt, this spelled irresistible temptation. She likely wouldn't miss an opportunity to nudge and jiggle the thing whenever she sensed their attention to her flagging.

On top of this, Lydia had no especially fond memories of
Matt's aunt, the Buckhead dealer, whom she'd met once before. The toad-like woman with flat straw-colored hair was
so absorbed in recent acquisitions that she hadn't glanced at
Lydia when they were introduced. Lydia, a college professor,
was accustomed to deferential treatment from students and
colleagues, no less from family members—hers and Matt's.
But the woman barely even acknowledged Matt, her nephew
whom she hadn't seen in years. They would have elicited a
warmer welcome from her, Lydia was sure, if they had come in
coveralls to clear out the rain gutters. She didn't even admit
them to the house. Instead she maneuvered her large, pale
body around the paintings stacked in her garage, straightening here and there, as though they'd arrived to a garage sale
she was holding. It was a good thing the woman was an art
dealer, Lydia thought, and art enables people to transcend self
because if ever there was a self that needed transcending—

Another rumble from the backseat, a crashing sound and
Matt said, "You're not touching that painting, are you?"

"No, I was trying to get my coloring book. I can't ... *reach*
it."

"I'll get it." Matt reached behind his seat. "Where is
it?"

"There, there, you're almost touching it," Roxanne said.
"There!"

He jerked his arm back and howled like he'd been
stabbed.

Lydia pressed on the emergency lights. "What happened?
Should I stop?" They were about to veer onto Interstate 24,
so there was no place but the shoulder to park.

"Keep going, keep going," Matt said, his voice taut with
strain. "I pulled a muscle, that's all. I'll be okay in a minute."
He clutched his shoulder, massaging it.

"You almost reached it, Matt," Roxanne said. "Just a little more that way."

"He can't get it now, honey." Lydia flicked off the hazard lights and sped onto I-24. "He hurt himself. Let's do something else."

"I know," the little girl said, "let's tell ghost stories."

They had timed the trip so as to depart just after lunch, hoping Roxanne, who grew cranky being confined in the car, would nap through most of it. Perhaps a long and tedious ghost story would be just the thing. If only Roxanne didn't insist on telling one herself. Her ghost stories always went the same way: People left their house, ghosts came in and helped themselves to potato chips from a blue bowl on the kitchen table, people returned and noticed the chips missing, they ate some themselves and departed again, the ghosts reappeared to devour more chips, and on and on in this vein. These were lengthy and repetitive, but instead of lulling Roxanne, as they stupefied Lydia and Matt, the tales excited her, triggering her appetite for chips and her grievance against Lydia for refusing to pack junk food in her lunchbox.

"Torvah gets potato chips in her lunch." Just the mention of ghost stories sparked Roxanne's grudge.

Matt fumbled for the insulated bag, in which they kept vitamins, bandages, and antiseptic cream. "Did you remember the aspirin?"

"No, I forgot," Lydia said.

"Even Daniel gets chips."

"I put them right on the counter for you. I said, 'Don't forget these.'"

"I know, I know. I'm sorry. We can buy some when we get gas."

A rapping sound came from the back seat.

"You're not kicking that painting, are you?" Matt started to turn and yelped. "Man, that hurts like a mother—"

"I'll tell the first story," Lydia said. "Listen closely because it's very scary, and it's a secret story, you can never, ever, *ever* tell anyone." She dropped her voice to a stage whisper. "*It's a true story.*"

Matt sat in silence, twisting his ring.

"What's it about?" Roxanne asked.

"Well, there was this woman who was watching a house for some people who had gone to ..." Lydia paused to come up with a faraway place that Roxanne would know.

"Israel!" Roxanne said.

"Yes, Israel, they'd gone to Israel for a vacation, and they told her to take care of their house and feed the cat while they were away. And so she did. She moved into their house, a big old-fashioned house with lots of hidey holes and cupboards." Lydia was drifting into a story that once happened to her, so she hastened to change it some. "There was a big fireplace with an ugly painting hanging over it. A really yucky painting taking up the wall, crowding everything out, just a stupid, stupid painting—"

"We get the picture," Matt said.

Lydia winced, as she usually did when Matt made a pun. "Ha-ha—very funny."

"What's funny?" Roxanne asked.

"Nothing, honey, trust me," Lydia said. "Let me tell the story, okay? So after the couple left for Israel, and the woman was in the house alone, she decided to take that picture down and hide it in the basement while she was staying there in the house."

"What was in the picture, Auntie?"

Lydia thought for a moment. "It was a deep, dark, lonely room filled with shadows and cobwebs, and in it was a bony hag reaching out, like to *grab* someone."

Matt put his hand on Lydia's knee, squeezed it in a gentle, but warning way.

"Of course, it was just a picture, but it sure was ugly, so she took it down, just for while she was there. Well, that night, after she fell asleep, she heard noises in the house, like someone bumping around on the stairs and then scraping sounds."

Roxanne gasped, and Matt put a little more pressure on Lydia's knee.

"Now, the woman was scared, but she got up, grabbed a flashlight, and went downstairs to look. She didn't find anything. The house was silent again. Still, she searched every room, flashing the light over the furniture and the carpet. Finally, in the living room, she raised the beam over the fireplace, and there it was."

"What was it?" Roxanne's voice quavered.

"The painting, the ugly, ugly painting, that's what. Someone had put it back over the mantel. This was weird, but then she told herself, hmm, maybe I didn't really take it down. Maybe I just thought I did. She wasn't sure anymore, and besides the rest of the house was quiet, and she was sleepy, so she just went back to bed. The next morning, first thing she did was to take that painting downstairs and *lock* it in the basement."

"I bet a ghost moved it!"

"Maybe so." Lydia beeped the horn at a van that cut her off, causing her to brake. "Because the next night, the same thing happened again—noises from the stairs woke her up, and she went down to find the painting back in its place over the mantel. This went on every night until the couple returned from Israel. They'd taken an early flight home, so she wasn't expecting them, and she had the picture hidden away when they came through the front door. The first thing they said when they stepped in the house was, 'What happened to our mirror?'

"Well, the woman was surprised. She said, 'You mean the *painting*?'

"'Painting, what painting?' they asked. 'We have no paintings—just our mirror.'"

Lydia took pride in this extemporaneous twist. "So they went downstairs to get it, and guess what, it *was* a mirror—not a painting, and guess what else, that hag in it—"

"Ooh! That was *her*, the lady!" Roxanne's voice was rich with satisfaction.

"Correct."

"But what if it was the cat, Auntie? What if the cat moved the painting?"

"Think about it. Could a cat move a painting?"

"Maybe with a step-stool," said Roxanne, who'd used her step-stool to reach butterscotch discs from the crystal dish on the mantel until Lydia caught her at it and replaced the candy with unsalted soy nuts.

"Well, if the cat did it, then it wouldn't be a ghost story. It'd be a cat *tail*, right?" Matt stroked his chin. "Gives one pause—get it? *Paws.*"

Neither Lydia nor Roxanne laughed. Really, it was wrong to encourage him.

"I'll tell one now," and Roxanne plunged into an unabridged version of the potato-chip-eating ghost tale that lasted past Murfreesboro, Manchester, and almost to Monteagle, putting Matt to sleep—still holding his shoulder—just outside of Beech Grove and driving Lydia to bite the inside of her cheek to keep alert.

At the end of her story, Roxanne complained only briefly about potato chip deprivation before pulling a blanket—from the painting?—over her head and emitting muted snores from under it. They had just begun to climb the mountain toward Monteagle, the little car whizzing past the eighteen-wheelers that had thundered by earlier. Stony ridges on both sides of the highway resembled the bristled backs of prehistoric creatures, and the dynamite-sheared rock, iron-stained deep russet, offset shady patches of loblolly and oak. Ordinarily, Lydia enjoyed such a drive. But this time, she barely glanced at the landscape, and when she did, it struck her as remote and desolate, nowhere she'd want to be stranded. Thunderheads crowded the sky, casting an inescapable umbra. She fixed her gaze on the highway and thought about the parts of the story she hadn't told.

It had been a doll, not a painting, a doll given her by a man she picked up in a bar and brought to the house she was watching for her professor and his wife while they were in South America. The man, an antique hobbyist, had presented her with a doll on their second date, a porcelain-faced baby doll. She'd thought it an insipid gift for a grown woman and left it in the trunk of her car. But in the night, somehow, it had gotten in the house, and Lydia found it when she went downstairs for a glass of water. She had been drinking that night and wasn't sure she'd left it in the car, only that she'd *meant* to leave it there. But the doll was out of its box, and she certainly hadn't removed it from the cardboard and cellophane casing—had she?

In the morning, clearheaded and caffeinated, she re-boxed it, placed it near the spare tire, and slammed the trunk shut. The next day, she woke to find the doll, again, in the house, seated in fact, at the dining table with a tea-setting laid before it. That was it. She packed her things and moved back to her apartment, returning to the house twice daily to feed the cat and turn lights off and on to make it seem inhabited. When she told the man who'd given her the doll about this over the phone, he made an unkind remark about her biological clock and broke off their next date. She never saw him again.

After the professor and his wife returned from Peru, they thanked her with a small woven rug, and she, in turn, gave them the doll.

"Our little ghost will like that," her professor had said with a wink at his wife.

"Ghost?" A chill raised the fine hairs on Lydia's arms.

"Yes, didn't we tell you?" the wife said with pride. "Our house is haunted."

"It's the ghost of a child, a little girl." The professor had cupped a hand over his mouth and whispered in Lydia's ear. "*She likes to play.*"

Lydia stopped for gas in Dalton, Georgia. She pulled the blanket off Roxanne and tossed it over the painting before Matt woke up, without much glancing at it, except to see that it was dark under the bubble wrap—a deep brown or blackish thing. She hoped it was an abstract. Still-life and landscape paintings struck Lydia as dated, even corny.

Roxanne grumbled, waking. "Are we here yet?"

"Sure are," Matt said, and he yawned.

"We *are*? We're at Mama's house!" Her excitement stung Lydia like a slap.

"No," she said. "We still have a ways to go."

"But Matt *said* we're here."

"Everywhere we are is *here*," he said. "Everywhere we aren't is there. We're here, and there is where we're going, but when we get there, it'll be *here*."

Roxanne groaned, and Lydia rolled her eyes. "Come on, then, pumpkin. Stretch your legs, while I get some gas. I'll take you to the restroom after we fill up." And to Matt, she said, "Do you still need aspirin?"

"In a big way," he said. "I think I've thrown out my frigging back." His angular face was clenched with pain, but when he grimaced, the gap between his top front teeth struck Lydia as absurd, even comical.

Roxanne hopped from the car, banging her knee on the painting. Lydia would have liked to give it a solid kick herself, but instead she shut the back door and leaned in the front passenger window to whisper, "Do you think we ought to phone Shirley on the cell? See if she hasn't changed her mind?"

"I'll call in a bit," he said, "to check the directions, see what she says."

"You want anything else?"

"Just the aspirin—please don't forget this time."

The gas station housed a souvenir/candy shop. Inside, Roxanne and Lydia wandered its full shelves and displays: mason jars filled with chow-chow and peach salsa, rubber snakes, Indian dolls in buckskin and dyed feathers, postcard displays, satiny pillows with embroidered sayings, shot glasses, ashtrays, and racks of candy—everything from orange marshmallow peanuts to divinity squares. Roxanne held up a lifelike cat novelty. "Can I have this?" she asked. The thing was realistically furred and cat-sized, but oddly flat on the bottom, like a doorstop.

A heavy woman, gray wisps straying from her rain bonnet, overheard this and said, "I bought me one of them fake cats, and the durn dog tore it to shreds." She laughed. "He thought it was the real thing."

"Please, can I get it as a souvenir to remind me of you?" Roxanne said.

"How would a fake cat remind you of me?" Lydia asked, disturbed by the idea.

"How about this then?" She held up a bag of salt-water taffy. This was a familiar tactic—to ask for something outrageous and settle for what she really wanted all along.

"Bad for your teeth," Lydia countered and reached for a small sack of pistachios. "Here, I'll get you these." She had a few strategies of her own.

"Thank you, Auntie. Every single nut I eat, I will think of you."

The older woman squinted at the two over the top of her glasses, and Lydia wondered if she'd ever get used to the looks she got from strangers puzzled by her relationship to the biracial child. She supposed not. No chance of it now that Roxanne was going home to her mother.

"Are you okay, honey?" the older woman asked, and she touched Lydia's elbow.

Lydia stepped back, fanning her face with one hand. "Allergies," she said. "Maybe I'm allergic to all these cats." She made herself smile.

"That's *not* the problem." Roxanne wagged a finger. "They're not even for real."

Back in the car, Matt reported that Shirley was anxious to see Roxanne and she'd given straightforward directions for when they hit Atlanta. Lydia pulled out of the gas station and headed back to the highway. As they sped up the on-ramp, Matt said, "Say, where's the aspirin?"

Heat suffused Lydia's face. "Shoot, we can go back."

"I can't believe this. You forgot?"

"I can turn back."

"*How?* How are you going to turn back? It's at least five miles to the next exit. You know what," he said, twisting his ring this way and that, "just forget it."

"Listen, if it's so bad, maybe we ought to head home, get you to the doctor in Nashville. I'm sure Shirley will—"

"No, no, no, no," he said. "You're not doing that."

"Doing what?"

"Using me to get what you want."

"I don't want to go back," Roxanne said from the back-seat. "I want to see my mama," and she started to cry.

Matt gave Lydia a sidelong glance.

"Hush, honey, hush," Lydia said. "You're going to see her. We'll be there in just a short while." The past year she had thought, had *wanted* to believe that Roxanne had no desire to return to Shirley. The little girl never asked when she would be going home or complained of missing her mother. She didn't even ask to call Shirley on the telephone. Now, Lydia understood that Roxanne—a four-year-old child when she came to live with Lydia—was just being brave, steeling herself not to cry for what she wanted most until now that her ordeal was nearly over. But had it been such an ordeal?

Being separated from her mother, that was the ordeal. Lydia remembered the way she herself would cling to the chain link fence of the kindergarten yard long after her mother had dropped her off, until the teacher pried her loose—one rust-stained finger after another—to carry her into the classroom. The other children teased her for crying, called her a baby, but Lydia couldn't help herself. She barely managed a half a day of separation from her mother at Roxanne's age. A year would have been unendurable for her. She would not have survived it.

But Roxanne had flourished during this time, grown taller, stronger, and smarter than ever. Shirley would hardly know her. Her wild mass of crinkly hair neatly combed and braided, her nails clipped and carefully painted shell pink, her brown eyes clear and wide—she would surprise her mother, Lydia felt sure. *If* Shirley noticed, that is, if she were sober—

"Shirley sounds good," Matt said, nearly reading her thoughts.

"I'm glad," Lydia said, looking straight ahead.

The house was a large two-storey with yellow vinyl siding, set in the middle of a smallish lot. It belonged to an aunt of that doper—as Lydia thought of him—that Shirley had ended up marrying, the one she'd been arrested with a year ago. Supposedly, they were both straight, now, working, and living with the aunt until they found a place of their own. Lydia pulled into the gravel drive behind two other cars.

For all her eagerness to see her mother, Roxanne made no move to release her seat harness. Matt was the first to heave himself out, and this he did gingerly, favoring his sore shoulder and moaning. "I won't be able to help with her stuff," he told Lydia.

"I'll unload. Let's go inside first, visit for a minute," she said, meaning let's see if Shirley's actually here and what condition she's in before we bring in anything.

He opened Roxanne's door. "We're really here, sweetie. I can't help you out because I'm hurting too bad. Can you get yourself out? Now don't bang that thing."

Lydia stepped out of the car and brushed the wrinkles from her skirt while Roxanne unclasped the strap buckle and climbed down. "My mama's in *there?*"

"That's right," Matt said.

The little girl shuffled up the drive, Lydia and Matt trailing her. At the threshold, Roxanne waited for Lydia to press the doorbell. The door swung wide, and Shirley, plump and smiling, stood before them. "Oh, Roxie, you're so big!"

Roxanne smiled, looking shy, but pleased. They all stepped into the hall and from there into the living room. The carpet had been freshly vacuumed, Lydia could tell by

the stripes in the shiny beige pile, the coffee table polished
and porcelain knickknacks dusted, but the house had a
peculiar fishy smell.

Matt sniffed. "Is there a baby here?"

"Damien's cousin has a baby. They're staying here, too,"
Shirley told him.

Lydia wondered why Shirley hadn't embraced Roxanne,
as she stepped forward to draw her cousin close. "You look
terrific."

And Shirley did appear well fed—her pink cheeks filled
out and her mid-section bulging over the waist of her faded
blue jeans. She took Lydia's hands in hers and beamed. "I
want you to be the first to know, but you can't tell anybody. I
haven't even told Mama yet. Damien and I are expecting."

Lydia's smile ached as she waited a few moments for her
cousin to finish the sentence—expecting *what?*—before she
realized Shirley had finished it. Then she pulled away, wanting to stamp her foot like a child and shout: B*ut that's no
fair!*

"Congratulations," Matt said, and he turned to Roxanne,
raising his eyebrows. "You hear that? You're going to have a
baby sister or brother. How do you like that?"

Roxanne, kneeling before a coffee table laden with ceramic angels, rabbits, and poodles, fingered these with care.
Her spine was rigid and shoulders taut as she listened, but she
made no answer.

Lydia breathed deeply and hugged her cousin again. "I
hope things work out for you, Shirley, but if you ever need me
to take care of Roxanne again, I will."

Lydia brought in Roxanne's suitcases and boxes from the
car while Matt, still cradling his shoulder, made small talk
with her cousin. Lydia overheard him telling Shirley how

well Roxanne was doing on the swim team. He liked that the little girl was athletic and competitive. Who'd go to the driving range to hit golf balls with him, Lydia wondered, carting in a crate of books and art supplies. Who'd toss the Frisbee with him now? Certainly not me, she thought.

Roxanne spent the whole time arranging and rearranging the figurines on the table. And Damien, if he was in the house, never showed his face. Lydia brought in the last load—Roxanne's carton of games and her backpack—and Matt excused himself for the bathroom. Lydia sat on the couch beside Shirley, struggling to unzip the backpack. From this, she pulled out a file sleeve. "Here are her medical records and a copy of her birth certificate. I had to send away for that, and you'll need it to get her in school. Her vitamins are in here—one a day of the calcium and two of the multi-vitamin with meals, okay?" She wanted to add: Roxanne's favorite color is pink, and she likes smoothies for breakfast—you make them with protein powder and frozen fruit, no ice cream—and she loves peanut butter sandwiches, and she's crazy about bowling and playing Candyland, though we changed up the rules some—

But Shirley's eyes glazed over, and she yawned.

"Oh, well." Lydia re-zipped the pack. "You'll see where everything is when you unpack." She set the bag down. "Thank you," she said. "Thank you for letting me—"

Her cousin flushed. "No, gosh, thank you. You were great to take her like that."

Matt reappeared in the doorway, flicking water from his hands, and Lydia rose. "We've got to do an errand in Buckhead," she said, "so we'd better get going."

Matt mussed the nimbus of hair that had escaped Roxanne's braids. Lydia knelt beside her. "You know what," she said, "I'm going to miss you." She kissed the girl's smooth forehead and embraced her, inhaling her strawberry-scented shampoo and salty pistachio breath and locking the child's smell and warmth in a deep vault of memory.

"Bye-bye, Auntie," Roxanne said without looking up.

Matt, still too sore to drive, directed Lydia back to the interstate. Otherwise, they were silent, Lydia steering through dense but fast moving traffic and Matt staring out the window. As they neared their exit, Matt made a strange chuckling sound. Lydia thought he was laughing to himself, but when she glanced at him, she saw his head was bent and his hands covered his face. Was he weeping? They had been married less than a year. They'd hastily wed when they hoped to gain custody of Roxanne, and they hadn't dated but for a few months before that. Lydia had never seen him—or any man—cry before.

"It would be different," he said, "it would be different if we knew she was going to be well taken care of. Then I wouldn't feel so bad."

Lydia reached for a tissue from the console and handed it to him. "I know," she said, and she clicked on the signal and accelerated to pass a slow-moving trailer. She blinked rapidly, cleared her throat.

"They didn't even have soap in the bathroom or towels. I had to wash my hands with some shampoo I found under the sink."

Lydia clucked her tongue, her throat thick and burning, and she wished Matt would go back to gazing morosely, and silently, out the window.

"And that medicine cabinet had everything from Percocet to Valium—all prescribed to Damien's aunt, but still. It's going to be hard to stay clean with all that—"

"Did you find an aspirin?" asked Lydia, remembering his back.

Matt shook his head. "No soap, no towels, no aspirin."

"We'll stop at a drugstore in Buckhead," she promised.

"No need. I took a couple Oxycontin."

"*What?*" Lydia turned to face him.

"I took some Oxycontin. I was curious. You hear all that stuff in the news."

"You're not supposed to take other people's medicine. What if you're allergic? What if she's counting pills and thinks Shirley or Damien took them?"

"Relax, will you? Anyone who's popping all those pills doesn't have the wits to count them, believe me." Matt rotated his shoulder. "My back feels better already."

Matt's aunt had fixed up her place to look like a French *maison* with pale yellow and orange paint marbled on the exterior walls of the house and a trellised courtyard that had a fountain. But a *faux maison* in Atlanta, Georgia, of all places, struck Lydia as phonier than vinyl siding. She lugged the bundled painting over the pebble-strewn walk. Matt, no doubt already high on Oxycontin, stumbled after her. "We're *not* staying long," she hissed over her shoulder, and she rang the doorbell.

Matt's aunt—Lydia struggled to remember her name— cracked the door open a few inches. "I'm not sure how much this will open," the woman said. "We've got paintings every- where." But she managed to pull it a few more inches wide, and Lydia handed her the framed canvass and slid in after it. Matt followed. Lucky, thought Lydia, they were both thin, or they wouldn't have been able to fit through the opening.

"Good to see you, Aunt Belinda," Matt said and gave a loopy, Oxycontin grin, his eyes still red-rimmed from weeping.

"Is this the painting?" Belinda asked, holding the framed canvass. She wore a dingy turquoise running suit and her large rough-looking feet were bare.

Lydia nodded and helped Belinda unwrap the blanket and plastic covering the picture. The woman didn't even bother to offer them a seat, let alone a glass of water. True, in addition to blocking the door, paintings leaned against every piece of furniture. The one chair that propped no artwork was occupied by her current husband, who sat at a computer in an adjacent room. He hadn't troubled to glance up from the monitor at them.

When she and Belinda finally unveiled the painting, dropping the blankets and bubble wrapping to the floor, Lydia managed a sideways view of it. It was darker than she'd thought.

"Uncle Ben's trying to sell the thing. He just wants to know what you think it's worth," Matt said, squinting at the canvas himself.

"Oh, I don't know." Belinda bit her lower lip and peered through her goggle-style glasses. "Will you and she hold it, so I can get a better look?"

She! The woman didn't even know Lydia's name.

"I can't, Aunt Belinda. I threw out my back this afternoon and—"

"Let's just put it against that group of paintings there, then." She pointed to a stack leaning against a wall, and they set the picture down.

They stood back to regard the work. It was a landscape after all, a shadowy rendering of some body of water—a swamp?—surrounded by morbid-looking trees under a dull sky. A feeble light emanated from the center, but the darkness threatened to overtake this as surely as death punctuated life. The painting was so dismal that it disgusted Lydia.

Gloom for gloom's sake, she thought, gratuitous gloom. She'd never seen such a depressing view.

"Here's some crackling." Belinda fingered the canvass, "and flecking."

Lydia flashed on Roxanne's nudges and taps.

"And it's unsigned," Belinda said.

Of course, it is, Lydia told herself. After finishing it, the artist probably threw up his hands, saying "What the hell have I done? I'm not putting my name on this thing" before he set it out on the curb. She couldn't imagine what would inspire anyone to capture such dreariness, let alone to share it with others.

"I don't think it's worth much." Belinda shook her head. "Maybe five or six hundred dollars tops. *We* don't want it. Tell Ben we don't handle anything less than—what does our cheapest piece go for, hon?"

"Forty-eight hundred dollars, love," piped her husband from the computer.

"Well, he just wanted your opinion," Matt said, but surely his uncle had hoped Belinda would buy the painting and get it out of his sight. "We'll take it back to him."

Belinda made a hasty move for the door, and then somehow remembered her manners enough to stop herself. "What brings you to Atlanta?"

"We had to drive Roxanne back," Matt told her.

Lydia doubted Belinda had any idea who Roxanne was, but the older woman looked, for the first time, into Lydia's eyes. "*Oh*, how was that?"

Lydia tried a smile, but her lips quirked and her cheeks flamed.

"Are you okay?" Belinda asked her. "You look—"

"Fine, I'm fine." Lydia pulled the keys from her purse.

"We'd better go." She wound the wrappings over the painting in a clumsy way.

"I'm learning all I can about art and art dealing," Matt told his aunt. "You know I'm taking an appraisal course this fall to get certification."

"Listen to this, dear. He wants to be an appraiser. This from a sociologist," she said, meanly.

"I think he finds it diverting," Lydia said, "from his *real* work. Besides he wants to help out his uncle, who hasn't been well lately. It's a good hobby for someone like Matt who does so much important work that is meaningful to others." Take *that*, she thought, glancing around at the paintings as though they were trifles, worthless extravagances. This hardly reflected the way Lydia felt about art, but she had to defend poor, stoned-looking Matt, who stared at her now as though she'd spoken in tongues.

"My," Belinda said, clearly satisfied for having struck a nerve here. She was free to usher them out now, and so she did, saying with insincerity that Lydia found appalling, "You must come and visit us again."

"Oh, we will," Lydia said, her voice edged with threat. "You can count on it."

Back on the interstate, Lydia hit a wall of traffic. Minutes trickled past, and no car moved. Matt sat mute, but he wasn't sleeping. He was twisting that wedding band so vigorously she felt sure he'd chafe his finger. Lydia resisted observing that they might have missed this congestion if they hadn't had to stop at his aunt's. She drummed her fingers on the steering wheel lightly and thought to turn on the radio, but they never agreed on stations. He liked classical music and inflectionless discussions about politics or the economy, while she preferred raucous garage-band music. Lydia thought of Roxanne. Lately, the little girl insisted on listening only to women vocalists. Lydia would set the system on scan, searching for female singers to please Roxanne and finding them most often on country-and-western stations. Roxanne—what was she doing now? Lydia checked her watch: dinner time. She hoped Shirley would put some fresh vegetables on her plate. Broccoli, steamed broccoli was Roxanne's favorite. She ought to have mentioned this. Maybe she could slip Matt's cell phone from his belt—

"You don't seem to care much for my aunt," Matt said.

Lydia snorted, but then said, "I have nothing against her. In fact, I like her more than ever now. Today, she actually made eye contact with me."

"I was very uncomfortable to see you like that with her," he said.

"Like what?"

"Like you couldn't wait to get out of there."

Lydia regarded her husband out of the corner of her eye, amazed she could feel such tenderness towards him as he wept not an hour ago, and now, wonder why on earth she'd ever dated him in the first place—that bony face, those thick glasses. Matt was a slight man, and Lydia was on the small side herself, so if they ever had children, they'd be dwarfish, spindly things, nothing like the splendidly tall Roxanne. Like him, they'd no doubt be legally blind, and they'd inherit that gap between his teeth that made it so hard for her to take him seriously. How would she ever be able to love them?

Finally, traffic flowed around a knot of squad cars and an ambulance. When a lane freed for them to pass, Lydia caught sight of a mangled gray sedan, the front end smashed accordion-style nearly into the backseat. "Surely, no one survived that."

"But they did." Matt pointed out an ashen-faced man and woman, wearing blankets and holding onto one another, as they perched on the median divider. "Look."

Matt fell asleep just before they crossed into Tennessee, and Lydia's seatbelt pressed against her full bladder so uncomfortably that her eyes teared. She knew there was a rest stop just past Lake Nickajack—all that water!—so she unfastened her seatbelt and aimed for it, driving as fast as she dared. At the rest stop, Matt still slept, undisturbed by the slammed door and the heat filling the car in her absence. Back in the car, she pulled out her checkbook—she and Matt still kept separate accounts—and scribbled out a check to Uncle Ben for six hundred—no, make that six hundred and *fifty*—dollars. Then, she pulled the painting from the back seat, propped it against the drinking fountain, returned to the car, and drove off, feeling lighter than she had in weeks.

Matt roused himself about twenty miles from Murfreesboro. "Where are we?"

"Not too far," Lydia said, "but we need to get gas."

"How long have I been asleep?"

Long enough, Lydia thought, but she said, "Not that long. We're coming up on Luv's—that gas-station/fast-food place. Are you hungry?"

"I don't know. I suppose I should be."

"Maybe we can get a salad or something there." She veered for the exit and was soon bumping the car up the drive to the pumps. As she fueled the car, Matt staggered across the blacktop. "Whoa, there," she said. "Can you manage by yourself?"

"I'm okay," he said. "I'm headed to the restroom. I'll meet you inside."

He took slow deliberate steps, like a careful drunk, all

the way into the store. As she waited for the tank to fill, an elderly black couple pulled a powder blue Cadillac alongside her car. The man, who was driving, rolled down his window and said, "Thank goodness we caught up with you. I didn't think we'd make it."

"Are you talking to me?" Lydia asked.

"Why, yes, ma'am, I am." He smiled broadly, revealing an uneven row of longish yellowed teeth.

A thin woman with a cap of blue-rinsed curls stepped out of the passenger seat and rapped on the roof of the Cadillac. "Open up the trunk, Seth." She was wearing a navy blue and white polka dot dress with a white collar.

"Forgive me for not stepping out," the man said, after pulling the trunk release. "My knees are bad."

The old woman struggled to pull the familiar blanket-covered bundle from the trunk. No, thought Lydia, not the painting, but of course, it was.

"You left it behind at that rest stop in Nickajack," Seth said. "We tried to stop you. I honked and honked, but looked like you had something else on your mind."

Lydia hurried around to help lift the thing.

"I had a look at it," the woman confessed. "Not real cheerful, is it?"

"We were headed for Monteagle, the chapel up there, you know, but I told Alma we'd better follow you and give this thing back. Looks valuable," Seth said.

Hearing that the woman found the painting none too "cheerful," Lydia realized there was no way she could offer it to them for driving a good hour or more out of their way. She glanced over her shoulder toward the station before shoving the painting into the back seat. "I don't know how to thank you. This is so nice of you."

"Random axe," the man said.

"Excuse me?" Lydia said.

"Random acts of niceness," the old woman explained with a grin. "The Lord sees them. We ought to thank you. You're helping us get into heaven."

"Well, I'm sorry you went out of your way, but I'm very grateful." Lydia hoped they'd be satisfied and leave before Matt came out to see what was going on.

"Save your gratitude for the Lord," Seth told her, as the woman slammed the trunk and climbed back into the car. "He's the one works through us." He rolled up the window, and both waved at her as the blue Cadillac pulled away from the pumps.

Lydia locked the car, stuffed the gas receipt in her purse, and made her way into Luv's. The shelves, like those in the souvenir shop earlier, were laden with cheap toys and mementos. As she strode past an aisle of dolls wearing frilly, feathery umbrella dresses in neon colors, she nearly stopped to point these out to Roxanne before she remembered where the little girl was. The store was filled with customers, but no one seemed to notice her. That is, no one looked at her the way Roxanne did—the intensity of that attention missed now like a phantom limb. This is what the dead would feel, she thought, if they walked among us.

She found Matt standing in line behind a family of overweight tourists, all in wrinkled khaki shorts, at the fast-food counter. "Who were those people?" he said. "Those people you were talking to outside?"

"Just some folks who wanted directions." Lydia stared at the posted menu.

"Oh, really," he said. "Then what were they doing with the painting?"

"I don't know what you're talking about."

Matt glared at his ring, as though it mocked him, daring him to twist it—come on, just once—and he was doing everything he could to resist. "I saw them take my uncle's painting out of their trunk and give it to you. That's what I'm talking about."

Lydia wondered if she could get away with blaming the vision on the Oxycontin, but decided that would not be fair. "Oh, that," she said.

"Yes, that. What the hell was that about?"

The heavy woman in front of them turned to give Matt a curious look.

He dropped his voice. "How did they get hold of the painting?"

"Listen, this is very complicated," Lydia said. "I can't possibly explain it here." She shook her head, frowning, and to her horror, she heard a great choking sob tear from her throat. She inhaled noisily, struggling to force it back, but it was too late. "I hate that fucking landscape! It's ugly and lonely, and it's depressing, and I can't bear it another minute!" She bolted for the women's restroom, where she sat in a locked stall, blotting her eyes with toilet paper and blowing her nose, until Matt, from the door, coaxed her out, saying, "Come on, honey. I didn't know you felt that way. Let's go home."

The rest of the drive home, Matt refrained from mentioning the painting, and in fact, when she glanced over her shoulder, Lydia saw that it was missing from the back seat. Maybe he had thrown it out. She hoped so, but after they pulled into their garage and he opened the trunk, he removed the blanket-wrapped parcel, saying, "Now, I'm going to put it in the basement, okay? I'm going to lock it down there until I can drive it back to Ben's. Unless you'd rather I take it right now."

"You can take it later, I guess. I don't have to look at it in the basement."

They'd left the house in a disheveled state that afternoon. Now Lydia gathered newspapers and collected cups and glasses, while Matt washed the dishes. The night was moonless, deep and dark. Lydia started, catching sight of her reflection in the living room window as she moved about the house tidying up. She looked like a hologram image in the shadowy glass, like a wraith. Lydia yanked the curtain shut. The phone rang, and she jumped, spilling water from the overfull glass she was carrying to the sink.

She set it down to pick up the receiver. "Hello?"

"Lydia, it's me Shirley."

"What's wrong?" Lydia asked, peering around for the car keys.

"Nothing, nothing's wrong. Roxanne asked me to call."

"Is she okay?"

"Roxanne's fine, really fine. She just wants to talk to you."

After a long conversation with Roxanne, Lydia finally said goodnight to the little girl, replaced the phone in its cradle, and finished straightening the house. Then she curled up on the couch with Matt to watch a movie on television. It followed a complex plot—full of twists and turns, betrayal and reconciliation and more betrayal. It was a love story that ended in a tragic way. Lydia had seen it before, but watched it again with the comforting satisfaction that at least she knew how this one would play out in the end. And though the movie ended sadly, the flickering images on the screen were much less haunting to Lydia than Roxanne's whispered words to her before they said goodbye on the telephone: *Auntie, when are you going to pick me up? I want to come home.*

Lorraine M. López lives in Nashville, Tennessee, where she teaches at Vanderbilt University. Her awards include the Independent Publisher Book Award for Multicultural Fiction, the Paterson Prize for Fiction, the International Latino Book Award for Short Stories, and the inaugural Miguel Marmol Prize for Fiction (selected by Sandra Cisneros and awarded by Curbstone Press, for a first book-length work of fiction of a Latino/a writer). She has written a book for young adults, *Call Me Henri*. Her latest novel is *The Gifted Gabaldón Sisters*, which was a Los Compadres/Borders selection. Her forthcoming books include a new novel, *Limpieza*, and an edited essay collection, *An Angle of Vision: Women Writers on Their Poor and Working Class Roots*.